By Karen Gass Saari

Copyright ©2013 Karen Gass. All rights reserved.

http://www.cottonspice.net

email: karengass144@gmail.com

All rights reserved. No part of this book may be reproduced or transmitted in any form by any means, electronic, mechanical, photocopying, recording, or otherwise, without the prior written permission of Karen Gass.

Preface

This book began in 2003 as a short story for my website newsletter. I had just had some major surgery on one of my feet, and I had a week to be flat on my back, foot elevated and only being allowed up for bathroom breaks. I figured this would be a great time to start that newsletter I'd always wanted and thought a little quilting story would be nice content.

Well, the story took on a life of its own, and grew into a book. It languished in my computer for about 10 years. I had shared it with various friends, and they all encouraged me to publish it. With one thing and another and life in general, it just never happened.

I think it's possible this story has a sequel. In fact, I'm pretty sure it does. I hope you enjoy reading it, and I truly appreciate that you've chosen to read my story, I thank you from the bottom of my heart. I wish you many hours of enjoyable reading as you are transported to Spring Street and into the lives of the women who make up this story.

Dedication and Thank You

I am dedicating this book to my friends and sisters in my Fibromyalgia Support Group. They encouraged me, reminded me, and generally harassed me to finish this book. It was what I needed.

My most important Thank You goes to my Lord and Savior, Jesus Christ, who I believe planted the seed for this book and gave me many of the ideas. Some of the events in this book were a surprise to me! I didn't know what was going to happen until the words came out of my fingers!

Thank you to my husband, Mike. He loves me and gave me wings. He's the one who made it possible to finish this, and to dare to dream of another one.

Thank you to my family, who read the first chapters and told me to write more!

Thank you to Cynthia Martin, for your encouragement and gentle prodding to finish writing. You are a treasure in my life.

Thank you to Karen Bush, for your friendship of too many years to say, and making me work on this book, when I should have been working on yours. And thank you for the tea parties under the table.

Thank you, dear readers, for embarking on this adventure with me.

Chapter 1

Carrie Barrister carried the wicker laundry basket from the back porch into the yard. Taking clothespins from the cloth bag on the line, she hung up shirts and blouses, nightgowns and underwear, jeans and Joe's work clothes. They stretched the length of the clothesline, one after the other, snapping in the breeze.

It was a late spring day, and she was glad to be hanging clothes on the line again after a cold winter. In the soft spring air the scent of line-dried clothes was irresistible. Happy birds built nests and a lawnmower rumbled in the distance. A lazy bee buzzed by in search of a flower.

Today was quilting day, the first one of the year to be held on the porch, and there was still a lot to do before everyone arrived.

Breakfast dishes had to be done, and the living room floor needed the carpet sweeper.

As Carrie reflected on her love of her home and her life, she realized again, how blessed she was and wondered what she had done to deserve it. As much as she tried not to think about it, she knew it was still there. The *secret* -- hidden away and locked into the smallest room of her heart. How could God have blessed her, when she kept this secret, even from her husband, whom she loved with all her heart? Her burning ambition was to make up for the sin and make things okay. It was a mystery why God had blessed her so abundantly, when she was such a liar.

Joe and Carrie's house was on the old and perhaps even shabby side, but they loved it. After their daughter Abby left home, it became quite empty. Their house which had been filled with a child's laughter, tears and chatter for many years was now silent and devoid of her clutter. Some days it was hard to face.

The neighborhood had once been a pretty ritzy place to live. Anyone who was anyone could proudly say they resided on Spring Street. The houses were large and set back on their generous lots, with an abundance of green grass and large gardens. Most were two story and some, although not theirs, had small guesthouses. But time had moved on, and the rich and well to do had moved to other neighborhoods, leaving this one to regular people. As far as Carrie knew, there was only one original resident, Mrs. Reginald Truesdale, and she never talked to any of the newcomers.

Inside, Carrie cleaned quickly, giving most of it a lick and promise. Today was quilting day and she didn't want to waste any more of it with cleaning. She swept the front porch clean. After a long winter, its corners were filled with dried leaves and a few dead bugs. This was their meeting place, for quilting and conversation. It was a lovely thing to be sitting on the front porch, stitching and quilting and visiting. There were only six of them, ladies who had stitched together for the past twenty years or so. And always on Carrie's front porch.

There was a large round table, and mismatched chairs placed around it, with comfy cushions, and a few extra pillows to add support to aching backs. She shook out all the cushions, ridding them of any unwelcome visitors ... like that earwig that just fell to the floor. She stepped on it quick, before it got away. Earwigs made her shudder.

All the quilters lived on Spring Street. They had no formal name, and just referred to Thursday afternoon as quilting day.

Carrie would make iced tea, Martha would bring her raisin cookies, and she supposed Gert would bring her mud cookies, so named for their mud-like appearance. In truth they were supposed to have a rich velvety texture and creamy chocolate goodness that was to die for. However, in Gert's case, they did taste exactly like mud. Gert was sure that everyone loved her mud cookies, but no one did. They were dry and tasteless and were only eaten out of politeness. Gert was their friend and if eating a few muddy mud cookies could cement a friendship, well then, it was a small sacrifice. The saving grace was that Gert was frugally minded and made small batches of small cookies.

Sometimes Martha's sister, Esther, would bring her chocolate cake, which was moist and delicious and tasted slightly of coffee. They shared a house, now that both their husbands had passed away.

Carrie ate a quick lunch of leftover vegetable soup and a few crackers. She changed her dusty clothes for a fresh plaid blouse woven in the colors of the rainbow, a soft blue denim skirt and tennis shoes. She ran a comb through her graying hair, fastening it in a ponytail to keep it out of her face as she worked and then ran downstairs as the front door knocker sounded.

"Hi Gert! I'm on my way down, come in and help me carry out the iced tea!" Carrie called.

"Hello?" Gert stuck her head through the door. "Carrie, are you here? Oh, there you are." Gert came in, carrying her quilting bag. She took the pitcher of iced tea

Carrie handed her and they both went out onto the front porch.

"How's your garden coming? Did you get it planted?" Carrie asked.

"Yeah, I got it planted. Then that durn dog next door got loose and trampled through the whole thing," Gert snorted. "Now all the seeds are willy nilly, and who knows what's gonna come up where!"

Carrie hid a smile at the thought of the jumbled garden.

Gert, now 63 yrs. old, was a sparse woman and mostly colorblind. It was a good thing she cared naught for fashion, as her clothes were mismatched in color as well as texture and design. She thought nothing of wearing an orange skirt with a pink T-shirt that said, "Gus' Bowling Alley – Knock A Few Down!" printed on it, with an over shirt of green plaid. Her socks were often different colors, and one time she had worn two different shoes to the market. She was very opinionated, and it never occurred to her that those opinions might sometimes be hurtful or taken the wrong way, as she really did have a heart of gold, and wanted, for the most part, to do what was right.

Martha was on her way up the walk with a plate of raisin cookies and Esther was a step behind but carrying no cake.

"Hi you two!" Carrie smiled, "Come on up ... isn't it a beautiful day?"

They each found their usual chair and settled their quilting bags on the table.

Martha smiled, "Oh yes, it's a gorgeous day! I just love spring. I'm so glad to be done with shoveling snow."

Esther nodded.

"Hi Connie!" Esther called, as she saw Connie coming up the walk. "Do you see Eleanor coming down the street?"

"She's on her way," Connie said as she settled into a chair. "I saw her come out of the drive a few minutes ago."

"Gert just told me her neighbor's dog got into her freshly planted garden, and now she won't know what's coming up where!" Carrie said.

"Oh no!" Martha, who was not an animal person, screwed up her mouth in disgust. "I guess there's no way to fix that is there? Did you go over and give them a piece of your mind?"

Gert snorted out a laugh, "Haven't got much left to give!"

Eleanor arrived to hellos, and a few seconds later Lydia arrived, and they all got out their thread and thimbles, and blocks they were working on. Stitching began in earnest.

"Anything new?" Esther asked, carefully holding her needle up to the light.

They began to share their news, each one having something to tell. Connie told of her teenage boys' baseball games, so far they were first in their league. Martha told of the door-to-door salesman who had come by trying to sell household cleaners. He wouldn't take no for an answer. She ended up shutting the door in his face. Esther told of the sale on cupcake holders at the market. Summer was nearly here and it would be time for bake sales to raise money for any number of church activities. Lydia told about their new computer and how she was learning to email.

"Lydia, who are you going to email? Do you know anybody who has email?" Martha peered over her glasses.

"Well, not now I don't. But I've heard there are all kinds of places to go on the Internet to meet people. I might just go exploring!" Lydia looked adventurous.

"Ahhhh, you better be careful of that internet," Gert scowled, "It's full of bad stuff. Nothing good will ever come of it."

"Oh, I don't know Gert, I've been to a couple quilting places. They seemed really nice. I emailed to one lady, and she told me about a nice Christian place where they give prayer requests and talk with each other about the Lord. I haven't had time to go there yet, but I will," Lydia said.

Gert snorted.

"Eleanor," Carrie asked, "Anything new with you? How's your husband?"

Eleanor startled, and looked up, timid as a mouse. "Oh, he's fine. There's not much new with me."

"Have you noticed that house lately? Did you see that baby running around in nothing but a diaper, early the other morning? No sign of his mother around." Connie said, clearly disgusted.

They all agreed, that house was the limit. Each of them had seen something shameful going on there at one time or another. At the very end of the street was the smallest and shabbiest house on the block. It was owned by a realtor and rented out to anyone who could afford $150 a month, which was an exorbitant rent for such a place.

"I just don't see why they can't keep it at least picked up around there, the yard is full of trash and the weeds don't even dare show their faces in that yard! And Lord knows they could manage to put some clothes on those children if they didn't spend so much on beer and cigarettes." Gert was on a roll. "Do you think they're selling drugs?" she asked abruptly, after a moment of silence.

"Oh my goodness, Gert! I'm sure they aren't selling drugs. Where would you ever get an idea like that?" Carrie half laughed.

Gert mumbled under her breath.

"Look!" whispered Martha, "here comes Mrs. Truesdale. She won't even look over here, you know, she's so snooty!"

They all looked and sure enough, here came Mrs. Truesdale, dressed very neatly in a light blue suit, black pumps, and little white pillbox hat, with a veil. She walked by Carrie's house without even turning her head the teeniest bit.

"See?" Martha said smugly, "She's as snooty as they come!"

Martha cleared her throat, "So, do y'all think the blocks will be ready by next week? Can we plan to put the top together?"

Each lady agreed they would be ready; they were almost done now.

"Good!" Martha smiled, "then let's plan to complete the top next week, and then the next week, it'll go in the frame." Martha liked things to be planned and to go according to that plan.

The iced tea pitcher was empty, as was the cookie plate. Even the mud cookies were dutifully eaten.

Carrie stood up and stretched. "Well, I'm going to save the rest of my blocks to work on when Joe goes to his bowling league tonight. That will give me something to look forward to while he's gone. Besides, my hands have had it for now!" She stretched out her fingers, flexing her wrists.

All their quilts were hand stitched and hand quilted. They had been stitching together since they were young brides, and through the ages of time, no one could tell Gert's stitch from Carrie's or vice versa. The quilts looked as consistent as if one person had made them, from seams to a hand quilting stitch at a fairly constant 9 stitches per inch. They didn't go in for fancy new patterns, they much preferred comfortable, easy-to-piece older quilt patterns, which had certainly been good enough for their grandmothers and were good enough for them as well.

They went to the fabric shop together and split the cost of the materials evenly. After the first few years of quilting together, each member of the group had several quilts in her own home due to the efforts of each lady. Not wanting to give up their quilting afternoons, they decided to give the rest of them away as gifts. There was no rhyme or reason to the deciding factors as to who got a quilt, it simply turned out that while they were hand quilting, a lucky new winner was selected. The system worked and the guiding philosophy was, "if it isn't broken, then let's not fix it."

Connie put her work down on the table. "I've got to get going too, the boys are each bringing a friend home for dinner, so …"

Eleanor said a quiet, "Goodbye, I'll see you next week." And she quickly walked down the street.

The other ladies gathered their things together, giving good-byes and a few hugs.

"Hey, don't forget we have Women's Club next week. We have that special speaker from Indonesia ... you know, the missionary," Lydia reminded everyone.

All the ladies returned to their own homes; another quilting day had passed into history.

Chapter 2

"Joe, look! We have a letter from Abby!" Carrie walked in from the mailbox and plopped on the couch next to her husband. Joe had just come home from a long day's work at Grover's Sand and Gravel Pit. He'd worked there for twenty some years, and was the foreman. He was a good employee, loyal to his employer, and he put in his time, but was eager to come home to his real love. That would be Carrie and gardening. He was a master gardener and they had the best vegetable garden and nicest flowers on the block. He kept his own compost pile, and raised all their own vegetables, all organic of course. Winters were spent poring over seed catalogs and plotting out new gardens. His gardens changed every year, as he still had many things he wanted to try, so many plants he hadn't grown yet, so many seeds yet to be planted.

"Looks like an awfully thin letter." Joe commented. "We haven't heard from her in so long, I'd have thought she woulda had more news than this." He reached for the letter. "Where's my glasses?"

Carrie reached over his shoulder and grabbed them off the table behind the couch. "Here ... hurry!" she was impatient to hear the latest from their wayward daughter.

"Ok!! Let's see now," Joe opened the letter and cleared his throat.

Dear Mom and Dad,

Well, I'm doing ok, here. I love New York, it's always fun and interesting, you can never be bored here. I don't know how you stand it, there in that same old house, it was soooo boring. Well, anyway, the super finally did fix the plumbing, so now the pipes don't rattle quite as loud. And the people upstairs moved out, Thank God!!! They were as noisy as an army up there, I never could figure out what they were doing.

I got a new job at Derry's, it's a new coffee shop around the corner. They needed a waitress quick, so I grabbed the job. I had a commercial lined up, but it fell through. I'm still working at the market, got a raise too!

It's been raining a lot. I had to sell my car to pay rent. Well, what good is a car in NYC anyway? Can't afford to park it anywhere safe and it gets trashed if you park on the street. So, now I take the subway. It's terribly noisy and dirty.

I got a new boyfriend. He's a bartender in a swanky place not far from where I live. His name is Rod and he's soooo cute! All my friends think he is the cutest thing, but I told them hands off!!! ha ha I'm so lucky! He's awfully sweet to me and takes me out to the coolest places.

I really need to get a computer so I could email you instead of writing these letters, well, I guess that would mean you'd have to get a computer too. Hint, hint!!!

Well, not much going on here, busy working and going to calls. If you have any extra money I sure could use it, barely have enough to buy food. You know, someday I'll be rich and famous and will be paying you back! Love ya, Abby

Joe and Carrie were silent for a moment. They had hoped for so much more. But it appeared their prodigal daughter was still unrepentant.

"Joe? Should we send her money?" Carrie was hesitant to ask. Over the several years she had been gone, they had sent her so much money.

Joe sighed. "You know? I think it's time we stop sending her checks. She's a grown woman who chooses to live the way she does and in that expensive city … we've sent her enough money."

Carrie let out a sigh of relief. "Joe, I'm so glad you said that! We've been saving for so long to get that air conditioner … I could just see it going out the window!"

"Well, sending her money isn't the answer to her trouble anyway. We've just got to pray for her more!" Joe touched Carrie's arm and together they knelt before the soft old couch and boldly took their daughter to the throne of grace.

****

The room was lit only by the television, which cast a blue flickering light into the room. Violence was the scene on the television screen, and profanity blared from the speakers. There were three people in the room, a man, Dennis Oster, his girlfriend Liz MacKenzie, and Dennis' brother, Doug, who lay sleeping on the floor behind the couch. Doug had been out for the past three days, who knows where. Dennis was a large man, who at one time had been muscular and well built. Years of drinking and drug abuse had taken their toll on his body. Now, he was just a large man with a pot belly and flabby arms. Liz had once been a beautiful girl. When she and Dennis had run away together on his motorcycle, she'd had long brown hair with golden highlights. Deep green eyes, a ready smile with lovely white teeth. She had always been slender with a nice figure, but now she was simply thin to the point of emaciation. Her hair, once full and shiny was now dull and limp. Years of abuse in general had exacted their price on her body as well. She and Dennis had two children in the twelve years they had lived together: Katie who was four, and Danny was six. Although they were only in their late twenties, they looked ten years older.

They lived in this small shack of a house, with Dennis' brother, Doug and his three children, Trevor, Cindy and little Dougie, the baby who was only eleven months old. Last year Doug's wife Rachel had died in a car accident, and he had been left with their three children. At one time he had been a responsible father and husband, working and paying a mortgage. But with the death of his wife, he no longer knew how to cope, and had lost everything – his house, his car, most of the furniture. He was jobless, as was Dennis, and the three adults and five children barely survived in this small, two bedroom house. The children occupied the small bedroom off the kitchen. There was a double mattress on the floor and a playpen for the baby. Dennis and Liz used the bedroom off the living room, and Doug usually slept on the couch, if he came home at all.

More and more Doug stayed out for days at a time, leaving Liz to take care of his three children. Not that he asked her if she would mind, he simply didn't come home. He roamed the streets, looking for anything to dull the pain, be it drink, drugs or sex. He wasn't picky, and he wasn't exclusive either. He'd indulge in one or all three, if it would dull his mind to pain and guilt.

Liz lay on the couch, staring at the ceiling and Dennis sat in a broken down recliner with a bedspread thrown over it, his eyes fixed on the TV, a beer in his hand, and cigarette hanging from his lip. There was a blue haze of smoke in the room. Three small children sat in the kitchen doorway.

"I'm hungry," Cindy whispered. "Go ask Aunt Lizzie for some dinner." She pushed her little brother, Trevor into the living room.

"Stop it! Don't push me ... YOU go ask her." He scampered back to his relatively safe place in the doorway.

"Hey ... You go, she's your mother." They pushed Katie into the room. She glanced back at them with fear in her eyes.

Katie hesitantly approached her mother, lying on the couch. "Mommy?" she said quietly, hoping not to disturb her daddy while he was watching TV. "Mommy ..." Katie reached out for Liz's shoulder.

Liz jumped. "What?" she yelled. "What do you want? And why are you sneaking up on me like that?" She sat up, and grabbed hold of Katie, giving her a shake.

Dennis looked up and scowled. "Shut up!" he yelled, "I can't hear the TV!!!"

"You can hear that TV all the way down the block!" Liz yelled back.

Katie began to cry. "Mommy ... I'm hungry. My tummy growling." Her lower lip trembled.

"Go get some cereal. It's on the table." Liz sank back into the couch, glassy eyes staring at the wall. She pushed her limp hair back from her face. Why couldn't these kids just leave her alone? She didn't have the energy to deal with them. And Dennis, he was no help. Even if she could pry him away from the TV, what would she do with him? He was of no earthly use to anybody ... except for making babies, and once they were made, he completely lost interest. She just wanted to curl up in a little ball and die in peace.

"B ... but there's no milk ..." Katie's tears were falling fast now.

Liz sighed loudly. "Then I guess you'll have to eat it without milk!" She had carefully measured her words, and her voice rose as she talked. "Now get"

"If you don't stop that crying, I'll give you something to cry about! Get out of here!" Dennis raised his arm in a menacing gesture, but never took his eyes off the TV.

The three children took the box of cereal into the bedroom, where they shared it with the other two. It was a dismal night in this house. It couldn't be called a home because there was nothing homelike about it. Their clothes lay around on the floor in so many heaps. There were dirty diapers stacked here and there. They sat on the mattress and shared what was left in that cereal box, getting crumbs on the dirty sheet. There was a hopelessness about them that could not be missed. There was no laughing, or singing, or telling stories. There was only another dismal night, in front of another dismal day. Finally they lay down and went to sleep, cuddling with each other for comfort.

Out in the living room, things were even more desolate. The horrid images flashing on the TV screen seemed to amuse Dennis, and the crude and lewd jokes brought shouts of coarse laughter from him.

"Hey baby! I'm hungry too. What's for dinner?" Dennis looked over at Liz, raising his eyebrows.

"I don't know, and I don't care. Get it yourself." Liz went into the bathroom, hoping to escape him for five minutes.

Dennis looked after her, considering getting up and showing her who was boss, but shrugged it off. He wanted to see the rest of the movie. He'd deal with her later.

Liz turned on the water full force, sat down on the toilet and let the tears flow.

Chapter 3

The next week passed uneventfully. Connie ran into Carrie at the market. Connie had a cart full of 4 gallons of milk, compared to the one quart in Carrie's and they laughed over the incongruity.

Gert went out every day to check her garden, to see what was coming up where. A few brave green shoots, as tiny as pieces of thread had poked their heads up, but she had no clue what they were.

Esther and Martha spent much time out in their yard, reveling in the spring days, and the end of the cold. They culled the flower beds of dead debris from last summer and stuffed it all in big brown plastic garbage bags, for the trash man.

Eleanor went about cleaning houses, as she did every day. Thursday was her day off, and it was reserved for quilting. She had to stay up late into the night to make sure her blocks were finished, but she never mentioned that to anyone.

Lydia was the only one who showed up to Women's Club to hear the missionary speak and was delighted to find out she had a website. She quickly found a piece of paper in her purse to write down her 'web address'… as she now knew it was called. She couldn't wait to get home to look it up.

Dennis and Liz continued much the same. Dennis went out drinking and came home yelling. What was new? Liz tried to cope with five children, but really had no ability to do so, and the children ran around as they pleased.

One warm spring morning, Doug said he was going to the store to buy diapers for little Dougie. While he was there, the clerk turned her head to answer a question from another customer. Doug considered for about 3 seconds, and then his hand quickly reached out and grabbed the stack of twenties from the register drawer. He left in a flash, never even picking up the diapers. When the clerk finished with her customer, she absentmindedly closed the register drawer, and put the diapers away, thinking someone had forgotten to pick them up. That night, her register drawer was $560 out of balance, and she was fired.

****

This quilting day dawned as bright and pretty as the last one. Bees were buzzing, the birds were singing, flowers had poked their heads up even higher to catch the warm rays of the sun. Spring had sprung and was wasting no time in making it known.

Quickly all the women finished their household chores. Today's meeting started early. Completing a top took extra time. Lydia and Esther prepared plates of sandwiches and Martha brought her raisin cookies. Gert had been too busy in her garden to make mud cookies, and everyone secretly breathed a sigh of relief. Eleanor arrived late and apologized that she hadn't had time to make anything. Connie fixed a plate of cut up veggies: carrots, cucumbers, broccoli, and mushrooms, with some ranch dressing for dipping.

Paper plates were set on the table, and they all helped themselves. Lydia said a blessing, and they all fell to eating. Lydia told about the missionary meeting they had all missed.

"So, Lydia, did you find someone to email with yet?" Carrie asked.

"Well, maybe. I went to the missionary's website and emailed them how much I enjoyed her talk. But I haven't heard anything back." Lydia said, around bites of ham and cheese sandwich.

"Well, I'm sure you will." Carrie smiled, "She's probably busy giving talks at churches! Hey ... we got a letter from Abby!"

"Wonderful! Any good news?" Esther asked, as everyone looked at Carrie with a question in their eye.

"Oh, just the usual, new boyfriend, needs money ... yada yada..." Carrie said, shrugging. For a moment she stared off into space, remembering and trying to forget at the same time. It was best to keep busy.

"Carrie, I'm sorry there hasn't been any change in her. I don't want to say anything against Abby, I know you love her to pieces, but sometimes it makes me mad. You and Joe were such good parents to her. What is her problem anyway?" Martha said bluntly.

Carrie sighed. "Martha, as I've thought over it, I've realized that we really weren't very good parents." She held up her hands as the ladies protested. "No, we really weren't. I'm not fishing for compliments here. We thought *love* would be enough, and we neglected any kind of discipline or character training. We never held her accountable for her actions. We thought our explaining what she had done wrong, and her understanding it, would be enough." *And besides, I had hoped to be able to make up for my past. I had hoped that enough love would redeem me. Seems I was wrong, very wrong.*

"I'm sorry, Carrie." Esther reached over and patted her arm. "We'll just keep praying." The ladies murmured agreement.

Everybody finished up the last crumbs of lunch, declaring it delicious. After going into the house to wash their hands, they returned to the porch, ready to work.

There was much shuffling as everyone adjusted their chairs and back pillows, got out their glasses, scissors, thread and pincushions.

"OK ... does everybody have their blocks ready? We're going to stitch them all together today for a complete top." Martha looked around the table at everybody, expectantly, hoping that no one was going to throw off the plan.

The blocks were finished, so they quickly set to work stitching them together until they had a length of eight blocks.

Again, the subject of the people down the street came up.

"You just would not believe it!!! The police were there for the third time in four days. I couldn't believe it!" Gert was getting all fired up. She had the best view of their house from her living room window, and she watched them like a hawk. She felt it was her duty and continued to tell hair-raising stories about what she'd seen going on there.

Carrie tuned out Gert's voice, but at the same time listened for an opening to change the subject.

"You know," Carrie said, at the first opportunity, "we're almost done with this quilt; we need to talk about our next project." They had been stitching a blue and white nine patch, for a friend in a nursing home, who was recuperating from a knee operation. Quilt projects were chosen with care and not everybody who thought they needed or deserved a quilt from these front porch quilters, got one. The blue and white quilt would be ready to go in the quilting frame after today, and then it would be a matter of two weeks before it was time to start the next one.

Gert kept up the diatribe against the people down the street. No one was quite sure if a family lived there, but there did seem to be a couple of adults and various children.

Carrie pondered the situation at the end of the street. It was indeed the most humble of abodes; one could barely call it a home. The children were unattended and dirty, rarely having their hair brushed. There were several cats coming and going, one mangy looking dog and a goat. The adults – two men and one woman – never seemed to go to work. They stayed around the house most of the day, doing what, Carrie couldn't imagine. She wondered how they did keep food on the table. Maybe Gert was right, and they were selling drugs. There was often yelling and screaming among the children, and the adults were worse. The police had been called several times. Carrie wondered why God had brought them into the neighborhood. And as soon as she wondered that, an incredible thought occurred to her. One she could barely think about herself, let alone tell the others.

Gert was saying, "Well, I just bet you the farm they're selling drugs! Somebody has to do something. They are a disgrace to the neighborhood, and an embarrassment! I'm sure they're bringing down property values, and … well, I think someone should go talk to them and tell them how decent people live." And with that, she set her mouth and everyone knew that she had decided – something had to be done about those low-class, good for nothing, and dirty to boot, people.

The others had said little other than a murmur of agreement here and there, or an, "Oh my!" a few tsks tsks, and shaking of heads. They were appalled at the conditions as well but had no good ideas for dealing with them.

"Well, maybe we should call the Welfare office." Connie offered.

Gert gave her a withering look. "I'm sure they're already on Welfare."

And nobody said anything else after that.

The lengths were finished, and one by one each lady reached for her iced tea or a raisin cookie, flexing tired fingers and necks. It was time for a small break. Eleanor excused herself to use the bathroom, and Lydia got up and went to the other end of the porch, looking over Carrie's yard and commenting on the primroses that were doing so well.

"Joe said this summer he was going to put up some ceiling fans for us … out here on the porch!" Carrie smiled, proud of her husband and his thoughtfulness. "Won't that be great?"

They agreed it would be heavenly to have a breeze on a hot summer day. No one considered for a minute going indoors to stitch, until it was too cold and fingers became numb.

Brushing cookie crumbs off themselves, they reassembled at the table. They stitched each length of blocks to each other to complete the top. Carrie breathed a quick prayer for wisdom and broached the subject of her incredible idea.

"I have a suggestion for who gets the next quilt," she stated quietly.

A few mmms and Eleanor ventured a quiet, "Good." It meant she didn't have to come up with an idea. Needles flashed and scissors snipped.

"Ok, out with it. Who is it?" Connie finally asked after no more information had been forthcoming. She smiled to soften her words, wondering if they had come out harsher than she intended.

Taking a deep breath, Carrie said, "I think we should give a quilt to the lady at the end of the street."

Needles stopped in midair, and Martha's scissors clattered to the floor. Gert's eyes popped open so wide Carrie feared they might pop out, and her chin dropped nearly to her freckled chest.

"You mean … you mean … that 'woman', those 'people'?" Gert said disdainfully, looking like she'd swallowed a lemon. "She wouldn't know what to do with a quilt … she'd lay it out in the dirt for the dogs and the goat to sleep on … she'd, she'd …" She sputtered with righteous indignation.

"Yes, those people, that woman." Carrie said. "I think we have a chance to minister to her, to make a difference in their life."

"What in the world gave you that ridiculous idea?" Gert snorted.

"Well," Carrie hesitated, "I think God gave me the idea."

Well, that shut up Gert's mouth for a few minutes. Carrie knew that Gert loved God, but Gert believed that God should be kept in church where He belonged, and she was supposed to go visit Him once a week, which she dutifully did. It was the least she could do.

The other ladies were beginning to grasp this idea and wonder about it.

"Carrie," Connie said, "what good would it do to give a quilt to these people? I mean, we don't even know their names! Are we just supposed to walk up to the front door and hand over an heirloom quilt?"

Eleanor was looking panicky at the thought of this completely new situation and looked to Lydia for support.

Lydia said, "Carrie, I don't understand. What would this accomplish?"

"I think we should minister to the people God brings to us, and He has definitely brought this family here, under our noses. Maybe they don't know the right way to live or how to take care of their children. But why can't we at least reach out to them? Have any of us said as much as, 'Hi' to them? No, we just walk right on past, not even looking left or right, not putting ourselves out one bit. We act to them the way Mrs. Truesdale acts to us." Carrie said.

That thought hit home. Mrs. Truesdale regularly snubbed everyone in the neighborhood.

"Well," Martha said thoughtfully, "I guess you're right about the way we treat them, and of course, I agree with you that we should be nicer, but *give them a quilt?*" Martha's voice rose just a tad nearer the end of her sentence.

Work on the blue and white nine patch had come to a screeching halt.

"Wait, I'm going in to get my Bible, I just read a verse about this very thing, this morning." Carrie went into the house. In her absence, the remaining five women looked at each other, speechless. Even Gert.

"Here it is, in James ..." she riffled pages, "– If a brother or sister is naked and destitute of daily food, and one of you says to them, 'Depart in peace, be warmed and filled. But you do not give them the things which are needed for the body, what does it profit?' That's what I'm talking about."

"Fine," Gert said, "Let's bring them a box full of food, but how in the world you can fit a handmade quilt into that verse is beyond me! Crimany!!" She snorted again.

"I think a box of food would be lovely, but a quilt speaks to the soul, and after all, isn't that eventually where we want to reach them?" Carrie said quietly. "They obviously don't know Jesus; they seem to live without hope. We have hope and we know Jesus, if a quilt can open the door for us to bring them eternal things, then why not?"

Eleanor, quiet Eleanor, spoke up, "Carrie, I agree with you. I'll work on a quilt for them, with you."

Everyone looked up in surprise. Eleanor was as quiet as a mouse, hardly ever saying two words to anybody, even though she'd been quilting with them for years. She was, for some unknown reason, very uncomfortable with new people or places. She dressed very quietly and modestly, mostly in browns and grays, as she tried to be as unobtrusive as possible. It was as if she didn't want anyone to notice her, or ... horrors, speak to her.

But now, she had a look of quiet resolve on her round face.

Suddenly Carrie realized that in all the years she had known Eleanor, she had never gone to her home. Now, why was that? Eleanor and her husband rented a guesthouse belonging to one of the bigger houses. Eleanor and her husband ... *what was his name? – I can't remember!* – had lived there forever. She used to see him coming home from work in the evening, but now realized she hadn't seen him in a very long time. And Eleanor hadn't spoken of him in years. *I wonder why not?* Thoughts were whirling in Carrie's brain faster than she could sort them out.

Connie and Lydia both agreed they would work on the quilt as well, and so Martha and Esther said they wouldn't go against the flow. They were willing.

Gert stood up and began packing her quilting bag. "I will NOT, no ... NEVER work on a quilt for white trash. God gave me a gift in quilting and I will not squander it on people such as those. It's to be used for people HE loves! Those who deserve it!" She threw things in her bag willy nilly, not stopping to wind her thread or cap her scissors. "I won't be a party to this foolishness!" She threw the straps of her quilting bag over her scrawny arm, hitched up her sagging elastic waistband with the other hand and stomped off down the porch steps.

"Wait!" Carrie called, and ran after her. "Gert ... please don't go. Let's talk about this! We don't have to decide today, we can all go home and pray about it! What do you think?"

Gert snorted. "Not on your life. I don't bother God with things like that. He's got important things to do. Don't call me, Carrie Barrister. I know you. You think you can wear people down by harping on things and praying about things ... but don't call me." And she continued stomping down the sidewalk, causing one sock to fall down over her shoe.

Slowly, Carrie walked back to her seat. Eleanor's face was white. Tears fell down Martha's face, and Esther was patting her back. Connie was dumbfounded and Lydia still held her needle in her hand.

"Oh, Carrie," Martha said tearfully, "what are we going to do? Nothing like this has ever happened before. We've always gotten along so well … what are we going to do? Should we forget this project and pick another person? Is it worth it if we lose one of our group?"

"I'm not sure," Carrie said slowly. "I was so sure that God gave me this idea … but was I too hasty? I just don't know …" Her voice trailed off. *Surely this act of kindness would bring me the peace I'm looking for, this would make up for the past. Wouldn't it?*

Lydia found her voice and suggested, "I think we should finish this top as quickly as we can, and while I do think Carrie's suggestion is good, I think we should go home and pray about it. We can decide next week. But in the meantime, I also think we should concentrate on being nicer to these people and at least find out what their names are so we don't have to refer to them as 'those people' all the time. But, let's not overwhelm them with kindness, I mean it would look funny, don't you think?"

"Yes, it would look funny," Connie finally said, "To have never spoken to them in the three months they've lived here and then all of sudden five women are falling all over themselves to be nice to them. Yup, that would be suspicious – and weird!" she added.

They were quiet for some moments. They still had about an hour's worth of work to do to finish this top, so it would be ready for the frame next week. The hour passed slowly, with not much conversation. Each woman was quiet with her own thoughts.

Chapter 4

Gert stomped around her kitchen, washing dishes, and breaking a few in the wild process. She was mad, oh she was mad! After returning her Yellow Ware bowl to its shelf, she slammed the cupboard door shut and grimaced as she heard a clunk.

How dare they exclude her like that? That Carrie Barrister was as self-righteous as they come, thinking herself better than everyone else, thinking that GOD had talked to her! Why the very idea ... God had better things to do than talk to Carrie Barrister.

Gert was certain of all the *better things* God had to do, although she didn't have a clue what they were. She suspected they had to do with native people, living in huts and wearing very little clothing. But this was America, for crying out loud, God wasn't needed here. Of course she went to church ... all good people go to church. But there was such a thing as carrying it too far. And that Carrie Barrister was the limit.

She grabbed her old straw hat, jammed it on her head, and stomped out to the yard to yank a few weeds out by their very roots.

****

Connie Watson rinsed each plate and leaned over to put them in the dishwasher. She had been very quiet on her way home from quilting, even passing the shabby house in question. It looked like no one was at home, and she had felt relieved. There had been no need to say hi or even to nod and smile.

Her boys were upstairs doing their homework, and her husband, Ron was in the living room watching a ball game on television. The kitchen was finally clean after a day of cooking meals, and boys grabbing snacks. Why did they need a clean cup every single time they drank so much as a teaspoon of liquid? She pushed back the hair that had fallen in her eyes, hair that had looked pretty good this morning, but was now limp and sticking up in places, in ways she couldn't explain. She sighed, and stretched her back, tired in every muscle. She was going to get some comfy sweats on, her favorite slippers and sink into the couch with a good book.

As she passed the hall table, she noticed her Bible, right where she left it after church last Sunday. She felt a niggling in her mind to pick it up and read it. Oh, she groaned to herself, I'm too tired. I'll read it later.

Half an hour later, in her comfy sweats and slippers, sinking into the couch, with a small pillow behind her back, her book in hand and even a few cookies to munch on, she sighed in pleasure. And tried to lose herself in her book. She read over the same paragraph three times and put down her book. What was wrong with her? She stared at the wall, wondering what it was she had forgotten to do.

Go get your Bible.

She started; it was almost as if someone in the room had said that. It was probably just her conscience being a tad too loud. Last Sunday, the pastor had talked about how important it was to read your Bible every day, and she was probably just feeling a little guilty. The last time she had read her Bible ... well, actually she couldn't remember. She was a busy mom, with two growing boys, a big house to take care of, a husband who liked a good meal when he got home from work ... she didn't have time to be reading!

Suddenly, she looked at the book in her hand. Realization came to her that she had time to read novels, but not the Word of God.

"Oh Lord ... I'm sorry." She prayed quietly, "I didn't realize." Quickly she went to the hall table and gathered her Bible, taking it to the couch.

"Lord, I don't know where to read." She prayed again. She looked at the Bible cover and wondered where to start.

"Well ... I'll just open it and see what happens!" she thought to herself. "I sure hope I don't get that 'and Judas went out and hanged himself' verse, I've heard of that happening. Ok, here goes!"

Her Bible fell open to the 4th chapter of Ephesians. She started reading at the beginning of the chapter.

"Oh, this is nice ... *walk worthy of the calling*," she thought, and continued. Her husband turned up the TV and the baseball game was now blaring. Halfway through the chapter, her mind wandered to the grocery list hanging on the fridge. Did she remember to write down Saran Wrap? They were almost out.

"Oh shoot, I'm supposed to be reading my Bible, why am I thinking about Saran Wrap?" she thought. "Ok, where am I? verse 17 ... ok ... *should no longer walk as the rest of the Gentiles walk* ... Huh? what does that mean? Ok ... just finish the chapter so you can say you 'read your Bible' if the pastor asks."

And suddenly, the words she read became crystal clear and seemed to even get up off the page and dance before her eyes. Instantly her mind latched onto these words, and she felt the presence of the Lord in the room. Tears slipped down her cheeks as she realized that God was speaking to her, that He had called her to this time, to this act of obedience, to read His word, because He had something to tell her. She slipped to her knees, wanting to get things right with Him before she acted on this verse He had given her. She was so guilty of putting Him last; it was time to start putting Him first.

****

Eleanor Beecham looked at her husband, Alfred, slouching in his worn armchair, his mouth open, his hair falling over his forehead. He was asleep, or was he just passed out? She was too tired to care or to try waking him, carrying him down the hall to bed. He could just sleep in his chair for all she cared. It had been a long day and all she wanted to do was go to bed and forget the sordidness of her marriage and her beyond shabby home. Her old clothes mended more than once, her absolute loneliness. She barely remembered the days when he had worked at the insurance agency and come home sober every night. Those days seemed like a million years ago. If only ... well, there was no point in going there.

There was no one she could talk to about all this, her quilting friends – and they were the only friends she had – wouldn't understand this. They had happy homes, with husbands who worked and came home sober. Her husband sat in his chair most of the day, watching TV and drinking from a whiskey bottle. There was nothing for her; there was no hope of any other kind of life. Even their children had left, once they were of age. They had moved as far away as possible. Wanting to get away from the utter hopelessness of living near their parents. Their father, drinking his life away, and their mother ... a resigned, tired, sad old woman.

The bright spot in Eleanor's life was the quilting afternoons. She went to those faithfully, even if Alfred complained, which he did regularly. It was the only thing in her life of any value. And why in the world had she agreed to work on a quilt for that woman? She sighed wearily.

Tonight, she felt at the end of her rope. This wasn't an unfamiliar feeling, she often felt at the end of her rope, only to discover there was more rope to hold onto and she had to go through with life anyway. But tonight, was different. She just didn't care. Truth be told, she could identify with those people in the shabby house. They seemed to have no joy in their lives, and neither did she. They were just existing, killing the pain of living with their beer and cigarettes, and maybe even drugs. What was the difference between them, and her and Alfred? She couldn't see any. Why was she doing this? Why was life dragging on day after day … for no reason? Alfred certainly didn't contribute anything to society, unless you counted the money he spent for whiskey, as an economic boon. He didn't contribute anything to their relationship, he only saw her as a ride to the liquor store.

For the first time ever, she felt like taking a drink from that whiskey bottle herself. Maybe it made things tolerable for Alfred, and maybe it would for her too. But not tonight, she was too tired to go back out to the living room and get it.

She sat on the edge of the bed and took off her shoes, dropping them on the floor, peeled off her socks and massaged her poor aching feet. Her eyes fell on her Bible. It was sitting on the floor, next to her nightstand, covered with dust. She gave a soft snort, "What in the world is that doing there? I don't remember seeing it there before." A thought entered her tired mind to pick it up and read it, but she quickly dismissed it. What had God ever done for her? She received precious little sleep as it was, she wasn't going to waste any of it on the ***Bible***. Maybe tomorrow she'd dust it off, seemed kind of sacrilegious to have dust on a Bible.

She lay down, and for the next half hour, tossed and turned. Unable to get comfortable or to fall asleep, she got up to take half of a sleeping tablet. Sometimes that helped. Again, her eyes fell on the dusty Bible.

"Oh, what the heck … it can't hurt to read a verse or two. This pill won't work for an hour anyway." She picked up the Bible and blew the dust off.

Before she could even think of where she was going to read, she noticed a small paper bookmark. Opening the Bible to that page--in Isaiah of all places--she noticed an underlined verse. How odd. She never remembered underlining a verse, let alone marking it with a bookmark.

She put on her glasses and read the verse, it was underlined in blue ball point pen, kind of crooked, like someone had been in a hurry to do it. The verse, and one word in particular, leaped up at her, and stared her in the face as if it was suddenly lit with bright light. It nearly glowed.

Suddenly she was aware of tears cascading down her face, and of the huge amount of hurt in her heart. Hurts she had buried and ignored for so long, now suddenly surfaced.

"Oh God … I can't stand this! Please make this pain go away … I can't take anymore," she sobbed into a tissue. Tears, not cried for years, came and came and wouldn't stop. Tears, running down her tired cheeks, splashing on her open Bible, finally opened her heart to let the Holy Spirit in, to do a work in her poor tired heart. Slowly and softly, peace came and with it a quiet – and a ceasing of tears. Gradually, she felt the hand of God on her and He spoke to her heart about His overwhelming love for her, and assurance that she was not forgotten. Not by any means. His hand had been upon her all along; He had let these things happen to her for a reason. He continued to speak words of love to her poor tired and worn heart, and she drank it all in like the starving woman she was.

Finally, she lay down to sleep, the most peaceful and restful sleep she had slept in years.

****

Martha and Esther had lived together for a year now. They had established a routine that was comfortable. Esther had moved into Martha's house after Esther's husband died. Martha's husband had died five years earlier. She was tired of living in this big house all alone, and happy her sister had come to live with her. Neither of them had any idea of remarrying, although, only in their early fifties, they were still fairly young. It simply had not crossed their minds to consider remarriage. They had their house, their quilting group, their church activities, their favorite TV programs – they both loved *Home Improvement* and never missed it. It was a happy day when the local TV station had started airing reruns. If they weren't home at the time it was on, they set the VCR.

Esther did most of the cooking, and Martha did the washing up afterwards. They shared household chores, but Martha handled the money, and Esther took care of the yard.

When Esther moved in, she brought with her some favorite pieces of furniture, and a beautiful Persian rug woven in deep red and green, with gold accents. The rug was old, but in good condition. The colors seemed to blend together in a wonderful muted tone that added beauty to the living room in a magical way.

She had also brought her cat, Ralph. Martha secretly couldn't stand cats, and especially Ralph. Ralph was completely gray, with green eyes, and always seemed to look at her in a menacing tone of voice ... if such a thing could be done. Ralph was the clumsiest cat alive. Martha had always thought cats were supposed to be graceful creatures. Not Ralph. Numerous times he had been sitting on the windowsill, looking outside, when all of sudden he would simply fall off. Of course, his claws would shoot out trying to grab hold of something. Normally it was the drapes. Martha was not fond of rips in her drapes. But Esther loved the creature and Martha held her tongue, realizing that cats don't live forever and hoping once he had gone to the hereafter – Esther would leave well enough alone and not get another one.

Esther enjoyed reading the Bible with Martha in the evening, before they went to bed. Martha agreed to it, it seemed a good thing to do, although if she still lived alone, she probably wouldn't have done it. But it made Esther happy, so Martha went along.

"Martha!" called Esther, "Are you ready for devotions?" Esther was getting situated in her chair, and finding their place in the Bible.

"Just a minute, I'm coming. Just getting a cup of tea, do you want one too?" came Martha's voice from the kitchen.

"I'd love one, thank you, dear." Esther leaned her head back and rested her eyes for a moment. "Oh Martha, could you grab my glasses, I left them on the kitchen table."

"You need one of those glasses necklaces to keep hold of them. I've never seen anybody lose their glasses as much as you do." Martha was slightly grumpy. Her glasses weren't on the kitchen table. "I don't know where you left them, I can't find them."

"Oh no, I can't read without my glasses!" Esther worried. "Where did I leave them?" She puckered her brow in thought and chewed on her lip … thinking.

Martha wondered to herself if Ralph had knocked them down behind something. She wouldn't put it past him. He would delight in doing that, probably thinking in his small cat brain that somehow Martha would be to blame.

"I can't remember where they are, would you read tonight, please?" Esther handed Martha the Bible.

Martha sighed. "I'd love to." And put a smile on her face. "Where are we?"

"Last night we read the first half of Matthew 25, so tonight, I believe we start with verse 31, but I'm not sure, you check. I put a little pencil mark right where we quit." Esther smiled happily, and again leaned her head against the back of her chair and settled down to listen.

Martha began reading. It was hard to read and drink a cup of tea at the same time. Then, she was dismayed to find her mind wandering, even though she was reading. This seemed to be disrespectful to God, if you were going to read His words, the least you could do is keep your mind on it. She tried to concentrate on the words she was reading, but they just meant nothing to her. When in the world had Jesus been hungry?

Ralph jumped up on the table next to Martha's chair. Martha could barely contain her annoyance. If that cat bumped into her cup of tea and knocked it over, well, even Martha couldn't think retribution on a cat and read the Bible at the same time.

All of sudden, Esther jumped out her chair. "Did you hear that?" she nearly yelled.

"Hear what?" Martha jumped out of her chair too. Was somebody trying to break in? "What did you hear? Should we call the police?" Martha ran for the phone.

"No silly." Esther laughed. "What you just read! Didn't it just shout out at you?"

Martha stopped in her tracks and looked at Esther, blankly. What she had just read? How could she admit that she hadn't been listening, even though she had been reading?

"Uh, I'm sorry, what shouted out to you?" Martha stammered.

"That verse you just read ... how could you miss it? I think God put it on a neon sign and planted it right here in the living room." Esther nearly danced around the room.

Martha hated it when this happened. It always made her feel so stupid. As if Martha wasn't good enough for God to talk to, so He only talked to Esther.

"No, I guess I didn't get it." She said testily. "Do you want me to finish reading or what?"

"Oh Martha, I'm sorry. Don't feel bad, I'll tell you about it. Come on, let's go upstairs, I think my glasses are on my dresser. I want to underline that verse and put a star by it! It's not every day God talks to us."

****

Lydia Whitman sat with her husband Carl, at the kitchen table. They were just finishing up a dinner of Saturday night meatloaf, mashed potatoes, and green beans.

It was a lovely spring evening, the kitchen window was open, and the curtain was blowing slightly in the breeze.

"Ah, that was a good dinner, love." Carl stretched back in his chair, leaning it back on two legs, and rubbing his belly with both hands.

"One of these days, that chair is going to break right off and you're going to land flat on your back. Probably have to take you to the hospital and put you in traction." Lydia said. "Do you want some coffee?"

"Yes, dear, I do. Got any cake to go with that?" he grinned at her.

Lydia bustled around the kitchen, making coffee, and getting cake. It was nice to sit here in the evening and talk with Carl. He worked so hard, and such long hours; it wasn't often he was even home for dinner. This was a special treat.

"You know, that's pretty interesting stuff you ladies talked about the other day at Carrie's house." Carl said, after his first bite of cake and swallow of coffee, "Oh, that's good stuff!" He gave her a big grin.

"You mean the people down the street? Do you know their name? Ever talked to any of them?" Lydia asked.

"I spoke to one of the guys there one time, just right after they moved in. He came over to borrow the phone, but that's about all I know. Didn't mention his name. Didn't even really seem all that friendly ... just wanted the phone." Carl remembered. "But I do think you ladies are onto something. I do indeed." He took another big bite of cake.

"Do you? How do you think is the best way to go about it? I mean, it would be weird if all of a sudden we started going over there and being friendly, wouldn't it?" Lydia wrinkled her forehead.

Carl took one last bite of cake, before tipping his chair back again. "Well, the way I see it, if God gave Carrie this idea, then I guess God will open a door for you ladies to say *Hello* or *How Do You Do?* or whatever. Don't you think?" he grinned again.

Lydia sighed. Carl always made everything sound so simple. She'd been worrying over this for the last few days, and Carl summed it all up in one sentence. She leaned over and kissed his cheek.

"Yes, dear, I do think so." She brushed a cake crumb off his shirt. "Why do I always make things so difficult?"

"Cause it gives you something to worry about, that's why!" he laughed out loud, and ducked as she chucked the dish towel at him. "I'm going out to catch a few minutes of the ball game."

Lydia filled the sink with warm soapy water and began washing dishes. She opened the curtain at the sink further and watched the birds at the feeder. The backyard was large and full of flowers, trees and bushes. Carl had spent lots of time gardening the first few years they lived here. As he had progressed in his job at the factory, he'd had less time to spend gardening, and had, for the most part given it up. They paid the neighbor boy ten bucks to come and mow the lawn every week. The flowers Carl planted had seemed happy enough to stay in their yard and uconsiderately re-seeded themselves every year, making a beautiful yard with a minimum of fuss and bother. Carl jokingly said he had planned it that way.

She finished the dishes and walked out into the backyard, to water some thirsty flowers. This was a special time of day for her, standing in the cool of the evening, watching water flow from the green hose to the green bushes and colorful flowers. The neighborhood was quiet, with soft home sounds all around. She could hear a phone ring a couple houses down. A screen door slammed, the rusty spring making that *screen door noise*, Mrs. Nelson's new baby cried, and next door a sprinkler made swooshing sounds as it revolved on its base.

The watering finished, she sat down on a patio chair. It was just too beautiful to go inside. She leaned her head back and closed her eyes. Praying a little, listening to see if she could hear Gods voice.

"You know, I may have something for you."

She jumped. God? Oh, her heart skipped a beat. "Carl! You scared me to death!"

"I'm sorry, honey, I thought you'd hear the door slam." He came and sat next to her. "Are you ok?" he laughed a little nervous laugh.

"Yes, I'm fine, I just thought ... oh never mind. What do you have for me?" she smiled.

"Well," his hand rubbed his chin, "The other morning I read a verse that I just can't seem to get out of my mind. Maybe it's for you and your quilt ladies."

Lydia sat up straighter in her chair. Maybe she was going to hear the voice of God after all. "What verse? Tell me!"

As Carl repeated his persistent verse, Lydia felt chills go up and down her spine. She leaned back in her chair and smiled a contented smile.

"Yes, Carl, honey, that was for me and my ladies." She reached for his hand.

Chapter 5

In another town, several hundred miles away, Laura MacKenzie sat at her quilting frame, in the living room of her farmhouse, far out on a country road. She was a professional hand quilter and had quilt tops waiting in the trunk to be quilted. Enough quilts to last at least a year.

Laura loved being in her home every day, sitting down to a quilt in the frame, and setting her stitches in it, making it a thing of beauty. She and her husband Dale had bought this old farmhouse 17 years ago. They had scrimped and saved and generally done without in order to save up the down payment. But it had been worth it. They both loved living out here in the peace and quiet of the country. Through the years, they had done a little remodeling, and they were pretty well satisfied with the way their home had turned out. Large windows let in lots of light, looking out over meadows in the back, and a small woods in the front. Heart of pine floors glowed, under braided wool rugs. Their furniture was old, but comfortable, like old friends. She had set her quilting chair near the front window. The light was excellent and she had a good view of the road to the house. If anybody was coming, she would see them right away. And she was indeed waiting for someone; she had been waiting for twelve years now.

Besides being a hand quilter, Laura was also an intercessory prayer. All those hours spent at the quilt frame were also spent in prayer. Praying for whomever the Lord laid on her heart, for prayer requests given at church, even for things she heard on the news. But most of all, she prayed for her daughter, Elizabeth. Gone from home these twelve years.

Laura didn't know for sure that Elizabeth was even still alive. Elizabeth–well, she insisted on being called Liz – but Laura always prayed for Elizabeth, had left home at 17 in a wild bout of rebellion, with a boy from up the road who rode a motorcycle, and had long hair and tattoos. Laura had heard from her from time to time, mostly when she needed money. But those phone calls had grown farther and farther apart until there had been no phone call or contact of any kind in the last three years. Laura's faith was wearing thin. She could feel it ebbing away, bit by bit as no discernible answer came regarding her daughter. In the last year she had been praying for the people who lived around Elizabeth , hoping they were Christians, and they would minister to her daughter, as she had been unable to do. But after so long without a word, Laura was wondering where God was in all this.

Next to her chair, the phone rang.

"Hello?" Laura said, hoping this wouldn't take long. She was under a deadline.

"Laura? Honey, how are you?" Laura heard the voice of Anne, her best friend and prayer partner. "I know this is a weird question, but have you heard from Elizabeth?"

"What?" Laura asked incredulously, "What makes you think something like that? Don't you think I would have called you?"

"Well, yeah, I know you would have called me, but I just couldn't help but ask. Elizabeth has been on my mind and heart so heavy all day that I couldn't help but wonder. But, nothing?" Anne asked.

"No, not a word. I wonder why the Lord didn't lay her on my heart. I almost feel left out!" Laura said.

"Well, honey," Anne laughed, "You've been praying for her for twelve years, and I'm just catching up!"

"Still…" Laura paused, "I wonder what's happening." It didn't occur to Laura to doubt Anne's word or God's prompting. "You know, Anne, this was just what I needed. I've been feeling so, well, faithless, this morning. Like God has just forgotten Elizabeth."

"Oh, we both know that's not true. Remember, God is in Control?" Anne named one of their favorite songs.

Tears came to Laura's eyes. "I know that's not true, I know He's in control and His timing is perfect. But I'm just so tired, and my mother heart just wants to hold my daughter in my arms and know that she is alive and well. And Anne, I'm just sure I have grandchildren…" Laura's voice broke, "that I've never held or kissed. I want them so badly." Laura cried quietly on the phone.

"Father," Anne prayed over the phone, "We need Your touch of healing right now, Your lifting up of my dear friend and sister in You…" And the prayers went up through the phone lines and caught a wind to heaven, to the Father's ear.

Chapter 6

Thursday, quilting day, dawned cloudy and a little chilly. It was the last tiny remnant of winter. Gert sat at her kitchen table, drumming her fingers on the plastic tablecloth. It was the first time in years she wasn't preparing to go to Carrie's house. What was she going to do today? Better yet, how was she going to get back in? Her anger had subsided, but she was unclear how to go about getting back into the quilting circle. She had left the group and painted herself into a corner at the same time. She could hardly go waltzing up the walk as if nothing had happened. Could she? She considered that for a few minutes, but pride wouldn't agree to that solution. No, she just could not go.

This made her mad all over again and she felt like kicking herself for even considering going back to that sanctimonious group. If they didn't care about her, then let them hang themselves with their ridiculous ideas, they'd see how foolish they were.

She jammed her straw hat on her head and went outside to swear at her garden, and then at the dog next door.

****

Carrie made a pot of coffee which she poured in a carafe to take outside. Some coffee instead of iced tea might be nice.

In preparation for this quilting day, she went out onto the porch and put the table in the corner, out of the way. She set up the quilting frame and placed the chairs and pillows around it. She brought out some coffee cups and set those on the table in the corner.

It seemed everyone arrived at once, except Gert. They were quieter than usual, but with a light in their eyes.

"Has anyone talked to Gert?" Martha asked.

"I wanted to call her, but I chickened out," said Lydia, scrunching her face in embarrassment.

Carrie said, "Well, I didn't call her, but I went over there. I figured she might hang up on me, and it's harder to shut the door in someone's face than it is to hang up on them!"

"Oh, what happened?" Lydia asked.

"Well, she really didn't say much. I told her how I wished she would come today, of course she hasn't, she wasn't very friendly, but she didn't ask me to leave either. I told her it wouldn't be the same if she wasn't here. She asked me if we were going to do this *foolish thing* and I told her we'd decide today. I kind of got the feeling she wanted to come but felt like she had backed herself into a corner. So ..." Carrie held open her hands in a helpless gesture.

The women were silent for a few moments, thinking. There was a lot to think about…Gert's refusal to participate, and the fact that they each had big news, even though each lady thought she was the only one with big news.

They set up the quilt frame, with backing and batting and the completed quilt top. They all got out their thimbles and scissors and thread and set to work.

Each woman was bursting to tell of her experience with the Lord this past week, but they had never discussed really personal things of the Lord. Sure, they talked about church things, and they exchanged prayer requests, they might even have shared a favorite verse over the years, but to actually admit that God had spoken to them? They were afraid.

The time passed slowly as they quilted and said little. After an hour, they took a break for a cup of hot coffee and some of Esther's chocolate cake.

Carrie decided to break the ice. "So, did you guys pray about this? Did you come up with anything?" She looked at each woman expectantly. There was silence. Who would start?

"Well," Lydia said, "I did pray about it and, well, I'm just kind of embarrassed." She breathed a sigh of relief. She had said it. She had admitted it.

"Embarrassed?" Carrie said, "I don't understand. Why are you embarrassed?"

Lydia sighed. "You know, we're not much for talking about these really personal things, I mean not about the Lord, anyway, and I guess I just don't know where to start!"

The others nodded in agreement.

"Then just say it! Who knows what the Lord has been doing this week on our little street. Did you all pray about it?" Carrie asked.

Heads nodded.

"And did you all get an answer?" Carrie asked.

Again heads nodded.

Carrie sighed. "Well, somebody has to start. I already shared with you how God spoke to me, I can't start."

Connie drew a deep breath and straightened her shoulders, "Ok, I'll start. But this is new to me, so …" She looked imploringly at her friends. "The other night I read my Bible, for the first time in a long time. I didn't want to, I was really tired, but it seemed like …" She hesitated, looking nervous, "well, it seemed like the Lord told me to read my Bible." And once said, she quickly looked at each woman's face for any signs of derision, but all she found were smiling, glowing faces, eyes alight.

Connie relaxed and went on, "I read in Ephesians, and some words just jumped up right off the page at me!" Confident now, she spoke firmly, "*And be kind to one another, tenderhearted, forgiving one another, even as God in Christ forgave you.* And I just knew that was the answer to our dilemma about giving the quilt to this lady. *Be kind to one another* … I just knew in my heart it was God telling me what to do." She finished but was unprepared for the reaction.

Each lady had tears running down her cheeks and Carrie said, "Oh Connie, that gives me chills. I believe God spoke to you!"

Now it was Connie's turn for tears as her faith was affirmed by the confidence of her friends.

Then they all started talking at once. They laughed. "Ok, who goes next?" Carrie asked, "I can see that you all have similar things to tell!" She gave a big smile. "I think I better go get a box of tissues!"

Esther said, "I'd like to go next. One night me and Martha were reading our devotions, when the Lord spoke to us through His word. It was amazing, as if He had erected a neon sign in the middle of the living room!" She gasped in awe, "We were reading in Matthew and the verse He used to speak to us was *inasmuch as you did it to one of the least of these, my Brethren, you did it to Me* ... Now that means to me, that whatever I do for them, I do it as unto the Lord, and actually also TO the Lord. It was absolutely amazing!" Esther wiped the tears from her eyes, and looked to Martha, "Wasn't it, Martha?"

Martha was embarrassed. "Well, yes, it was amazing. But," she hesitated, "I didn't see it at first. Esther had to explain it to me. Why doesn't the Lord speak to Me? Why does He speak to Esther?" She ended in tears and cried softly for a small minute.

Connie reached over and patted her hand, and said very quietly, "Martha, maybe it's because you weren't listening."

Martha's head snapped up, at first offended by this assumption on Connie's part. How dare she? Then, she just sank into her chair, "Oh Connie, you don't know how right you are." She reached for another tissue, as tears flowed freely. "Even though I was reading, I wasn't listening. I... well, I just don't like to read the Bible. It seems so boring and I'd rather watch TV."

Carrie touched Martha's arm, "Honey, is this boring? I know God spoke to everyone this week, I can see it your faces. This isn't boring! I have a feeling we are on a spiritual adventure and it's going to be very exciting!" and the excitement shone in Carries eyes.

Martha could only nod, unable to speak.

There was an electric buzz in the air, the Holy Spirit surrounding them, and encouraging them in this new found intimacy. It was almost a tension, although it wasn't stressful, it was exhilarating!

Eleanor nervously played with the hem of her blouse. "I..." she stopped. "I'll tell mine in a minute, someone else go."

"Ok, my turn!" Lydia was excited now. "Carrie, I think you're right! God spoke to me this week too, through Carl!!"

"Through Carl?" the ladies said, almost as one.

"What do you mean?" Carrie asked, excited/.

"Well, I told him about your idea, Carrie, and asked him what he thought. He thought it was a good idea, and then later he came out into the garden and gave me this verse. Said he had read it the other day and couldn't get it out of his mind. It's the verse in Philippians that says," she rummaged through her purse for a slip of paper, "*Let nothing be done through selfish ambition or conceit, but in lowliness of mind let each esteem others better than himself.* And I knew right away, that was God speaking to me. That's what we need to do ... esteem them as better than ourselves. After all, aren't we servants? And aren't we to have a servant's heart?" Lydia looked up over her glasses.

Sniffles could be heard, as each lady began to process all that God had shown them this week. God had been busy on Spring Street, but He had also found willing hearts. The breeze blew gently, ruffling a few curls of graying hair, tinkling a wind chime, blowing a piece of thread to the porch floor. Work on the quilt had come to a complete stop. God's Word was working its way into each lady's heart, doing a work to accomplish God's will in the life of a straying lamb. Prayers which had been prayed for years by a mother for her daughter, were coming to fruition. God was about to launch a mighty work.

Carrie turned to Eleanor, "Eleanor, you said you had something to share too." And Carrie gently touched her hand, to give her encouragement.

Eleanor turned red. "Oh my, I don't know if I should share…" She sighed. "My verse seems so different than what the rest of you got." She wrinkled her brow.

"Well, dear, I think it must be part of the puzzle, don't you?" Carrie asked gently, hoping to encourage their shy, quiet Eleanor to share her heart.

Eleanor spoke very quietly, "My verse was in Isaiah, in chapter 32, and I've thought of nothing else since then, so I know it by heart … *You will be troubled, you complacent women.*" She stopped and looked around uncertainly, wondering how much she could share.

Connie came over to her and put her arm around Eleanor's shoulders. "Go on, tell us the rest. Don't be afraid, Eleanor. We're here for you."

At that, Eleanor's tears flowed freely. She cried for a few minutes before regaining her composure. "Well, it means something to me, but I'm not sure what it means to this situation with those people…" Her voice trailed off. "I don't know when I've ever had nicer friends than you, I mean, well, I guess really, you're my only friends." She stopped and looked around. "The truth is," she took a deep breath as if she was about to jump off the high diving board, "my husband is an alcoholic."

As one, the ladies drew near her, and laid their hands on her in comforting gestures.

"Oh Eleanor, we had no idea," Carrie said, tears flowing again, for the pain and silence her friend had endured. "Can you tell us how the verse meant something to you?"

"Well," Eleanor sniffed, "I have been a complacent woman. I tried to tell myself I was being submissive, but the truth is, I was just complacent. I'm still not entirely clear on what the difference is, but I know ... I knew as soon as I read that verse, that God was telling me that a lot of the trouble in my life was because of my complacency." Eleanor had never spoken so many words at a quilting afternoon before, but she was gaining confidence as she spoke.

"And I don't know how this applies to our project, but I have decided, with the Lord's help, that I want to stop being complacent. And I don't know exactly how to do that, but I'm hoping that if He showed this to me, He'll show me how to do it." Eleanor looked around at her friends, wondering if there was condemnation on their faces, but found only love and compassion.

There were a few minutes of comfortable silence again, as each lady thought about the incredible events of this afternoon. There was a growing feeling of excitement and anticipation.

"Ladies!" Carrie said, smiling big. "I think we have our orders. Don't you?"

Women's voices cried *Oh yes!* and *You better believe it!* and *What do we do now?*

"Well, first of all," the ever practical Martha said, "We have to finish this quilt, so we can start on hers. Gosh, I wish we knew her name."

"And second of all," said Carrie, "I think we need to pray about the specifics, and ask God to guide us through this next step, actually meeting her and how to go about being her friend. Like we said last week, it would be awfully weird if all of sudden we just started showing up at her doorstep."

"I think we should also pray for protection," Lydia said. "The men that live there, well, they don't look all that friendly and there is the possibility that drugs or alcohol may be involved. We want to be wise as well."

They murmured their agreement, as needles were taken up again to finish the quilt.

"God is doing a new work with us and in us." Carrie said. "I know we've never done anything like this before, but maybe we could spend part of our Thursdays praying for her and asking for guidance." She looked around, a little embarrassed, wondering if she had pushed this new intimacy too far.

Softly they agreed, and one by one voices were raised to their Heavenly Father in prayer asking for wisdom, and guidance and hopefully some step by step instructions.

Chapter 7

A week passed. Nothing had happened. The ladies had been excited as they left Carries house last Thursday. They had looked eagerly at the little shabby house on their way home, hoping for a sign of someone so they could wave or say hi or something. But there had been nothing. And it was the same the next day and the day after that. They could see from their various kitchen windows or porches the children playing outside, the adults coming and going. But when they actually passed by the house, there was no one around. The ladies began to wonder if they had been all wrong. Had they somehow misunderstood? What were they supposed to do? They had agreed to meet twice a week, to finish up the blue and white quilt as quickly as possible, so they could start on hers.

Thursday morning, Carrie decided to make a quick trip to the market. She was out of coffee and knew she wouldn't have time to go to the market later. She combed her hair, grabbed her purse, and started out the door. It was a warm, almost summer day, so she walked. The market was only three blocks away.

As she approached the shabby little house, the woman came out her front door, followed by crying children. Carrie could hear yelling, but not what was yelled. The woman went through the front gate and headed in the same direction as the market. Then, the woman turned back to her gate, and took the littlest girl's hand and Carrie heard, "Fine, I'll take you, but shut up!" Carrie sent up a quick prayer. The woman was too far ahead of her to comfortably say Hello, Carrie would have to yell it out. Maybe they would meet in the market.

As the woman stepped off the curb, she suddenly fell. Carrie ran up to her.

"Are you ok? What happened?" Carrie knelt down beside her, reaching for her.

"I'm fine," the woman said angrily. "Leave me alone." The woman brushed Carries hands away.

"Are you sure I can't help you? Are you hurt?" Carrie asked again.

The little girl began crying at the sight of her mommy sitting on the ground.

The woman struggled to her feet, wincing in pain, then suddenly sat down again.

"Damn!" the woman yelled. Carrie could see her ankle swollen up like a small balloon.

"Oh, I think you've sprained your ankle. Let me help you get back home. Or … is your husband home? Can I go get him to carry you?" Carrie asked, taking hold of the little girl's hand.

The woman stared at her in amazement. "Carry me home?" she laughed harshly. "That'd be the day! No, he's asleep and wouldn't take very kindly to being woken up to carry me home." She ended sarcastically.

"OK," Carrie said pleasantly, "then we'll just do it ourselves."

There was no answer, so Carrie reached to help the woman up. They struggled, but finally the woman was hopping on her good foot. They slowly hopped to the shabby little house, as Katie followed and Carrie helped the woman inside to lie down on the couch.

"Now, we better get some ice on that," Carrie said, "I've had a sprained ankle before, and ice is the best thing. Do you have an ice bag, or maybe a Ziploc bag?"

The woman stared at Carrie as if she had lost her mind. "An ice bag? Are you kiddin'?"

"Well, I have one at home, I can get it real quick. Do you have ice?"

"What's the deal? Why are you bein' so nice to me?" the woman narrowed her eyes.

"Well, you're hurt and I just want to help, that's all." Carrie held up her hands, helplessly. "Do you mind?"

"No, I guess not," the woman muttered.

For the first time, Carrie noticed the surroundings. Five children stared at her as though she weren't real. The rooms she could see, the living room and the kitchen, were dirty. Dishes were stacked high, garbage overflowed the trash can, ashtrays were filled to capacity, newspapers and magazines littered the floor. Some of the magazines made Carries face turn red. Dirty dishes were scattered around the living room, and some clothes were in piles, as if someone had tried to do laundry, and then thought better of it.

"I'll be right back," Carrie said as she went out the door.

"Yeah, right." The woman cursed under her breath.

As she hurried home, Carrie prayed, "Father, thank you for this opportunity! Help me to do my best for her, and please keep the door open!"

Carrie reached her house, went for the ice bag and filled it with ice. Then she grabbed a few small pillows from the couch. She took five seconds to phone Lydia and quickly tell her what happened, and that she should phone the other girls to pass on the news, pray and be quick about it. She hurried out the door and back to the shabby little house.

"Hello? Can I just come in? I don't want to make you get up and open the door." Carrie called from the front step. She peered in through the screen door.

"Yeah, come on in."

"Here, I brought some ice in the bag, I wasn't sure if you had any. Can you lift your leg just a little; I'll put these pillows under it. It'll be more comfortable." Carrie helped her lift her leg and adjust the pillows. "Is that ok?"

"It's fine."

"What the hell is goin' on out here?" A voice thundered from the bedroom door. Carrie jumped, frightened. "Who are you?" he yelled rudely.

"Shut up!" The woman lying on the couch yelled right back. "I sprained my ankle, she's just helpin' me out."

A large man, in jeans but no shirt came stumbling into the living room. He was bleary eyed, and had hair sticking up in all directions. The odor of cigarettes and stale alcohol emanated from him. "Git outta my way!" he yelled, although there was no one in his way. "What's goin' on here?"

The children, who had been in the doorway, skedaddled into the bedroom. They knew better than to hang around for this. Carrie, frightened, tried to make herself feel brave. And before she knew it, she boldly went to the man, with her hand out, "Hi! I'm Carrie Barrister, I live a few houses down the street. I was going to the market, about the same time as your wife, and she fell and hurt her ankle. I just helped her home that's all." She smiled brightly the whole time, as if she was meeting a new member of her church.

He just stared at her in disbelief. He automatically shook her hand, not knowing what else to do.

"Uh, thanks." Some manners crawled out from somewhere in his foggy mind.

"Well, now, is there anything else I can do before I go home?" Carrie looked around, and then went over to the couch. "You know, I never did tell you my name, it's Carrie, what's yours?" She smiled.

"I'm Liz. He's Dennis, and he ain't my husband." She said, still not comprehending what was going on.

"I'm glad to meet both of you. I'm sorry I didn't come over sooner and introduce myself! I'll drop by later to see if I can help you with some lunch. Oh, you were on your way to the market! Can I go and get your groceries for you?"

"No, you can't. I got a food stamp card, and you can't use it, only I can." Liz sighed. They were out of just about everything, not even any toilet paper.

"Well then, just tell me what you need, and I'll loan it to you. You can pay me back in food when you can walk." She reached in her bag for a pen and paper and got ready to write.

Liz looked alarmed. "Oh, I couldn't do that. Just forget it, I'll figure it out."

Carrie was quiet for a moment and then said, "Ok, well, I'll see you this afternoon. Do you have enough ice to keep on there for a while? Don't get up now; you need to stay off of it."

Dennis and Liz both looked at Carrie as if she were from another world. And in truth, wasn't she? They had no idea what to make of kindness from a pure heart. They were so used to violence and harshness that kindness had become unknown to them.

"I'm sure I'm fine." Liz muttered. "Oh, and uh, thanks." She looked away, embarrassed.

"No problem! I'll see you later today. Bye." Carrie couldn't get away fast enough. What an awful place! And those poor children, five of them living in that tiny house. The smell had been enough to turn her stomach, the dirt and the mess, how could people live like that? Well, maybe that's the way they were brought up; perhaps they didn't know any better. *Lord, thank you for giving me this opportunity to serve You. Is it wrong to want to serve You and at the same time make up for what I did? I know You say I'm forgiven, but…I sure don't feel forgiven. Please let me be useful to Liz and her family.* She hurried to the market, bought her coffee and hurried home.

Chapter 8

Each lady arrived at Carrie's house with a box of food. Lydia had done her work well, explaining how Liz had been on her way to the market, and had been unable to buy her groceries. They all opened their cupboards and their pantries and gave to overflowing.

Carrie stood back and eyed all the boxes sitting on the porch in the corner. "My goodness! How am I going to carry all that over there?" she asked.

They had each been so enthusiastic in their desire to serve the Lord and help the woman down the street, they hadn't thought about the reality of little Carrie carrying six cardboard boxes of canned food, cereal, frozen meat, and cartons of milk.

"Oh my, I hadn't thought that far." Esther crinkled her forehead. "Should we all go with you?" the thought suddenly came to her.

The ladies all nodded in agreement. They were all dying to get inside that house.

"I think we better sit down and figure this out. They weren't all that crazy about me being there. I'm not sure what they'd do if we all trooped in, with boxes overflowing. We don't want to offend them," Carrie said.

The quilt was momentarily forgotten as they sat down to discuss this. Various solutions were offered. Maybe Carrie could take a box every few days, and just say it was some extra, and could they use it? That idea was discarded as too phony. Maybe one night their husbands could quietly drop the food on the porch and it would be there in the morning for them. That idea was discarded as none of the husbands had the same schedule, and they all couldn't get together on one night. And besides, Eleanor knew her husband wouldn't help.

"OK, we're not getting anywhere. Let's pray about it and work on the quilt. Maybe the Lord will inspire us while we're quilting," Esther said. And so, they gathered around the quilt frame, and each prayed a short prayer for wisdom. And work on the quilt resumed. For the most part they were quiet as each tried to listen for the voice of the Lord.

****

Liz lay on the couch, in considerable pain. No position was comfortable, and the ice had melted. She had asked Dennis to make some ice, which surprisingly enough, he had done. After Carrie left he had calmed down, and was for once actually almost pleasant. The kids were hungry and getting cranky. She was hungry herself. She couldn't remember a time when things had ever been so bad. There was literally no food in the house, except half a bottle of ketchup and a little pickle relish in an old jar. She remembered hearing stories of people during the Depression making soup with hot water and ketchup and wondered if she could do the same thing. But the truth was, she could do nothing, she could only lie on the couch and wait for water to freeze.

Dennis came in and sat down next to her on the floor.

"Liz, we've got to figure out something to do with Doug's kids. I don't think he's coming back." Dennis ran his fingers through his hair. He was more like the Dennis she had fallen in love with than he had been in a long time. "We can't even feed our own kids, let alone his."

"I know," she said quietly. "I don't know what to do though, do you know where he is?"

"I have no idea where that sonofa, no, I don't know. I've looked everywhere he could be. I think the jerk just took off and left his kids with us. It's been weeks." Dennis sighed, "Man, I could use a beer."

"Well, there's no beer, there's not even any food. So, get over it," Liz said irritated. "Figure out what we're gonna feed these kids, then you can think about beer."

"Chill out! I know, I know." Dennis yelled. Then he sighed. "Ok, ok, this isn't what I want to talk about, we've got to do something about Doug's kids." He paused, "I think I'm gonna call my mom to come and get them."

Liz looked at him in surprise. He hadn't spoken to his parents in years. They'd probably drop dead if they heard his voice on the phone. "Your mom?" she asked, one eyebrow raised.

"You got any better ideas?" he asked roughly.

Liz thought, man he must really be shook up if he's calling his mom. But she only shook her head. "Go ahead, call her, but what if she won't come and get them?"

Dennis got up from the floor. "Then we'll turn the kids over to the Welfare department and they can find foster homes for them. There's no other choice. I'm goin' to the market and use the phone."

****

Thoughts were stirring in Martha's mind and heart, so quietly and softly she could barely make them out. She continued quilting, not knowing yet what to say. She strained to hear that still small voice ... what was He saying? Then her fingers stopped and she just sat there, listening. She closed her eyes and listened to the voice of the Lord speaking to her heart. This had never happened to her before, she was amazed. Connie was right, this was exciting. Much better than watching TV.

"I know what to do!" Martha said excitedly, "It just came to me, just now while I was quilting. I … I heard the Lord's voice!" she was smiling broadly and her face was glowing. "Connie, you were right!!! When I listen, I can hear Him."

Work stopped on the quilt as the ladies waited eagerly for Martha to tell them what the Lord had said to her.

"Well, I'll try to explain it. It was more of an impression than actual words. But I do know it was the Lord! Ok, I was reminded of Jericho, where they walked around and around and the walls fell down? They weren't unobtrusive, they didn't go during the night, they didn't worry about hurting feelings, they just went and did what the Lord told them to do. Now, He's told us to give them this food, and I think we should just, all of us, walk over there and give them the whole kit and caboodle. And tell them it's from the Lord." She sat back and looked into their faces.

"Oh, I knew He would give us the answer. That's exactly what we should do." Connie said, and the other ladies all quickly agreed. Yes, this was the answer from the Lord. He says Ask for wisdom and it will be given to you, and it was. Now they were all talking at once. Should they go now? Finish their work on the quilt? What should they do?

Martha held up her hand. "I think, since He gave us the wisdom now, we should just go. Don't you?" She looked around uncertainly.

"Absolutely! We're such ninnies sometimes." Carrie laughed. "Let me go get some more ice for her foot. Oh and by the way, her name is Liz, and we'll get going. Put your needles away, ladies. We're marching!"

Chapter 9

Alice Oster was making lunch for her husband Bud. Bud had retired two years ago and had never really found anything for himself to do, except get in her way. She had taken care of him and this house for thirty years, and now he seemed to think Alice no longer knew how to do anything. He was making her crazy. Right now he was in the living room, working the crossword puzzle. But any minute now he was going to tell her the clothes on the line were probably dry, she just knew it. She put lunch on the kitchen table, opened the back door for a breeze and called Bud to come and eat.

He lumbered into the kitchen. "Don't you think those clothes are dry by now? I'd hate for it to rain on your dry clean clothes." He smiled.

"Thank you, dear," Alice said dryly, "I'd never have thought of it myself."

Bud was a heavy man, with a gray crew cut. He had a crew cut in the Navy and had never seen any reason to change. At least he still had his hair, which was more than he could say about a lot of his friends. He was a happy man with a smiling face. It was hard to get mad at Bud, but Alice was getting the hang of it, although she hadn't ever said anything yet. She was as small and thin as Bud was large and heavy. Her blond hair also had gray in it, but it was harder to see. She had kept it long and wound up in a bun on her head. She still wore housedresses, never having acquired the habit of wearing jeans like so many of her friends. They were old fashioned people with old fashioned values and they were happy. If only Bud would find something to do with his time.

They sat down to their lunch of tuna fish sandwiches, potato salad and cantaloupe spears. Alice had made some coffee. Bud said a prayer of thanks and they began to eat their lunch.

The open window let in the spring breezes which were fresh and cool. Their dog, Molly, scratched at the screen door to be let in for her lunch. Alice got up to let her in, when the phone rang. "I'll get it, Bud, I'm already up."

Alice opened the screen door at the same time as she reached for the phone on the wall. "Hello?" The screen door slammed and Molly ran in.

"Hey, Mom? Is that you?" Dennis asked.

"Dennis?" Alice's knees went weak. Bud jumped up from the table and went to her side, holding her up. He mouthed, "Dennis?" She nodded and he smiled heavenward. "Dennis! I'm so glad to hear your voice. Where are you? Are you here, in town?" She couldn't get the questions out fast enough.

"Ma, slow down. No, I'm not there. Listen, I need a favor. Some help with Doug's kids. Are you there?"

"What do you mean *help with Doug's kids*? Where is he? Where's Rachel?" Alice suddenly became very frightened and held onto Bud even tighter. His face was close to hers as he tried to listen to the phone at the same time. Alice was holding the phone away from her ear a tad so Bud could hear too.

"I thought you knew…" Dennis swore to himself. It was just like Doug to not even tell their mother his wife had died. "Rachel, well, she died in a car accident last year. I thought Doug told you." Bud had his arm around Alice now, as she was wilting. Tears ran down her face.

"No, son, I didn't know. Oh I'm so sorry, I'm…" tears choked her voice, "I … what's wrong with Doug? He's not …" Her voice trailed off, she couldn't even think the words.

"Doug? He's just a jerk. He's gone off and left his kids with me an' Liz. We can barely feed our own, let alone his. I got nowhere else to turn. If you and Pop can't come get 'em, I gotta turn 'em over to the Welfare department for foster homes." Dennis sighed. He hated talking to his parents, let alone asking them for help.

"Now, Dennis, don't you dare turn those children over to Welfare. You just tell us where you are, and we'll come and get them." Alice was suddenly strength personified, now that her dear grandchildren, whom she hadn't seen in far too long, were involved. "We'll leave today!" her voice was firm. Bud was next to her, nodding his head. He reached over to get a pencil and paper to write down an address.

Dennis gave them the address with some directions. "Ok, son, we'll be there as soon as we can. This is not a short trip you know." Alice was all business now. "We'll just be there as soon as we can get there. Are you alright? How is Liz? Her parents miss her so much."

Dennis sighed. He knew his mother would be like this. "We're fine Ma, Liz sprained her ankle this morning, but she'll be fine. We're all fine, except I can't feed five kids. I'll see you tomorrow. Bye." He knew from experience that if he didn't cut the call short he'd be there all day talking about all kinds of stupid things with his mother. He'd die before he got old and acted like them.

"Oh Bud!" Alice melted into her husband's strong arms, tears freely flowing. Molly sat at her feet, sweeping her tail across the linoleum, her eyes warm and loving. She knew something was wrong.

"Come on now, Alice, let's hurry and finish this lunch and get going." Bud led her across the kitchen. His mind was racing as he made plans. They needed to leave today. They'd have to spend the night at least twice, maybe three nights. They ate automatically, not knowing what it was they ate. In her mind, Alice was planning for children in the house again. School clothes, lunch boxes, pajamas, laundry, oh, the laundry. Both were quiet as myriad plans were made in their minds. Their lives were changing and would never be the same.

"Bud!" Alice suddenly got up. "I've got to call Laura MacKenzie. She'll want to know we heard about Liz!"

"Yes, of course, go ahead. Be quick though, I'm going to look over the car." His mind was already on such things as oil and spark plugs needed for the long drive ahead.

Alice quickly dialed Laura's number. "Laura? This is Alice, I have such good news for you!" Alice wasn't wasting time on small talk.

In the next town, Laura suddenly sat down on a kitchen chair. "Alice! What happened?"

Alice gave a small laugh, "Laura, Dennis just called! We're going to pick up Doug's children. Evidently he's taken off and left his kids with Dennis and Liz. Oh, Laura … he told me Rachel died last year in a car accident." Alice teared up. "And they can't take care of Doug's kids anymore. He said, Laura ... he said they could barely afford to feed their own kids, let alone Doug's." Alice could hear Laura sniffle, "Isn't that wonderful news? Liz is ok, they have children. Laura!! You have grandchildren!"

Laura asked, "How many children, Alice? And you got her address? What is it?"

"Well, I'm not sure how many children. He said he couldn't afford to feed five children, that's all I know. The last time I heard from Doug, he had two children, Trevor who was two and Cindy who three and a half so ... maybe they have three children. I just don't know, I'm sorry!" Alice knew how hard this was for Laura.

"Alice, please let me go with you. I want to see Liz so bad, and those babies I've never held. Can you squeeze me in?" Liz was practically begging. She wanted to go so bad, she could taste it. Her mind was already packing an overnight bag. Her arms ached to hold sweet and precious grandbabies and see her daughter again, in the flesh.

Alice paused for a minute, "Well, of course, dear, you can go with us if you want to." Alice quickly gained understanding, "I do understand, it was selfish of me not to invite you in the first place. Just be ready, Bud's rarin' to go!"

They quickly said goodbye, knowing they would have plenty of time to talk on the long trip.

Laura hurried into the bedroom, knelt down and reached under the bed for her small suitcase. As she was on her knees she heard the Lord's voice.

I want you to stay at home.

She jerked her head up. What?

I want you to stay at home.

Tears filled Laura's eyes. Why Lord? She asked in her heart.

It's not time yet. Elizabeth will come home to you, but it's not time yet. I still have work to do in her heart, and quite frankly, my darling Laura, you will only get in the way. I want you here, at home, praying.

"Oh Lord, how can you ask me to do this?" Laura prayed and cried, "For so long, I've prayed, I've wanted to see and hold my daughter again. And how long I've wanted grandchildren, and now I know they're here, I want them so badly!" She leaned her head on the side of the bed, soaking the quilt with her tears.

My grace is sufficient for you.

Laura was long practiced at obedience, but this was asking more of her than she was able to do. This was her daughter and her newly found grandchildren her arms and heart ached for.

She took a deep breath and prayed, "Lord, I don't like what You've told me, but ..." she paused, "nevertheless, Thy will be done." She crumpled to the floor, letting the sobs come. And in seconds, she was covered with a blanket of peace and grace, as the Lord poured out His mercy on her.

I love you, Laura and I love Elizabeth even more than you can imagine or understand. I also understand your mother's heart more than you do, and I want you to get some things together for Elizabeth, things that will show her that you still love her.

Laura breathed a "Thank you, Lord!" and flew to get a cardboard box. Think, think, Laura. What are you going to put in it? Ok, the box was on the kitchen table. Laura knew how Elizabeth had loved cosmetics and lotions. She put in her new bottle of Vanilla scented lotion, brand new bottles of a nice shampoo and conditioner. Elizabeth had beautiful hair. Laura had gone shopping yesterday and bought some new shirts, which she now put into the box. They had always been nearly the same size, and Laura was sure they would fit. Oh what a blessing that she had gone shopping yesterday. At the time, she wondered at all the things she had bought. It was completely unlike her, she was a thrifty person. But God had known, and now she was prepared to send her daughter a box of things she loved. The fact that Elizabeth wasn't deserving never entered her mind, she simply poured her mother love into that box. Some nail polish and new cosmetics went in, a new nightie, a pair of slippers, two packages of cookies for those sweet grandbabies she had never met.

When the box was full, Liz had another idea and asked, "Lord, is this ok?" Sensing no disagreement from Him, she slipped $200 in an envelope and hid it in the bottom. Hopefully Elizabeth would find it before Dennis did. She didn't know why she put in the money, but she did. God knew. Quickly she closed the box; she could see Bud and Alice 's car pulling in the driveway.

"Laura! You're not ready?" Alice was incredulous. She had half expected to meet Laura on the road.

"Alice, as I was packing, the Lord spoke to my heart and told me this wasn't the right time." Traces of tears were on Laura's face, and Alice knew how hard this was for her. "So I packed this box for her, would you take it to her? And tell her I love her, and give kisses and hugs to our sweet grandbabies? Please?" Laura's voice was cracking with emotion.

Laura handed over the box. Alice got out of the car and hugged Laura, and at the same time slipped her a piece of paper with Elizabeth's address on it.

"Oh thank you!" Laura held her hand for just a moment, "I'll be praying. You have a safe and good trip! Bye." They pulled out and were on their way.

Chapter 10

Carrie led the way, carrying her cardboard box and right behind her, like so many ducks in a row, came all the other quilting ladies with their own boxes. It was only a few houses down the block, but they felt conspicuous. They had never been to visit this family and now all of sudden here they were, descending upon them en masse!

Gert peeked out her living room window, through the curtains. She didn't want to be seen, but neither could she believe her own eyes. What did those foolish women think they were doing? All of them carrying a box, and good grief, there was Connie, carrying an economy size package of toilet paper. Right out in public, for goodness sakes! Well, they wouldn't catch her making a fool of herself for the world to see. No sirree, she was safe in her own home, where no one could laugh at her. Gert Gilbert had more sense than those silly women.

"Knock, knock! Oh, please don't get up!" Carrie pushed her way through the screen door. "Hi, Liz, how are you doing? Oh I hope you don't mind," Carrie continued before Liz could respond, "I brought some friends with just a little bit of extra stuff for your kitchen; since I know you couldn't get to the store this morning."

Liz stared in amazement as five women crowded into her small, dirty living room, each carrying a box. She felt suddenly ashamed at the condition of her house. These were real women, who kept house and cooked. She bet they never lay on the couch in the middle of the day.

"Liz, I want to introduce you to these ladies…" and Carrie named off each lady as she pointed her out. "We got together a few things we thought you might be out of and …

well, to be honest, Liz, God gave us the idea to bring this food over to you, and here it is! These things are not from us, they are from God." Carrie looked at Liz carefully to see what reaction there would be to that piece of news.

Tears slipped down Liz's cheeks. God sent them food? How could that be? She had nothing to do with God at all. Why would He send her food?

"I don't understand." Liz croaked, "Why would God send you over here with food? He doesn't have anything to do with me." She wiped her cheek with the back of her hand. The children stared from the kitchen doorway, unable to comprehend these new things which were happening.

"Oh, Liz, He has quite a bit to do with you. He loves you, why else would He send you food, when He knew you were out?" Carrie patted her shoulder. "Ladies?" She motioned with her head toward the kitchen.

The ladies set the boxes on the kitchen table, there was much hustle and bustle as purses were set down and then quickly picked back up at the sight of the dirty table. The children scampered to the bedroom door where they watched in fascination.

"We prayed for you because you were hurt today. Don't you ever pray, Liz?" Carrie asked on her way to the kitchen.

Liz snorted. "Not in this lifetime, I don't! God doesn't give a rip about me!"

"Well," said Carrie, "Obviously He does, or we wouldn't be here." She smiled her warm smile and went into the kitchen. *Oh thank you Lord, again, for this opportunity!*

All the ladies began to open cupboard doors, and the refrigerator to find new homes for this food. At the unexpected light forced into their little cubbyholes, roaches skittered into the cracks. There were a few mouse droppings in the corner.

"Carrie!" Connie whispered, "These cupboards are filthy! We can't put food in here. What should we do?" Martha looked on, waiting for an answer as well. As much as she had wanted to come here to see the inside of this house, now she was slightly sick to her stomach.

Carrie thought for a minute. If they pushed too far, they could offend or even embarrass Liz. They had to act like everything was just fine; they couldn't burst in here like housekeeping storm troopers.

"We'll just have to put the food away the way things are. We can't embarrass her. They haven't died yet from eating food out of this cupboard." Carrie's voice trailed off.

"Okay." Whispers came uncertainly. And soon the shelves were groaning with canned goods, and jars, bags of cookies and boxes of cereal. The old refrigerator was stuffed to capacity with eggs, milk, butter, and some fresh fruit and vegetables, some peanut butter and jelly, some bologna and cheese, some mayonnaise and mustard. The freezer gulped when it realized what a job it had to do with a few roasts, and packages of hamburger, and pork chops. This kitchen had never seen such bounty. On the table sat laundry soap, toilet paper, some cleaning supplies and some bath soap, even a bottle of bubble bath.

As each new item came into view, the children's eyes grew wide. They had had no breakfast and they were hungry.

"Liz, would it be ok if we made you all some sandwiches? Would that be a help to you?" Carrie asked, from the kitchen doorway, "We've about got everything put away, and I could even start dinner for you if you want. You'll probably have to be off that foot for a few days."

"Sure, whatever makes you happy." Liz seemed disgruntled, but there were also a few tears in her eyes. She was quite overwhelmed, nothing like this had ever happened before, and she didn't know what to think. God? No, they had to be on some charity mission for their stupid church or something. Or maybe it was some sort of scam, and they would expect her to pay for all of this. But, then she remembered the true kindness of Carrie in the street, and knew that wasn't the case.

Soon the children were happily munching on peanut butter and jelly sandwiches. In one hand they held the sandwich, and a glass of milk in the other. They were asking no questions; it looked like they could eat as much as they wanted!

Martha brought a plate out to Liz. "Hi, Liz, my name is Martha. My sister Esther is still in the kitchen. I'm glad to meet you." Martha smiled warmly and handed her a plate with a bologna and cheese sandwich, an apple that had been cut up and a few chocolate chip cookies.

Warily, Liz took the plate. "Uh, thanks." She took a bite of the sandwich. And tears filled her eyes, again. When was the last time someone had fixed her a sandwich? It had been her mom. This delicious lunch was dredging up memories Liz would just as soon not remember.

Connie handed the kids some cut up apple slices, and she held little Dougie on her lap, feeding him some peeled pieces of apple. He gurgled and kicked his feet and leaned back in Connie's arms. His little tummy was full for the first time he could remember – if he had been able to reason such thoughts. He just knew he was happy. He sucked on his apple and held another piece in his other hand. Connie held him close, what a little sweetie he was. Well, he would be if he could have had a clean diaper. She set him on the floor.

"Liz? Hi, I'm Connie. This little guy over here needs a clean diaper and I'd be happy to do it for you, if you tell me where everything is." Connie smiled, "I have two boys myself, and so I'm no stranger to changing boy's diapers!" She didn't mention that her boys were in Junior High School.

"Well, there might be a few clean diapers in the kid's room, probably near the window." Liz seemed embarrassed. She knew what that room looked like, and now that real women were in her house, she was very embarrassed. However, Connie made no mention of it, and came out with a clean diaper and a box of baby wipes. A few more tears crept down Liz's cheeks. She was seeing unconditional love in action and didn't know what to make of it.

Eleanor came quietly to Liz's couch. "Hi Liz. I'm, well, my name is Eleanor." Her voice was very quiet and timid. "I thought I'd get you some more ice. Is that ok?"

Liz looked at this shy little woman and felt a kinship with her that was puzzling. This little brown mouse of a woman; what would Liz have in common with her? But Liz smiled through her tears and thanked her. Then she smelled pork chops frying and could hear a potato peeler going full tilt. The tears came now, unchecked. Oh what was going on? Why was this happening? Was it a dream?

"Oh honey, what's wrong?" Carrie came out of the kitchen with toilet paper in her arms, on her way to the bathroom. She sat down on the floor next to Liz and took her in her arms. In some small way she was loving and ministering to her own Abby and making up for her wicked past all at the same time. The tears flowed and Carrie held her and let her cry. When had she ever had someone to hold her as she cried? Carrie reached over and opened the toilet paper, giving a length to Liz so she could blow her nose and wipe her tears.

****

Dennis stepped across the threshold and stared in amazement at a houseful of middle aged ladies and a crying Liz. What the heck was going on? There was food cooking, he could smell it. The children's faces were smeared with peanut butter and jelly. Although he couldn't put it into words, the atmosphere of his house had changed. The love of God had crept in on the feet of five slightly gray haired ladies he had never seen before in his life. Except for that one, who was sitting on the floor. She was the one who had brought Liz home this morning. None of the ladies had noticed him, so he backed out of the doorway. No way was he going to deal with five women, not after talking to his mother. Once was enough thank you very much! He ran his fingers through his hair and hurried down the street.

And for the first time, he noticed the other houses on his street. They were somewhat shabby, as was his, but they were clean. The lawns were watered and green. There were flowers growing in window boxes. There were clothes blowing in the breeze from a clothesline. Sidewalks were swept clean and there were no weeds growing out of the cracks. None of that could be said for his house. And a glimmer of shame began to grow inside him. He began to feel some guilt. He had not been a man, like the men who lived in these houses. No doubt they worked every day. He only worked when he absolutely had to. Working was for chumps. He couldn't have put these thoughts into words; his mind was dimmed by years of alcohol and drug abuse. Nevertheless, the impressions were strong. So intent was he on these unfamiliar thoughts, he bumped into a man turning into one of those houses. An older man, dressed in work clothes, which were dusty from a days work.

"Oh! Excuse me!" Joe said. "I'm sorry, I didn't even see you!" Joe stepped back. "Say, don't you live down the street?"

Dennis looked at Joe and saw respectability and hard work. "Yeah, I live down there." Dennis couldn't look him in the eye.

Joe held out his hand, "Well, I'm Joe Barrister, I live right here with my wife Carrie."

Dennis eyed his hand. In his world, men didn't shake hands. But he took it and shook hands with Joe, and with it came a feeling of his own respectability. He was a man, shaking hands with another man. He felt like he'd been let into a private club.

"Dennis Oster." And he looked Joe right in the eye. Dennis stood a little taller.

"Good to meet ya! Where do you work?" It was the first question every man asked of another man.

Instantly, Dennis was shorter. Dennis didn't belong in the club, he didn't work. He had no identification in the world except as a man who drank, smoked pot, watched TV and lived off his girlfriend's food stamps and welfare check. This Joe would never understand that.

Dennis hurried off, not even bothering to answer. He owed nothing to that Joe, whoever he was. His wife was a busybody and Joe was probably the same way. Dennis needed a drink, and the trick was to find it without having to pay for it. He needed a lot of drinks, to wash away these new and very uncomfortable feelings.

****

Martha had brought over an old pair of crutches and loaned them to Liz. She had even scared up an Ace bandage and wrapped her ankle handily. Liz limped out to the kitchen.

She opened the cupboard doors and found the shelves full. Similarly, the fridge and freezer were full. On the stove, sat her old dented fry pan full of pork chops, and a pot with a lid on it, full of mashed potatoes. There were little notes 'Add a little milk and warm up' and 'Turn on med high and fry again till warm through'. One pot held some green beans with bits of bacon in it. She looked at the table, oh it was so dirty. She felt her cheeks flame with embarrassment. She got a sponge, squirted soap on it and scrubbed the life out of that table. It was difficult going, standing on one foot, and keeping the crutch's handy, but finally she was satisfied. And the table shone as if new. Encouraged by the result, she took out plates and silverware and set the table for dinner. They would have a real dinner tonight. Dennis never came back from the market; she had no idea where he was. But she and the children would dine in style. Liz heated the food according to the directions left for her and brought the children in to eat. Their eyes were wide. This was a new experience.

"Oh Mommy, this looks good!" Katie breathed. "Can we have all we want?"

"Yes, sweetie, you can have all you want." Liz was happier than she had been in a long while. Perhaps Carrie was right, and God did care about her.

Liz cut up pork chops for little hands, spooned mashed potatoes onto mismatched Melmac plates and poured cups of milk for all of them.

Silence reigned at the little kitchen table. Little mouths were busy chewing and swallowing, and in general completely enjoying a feast. A whole big lunch, and now this whole big nice dinner? They had better eat while it lasted.

Liz was suddenly filled with energy and thoughts of cooking every day and making sure the house was clean all the time. Why, women did that every day, why couldn't she? She looked around her kitchen. She had never noticed before, but it seemed like there was a lot she could do to fix this place up. A few plants here and there, maybe a little red checked curtain over the sink. That wouldn't be hard. She could even wash these windows; she could remember her mom washing windows with vinegar water and newspapers. If she washed that throw rug, it would brighten up considerably and cheer up the whole room.

Then she noticed the children. Oh, they were so dirty. Their little faces were smudged with dirt, and their hair was sticking up and fuzzy in the back. She had not brushed their hair for so very long. Then she remembered the bottle of bubble bath!! That's it! They would all have bubble baths tonight. She was so excited she could hardly stand it.

"Everybody done?" Liz looked at empty plates and satisfied little faces. "How would you all like to take a bubble bath?" The children were all afraid this was going to disappear, but at the same time ... a Bubble Bath!!!!

Smiles broke out on their faces, and Trevor, who remembered bubble baths from when his mom had been alive, cheered. "Yea! Bubble baths!"

Liz herded all the children into the bathroom, wondering how many she could fit in the tub at once. Then suddenly she stopped. Oh my, this bathtub was filthy. She again felt shame and embarrassment. Those women had seen her house looking like this and they had never said a word, nor even made any indication they noticed. She realized they had treated her like one of themselves, as a real woman who was worthy of respect. But she wasn't worthy of respect, she had failed her little family terribly. She had neglected them.

"Trevvie ... do Aunt Lizzie a favor. Run into the kitchen and get me the can of Comet and a sponge ... and the big green pitcher." Her voice rose as he tore out of the bathroom. Carefully she settled herself on the floor, anxious to get this tub cleaned. She was barely even noticing the pain in her foot anymore.

The tub was scrubbed to within an inch of its life, and soon gleeful voices could be heard amid mountains of bubbles. Little belly laughs as bubbles were heaped on wet heads and shaped into cones and spikes. They took up handfuls of bubbles and blew them at each other, laughing the whole time. Liz took a handful of bubbles and blew them, too. How long had it been since she had played with her children? It seemed a lifetime ago.

Liz found a couple reasonably clean towels and wrapped up little wet, naked children. Their little cheeks were red with the warmth of the bath, and the fun in the bubbles.

"Now sit here and let me go find you some clean jammies." Liz limped off to the bedroom, only to be met with the disaster of dirty clothes, diapers and sheets. "Oh Lord, help me!" she breathed, not even realizing that for the first time in a long time, it was a genuine prayer, rather than a curse word.

Opening the dresser drawers, she found plenty of clean clothes and jammies. Now, why in the world had they gone about in dirty clothes, when a wealth of clean ones was readily available? Thankful for them now, she hurried out to dress these now sweet-smelling babies.

Half an hour later, she lay back on the couch. She was exhausted. The children clean from head to toe and wearing clean jammies, ran and played. They played in that silly three-year-old way, falling down on purpose, then rolling and laughing. They pretended to scare each other and then screamed with laughter. They had already forgotten the dismal past and were totally into the moment. This was now, and it was happy and joyous, and carried a full tummy along with it. They cared about nothing else.

Chapter 11

Bud and Alice pulled into the Holiday Inn. Tired and weary, they checked into a small room with one bed. They had eaten hamburgers in the car, not even stopping to eat a decent meal in a restaurant. Alice had helped Bud eat as he drove, wrapping his hamburger in the paper it came in, and handing him French fries. They were both tired beyond belief, and immediately got into bed.

"Bud, I'm so excited to see those sweet babies." Alice murmured sleepily. "I hope I can even get to sleep. What time do you think we'll be there?"

She was met by snoring. And, a few seconds later, she too, was asleep.

****

Joe and Carrie snuggled into their queen size bed, covered by a Log Cabin quilt, in lovely muted shades of blue, red and cream.

They were talking quietly about the day's adventures with Liz and Dennis.

"Carrie, where does he work? I ran into him today and asked him where he worked – but he just took off. Couldn't understand it …" Joe asked, puzzled.

"I don't know," Carrie said, "They never mentioned if he was working, or looking for a job. But they literally had no food in that house! Joe, those babies were hungry!" Carrie was still appalled by the poverty she had encountered that day. "I mean, there have been times when we didn't have much to eat, but I always made sure everyone ate and we never went hungry."

"Yes, you did!" Joe gave her a little squeeze. "You always kept the stew pot going!"

And slowly they drifted off to sleep.

****

At dinner that night, Connie was telling Ron about all the things that God was doing in their quilting group, and about taking the food over the Liz's house. He had looked at her as if she had lost her mind.

"What in the world do you want to do that for? They look plenty healthy to me, let them go to work. I work hard enough as it is, without you giving our food away to perfect strangers!" He said, irritated.

Connie sat stunned, unable to think of anything to say. Never in a million years would she have guessed he'd react this way.

They finished dinner in silence. Their two boys didn't say anything else either. Dinner was normally a fairly noisy event in their household, but tonight anger and resentment had crept in.

Later that night, Connie went upstairs to their bedroom, worried. She took her Bible with her, and spent some minutes in the Word and in prayer for her husband.

****

"Esther, hurry! I'm so tired, but I want to watch this before we go to bed!" Martha was dressed in her faded flowered nightgown, with a comfy chenille robe over it. She was wearing her favorite soft blue slippers. "It's the one where Tim glues the table to his head!!" Martha laughed in anticipation. She gave a gentle kick to Ralph who was winding around her feet causing static electricity.

"Ok, I'm here. Sorry ... I just wanted to get that last dish put away in the fridge. Ok, turn it on!" Esther was similarly dressed. They were watching today's episode of Home Improvement.

The clicked on the VCR, pushed Play and were transported to Detroit, Michigan.

****

"E'nor!" Alfred spoke to her, on her way to crawl into bed. "Tomorrow shtop at the liquor shtore. I'm out." His words were slurred. He took another sip. There was only enough whiskey to last until she got home from work.

Eleanor stopped at his words. She had a feeling that would be the exact wrong thing to do. But she had been doing it for so long; she didn't know how to say no. Then, the thought came to her, that she didn't need to figure it out, He would tell her how to handle the situation. She smiled, and patted Alfred on the shoulder. "Good night, honey."

Alfred looked up in surprise, through half closed eyes. How long had it been since she had touched him, let alone called him *honey*? And off he floated on one of his alcoholic breezes.

****

Lydia and Carl, on their way upstairs to bed, shut off the lights as they went. Carl locked the door and lowered the blinds. They had just finished a cup of tea, spending some time in their Bibles, and praying together over the different people in their life, and many minutes over the poor little family at the end of the block.

Lydia turned back the blankets, and opened the window. They loved to sleep with the feel of a soft breeze on their skin. It seemed to be a breeze of blessings, if blessings could have a feel to them. Quietly they crawled under the covers, turning to each other as one. Carl drew her into his arms. They loved each other with a passion that thirty-two years of marriage had never diminished.

****

Gert lay in her bed, alone, staring at the ceiling. Her room was dark, but the moon shone through the window, casting shadows on the wall. She had seen all her friends going to the little shabby house, and doggone it all if she hadn't felt left out. This feeling was quite puzzling to her and she couldn't figure it out. What possible good would it do to take groceries over there – if they needed food, let them work like everybody else. As far as she could tell, those men were able bodied – there were just lazy. She punched her pillow a few times, trying to get comfortable. She tossed and turned as these thoughts ran through her mind like so many dogs chasing their tails. And then her thoughts turned to the quilting group. She could barely admit it to herself, but she wanted back in so bad she could spit. How she was going to accomplish that, she had no clue. Then again, if she went back, she'd be working on that quilt, and there she drew the line.

Just as she was falling off to sleep, she saw the red and blue flashing lights of the police car, as it drove by her house. It seemed that Dennis had found his drink, and also his way back home.

Chapter 12

When Dale came home last night, he heard the news almost before he got out of the car. He held her while she cried yet again, and prayed over her, that God's grace and mercy would sustain them, while they waited for news. And they rejoiced over the fact that God told them Elizabeth would be coming home! When, they didn't know, but it was enough that God told them. They talked long into the night, about what they knew, speculating over what they didn't know, and wondering where Bud and Alice were now. Before long, Laura rested in the joy of the Lord, who had long been her strength.

During breakfast they talked about it all over again.

"Laura, I think I'll put the swings up in the backyard. We need to be ready." Dale was as excited as a boy. "I could drag out the old sandbox too, I'll stop by the lumber yard and have them deliver some sand."

Laura laughed. "Don't forget to stop by the toy store and get some dump trucks and loaders."

"Hey! I didn't even think of that." Dale laughed at himself, "Well, boys or girls, they'll like a sandbox."

"Dale. We don't even know when they are coming, I mean, for all we know, it could be years." Laura's chin quivered.

"We are going to plan and hope for the best and wait for the Lord to bring it about." Dale got to his feet, wiped his mouth with a napkin. "I've got to go. I love you." He kissed her and gave her a quick hug. "Stop worrying."

Dale left for work this morning with a spring in his step, and a smile on his face. He felt in his heart that their prayers were being answered this very minute. And perhaps, it would not be too long before their daughter was home. And grandchildren! What a blessing!! He was a grandpa, he couldn't keep a grin to himself.

With Dale gone to work, Laura took some time from her schedule and sat down to write a letter to Elizabeth.

****

"Bud, are you sure this is the right street?" Alice peered out the window of their green Chevy Impala. It was the last car they had ever bought, seventeen years ago, and thanks to Bud's excellent care of the car, it still ran like new. "These houses are kind of nice. I'm glad they have a nice house. What's the number again? 1244? Ok, here we have 1192 so it must be a few more houses, here's 1212 … keep going … slow down, Bud, I can't see the number on that house … 1226 … ok, a few more …" and Alice suddenly went quiet. They pulled in front of 1244 Spring Street and stared in stunned silence.

The paint was peeling off; the yard was bereft of any green living thing. A cat sunned itself on the windowsill. A dog was nosing around in the garbage can which had fallen over. The bench seat from a bus sat in the corner of the yard. There was a rusted old pickup truck alongside the house; wasps buzzed around one corner of the bed. And strangest of all, was the goat tied to the fence. A small girl, who appeared to be about 4, stared back at them.

Alice looked at Bud, and he patted her arm. "Let's go see what's what." Nothing scared Bud, he was a no nonsense, let's take care of business type of guy.

They let themselves into the yard, by a gate on rusty hinges. "Hello?" Bud called.

Alice bent down to the little girl, "Hi honey. What's your name?" Alice smiled, in her grandmotherly way. She was pretty sure it wasn't Cindy, she seemed too small.

Katie put her thumb in her mouth and backed away, and then ran into the house.

They knocked on the door. And waited. Again, they knocked, louder this time.

They looked at each other. They had to be home, the little girl had just run into the house. Dennis knew they were coming.

The door opened, and Liz stood there, on crutches. "Come on in." She pushed open the screen door. She looked none to happy to see them.

Bud and Alice entered the house, their eyes trying to adjust to the dimly lit room. Five pairs of eyes watched their every move. Dennis was nowhere in sight.

"Liz? Honey, how are you? Dennis said you sprained your ankle." Alice went over to give Liz a hug, noticing that Liz winced at the contact. "Liz, are you all right?"

Alice could now see bruises on Liz's arms, and an ugly bruise and a cut on her cheekbone. Surely this couldn't have happened along with the sprained ankle!

"Yeah, I'm fine. Dennis is still sleepin', but the kids are ready to go." Liz was again on the couch, with her foot propped up. She just wanted these people to leave.

Bud was crouched down on the floor, next to the children, getting to know who was who, and being introduced to his grandchildren. He was very gentle with them, sensing their fear and nervousness. These children hadn't the slightest idea what was going on. He could tell that Doug's children had no idea they were being picked up.

"Alice, come here." Bud motioned for her to come over to him. "Liz, we're going outside for a minute. Be right back."

"Hey! You're still taking these kids, aren't you?" Liz spoke harshly.

"Oh, yes, definitely, we're taking them. Don't worry, we'll be right back." Bud smiled gently.

Once outside, they breathed in great gulps of fresh air. The blue sky and the sounds of birds singing offered a glad respite, from the stale air inside the house, which reeked of cigarette smoke.

"Bud, did you see her? She's been beaten up. And I have a feeling I know who did it." Alice was livid. She stood on the front walk, her hands on her hips, and eyes flashing in righteous anger.

Bud took her hand and patted it gently.

"Honey, I know, I saw. But we have another problem. Those kids don't know they're coming with us. We just can't pick them up and take them out the door. They'd be scared to death. And Alice, there are three children … one of them barely a year old. What are we going to do?" Bud ran his hands over his bristly head.

"Oh Bud." Alice had tears in her eyes. "What will we do?"

Bud thought for a moment and then said, "Well, it's clear we can't just grab them and run. And it's also clear we are not welcome here except to pick up the kids. However," his mind started thinking logically, "the children are more important that Liz and Dennis. They have to come first. So, I say we stick around here today and maybe even tomorrow.

Let them get to know us and get used to us before we whisk them off to another home they've never even heard of."

"Allright! Let's do it. But, what about Dennis? Did you see what he did to her?" Alice's eyes turned dark.

"And that will give me time to talk to Dennis too, although he's never listened to me before." Bud sighed, "Let's go back in." Still holding her hand, they went back up the walk, stepping around the cat that had been winding around their legs, and went inside.

Once inside the house, Bud pulled two kitchen chairs up to the couch, so the three of them could talk.

"Liz," Bud began, "Did you tell the kids we were coming to pick them up?" He looked her straight in the eye.

"Well, uh, no, I didn't. I figured you could tell them when you got here." Liz couldn't meet his eyes. She fiddled with a stray thread coming loose from the couch.

"That's what I thought. Liz, they don't know us, we can't just pack them up and take them away. They'll be scared to death. They aren't prepared."

Liz glanced over at the children, at their big eyes, and unnatural quietness. It was true what he was saying.

"Liz," Alice said, "I think it would be a good idea for us to stay with you for a day or two and let them get used to us." Alice noted the look of alarm that crossed Liz's face.

"I'm not sure that's a real good idea, I mean, well, Dennis he wouldn't …" Liz broke off, not sure what to say.

"You leave Dennis to me, young lady." Bud stood up. "Now, let's get these grandkids of ours and give em hugs!" He held out his arms, smiling his big friendly smile, and one by one, the children came into his arms. He hugged them till they squealed, and tickled them till they giggled, and soon they were jumping on his back begging him to play Horsy. He bucked and galloped like the best of horses, and the children fell in love with their Grandpa. One by one, they crawled onto Alice's lap, for grandmotherly kisses and hugs. She smoothed their soft hair and hummed gentle songs for them. They relaxed in her arms and fear left the room on wings.

****

The peace was suddenly broken by a hung over Dennis in the doorway yelling, "What the hell is going on?" It seemed to be his normal morning greeting. At the sight of his parents, who hadn't changed one bit in twelve years, he groaned. He hoped they were on their way out … with the kids. At Dennis' appearance, the kids scampered to their bedroom doorway. Bud noted this and seethed inwardly. What kind of a son had he raised? One who beat his girlfriend and inspired fear in children? Even Alice seemed reluctant to go to him.

"Dennis. It's great to see you, son!" Bud clapped him on the back in that manly way, and if it was little harder than normal, who was to say?

Dennis winced, his head pounding. What had he done to deserve this? His bleary, bloodshot eyes tried to focus on Liz, lying on the couch with her foot propped up, a cut on her face, bruises on her thin arms. What in the world had happened to her? Realization hit him like a brick, well aimed. Good Lord, what had he done to her? And his parents here to see it all. He groaned. Life was not worth living.

"Son?" Alice tenderly cupped her hand around his cheek. "I'm so glad you called." She looked straight into his eyes. "How would you like some coffee? I'll make it for you."

It had taken Alice a minute of fervent prayer for grace to display God's love for Dennis. In her flesh, she was angrier than she had ever been. But years of living as a vessel that He could use had paid off in this minute, when her son needed a touch of human grace.

The four adult's chit chatted for several minutes while Dennis woke up and drank some coffee. Liz was so embarrassed by the conditions in her home, and Dennis she could hardly stand it.

"Well, ladies, we're going to leave you alone for a while … women talk and all that. My son and I are going out to breakfast. Dennis?" Bud's look gave Dennis no choice, but to follow. As much of a bully as Dennis was, he was still a little afraid of his father. And he knew his dad knew what he had done to Liz. It was time to go to the woodshed, and for once, Dennis decided the only thing to do was face it like a man.

Chapter 13

"Hello?" Carrie picked up the phone in the kitchen. "Hi Eleanor! How are you?" Eleanor had never called before, and Carrie was instantly as curious as a cat.

"Carrie, I'm sorry to call and bother you." Eleanor's voice was so quiet, Carrie could barely make it out.

Carrie interrupted her, "Eleanor! You are never a bother, and I'm so glad you called. Is everything ok?" She peeked at the cake in the oven and checked the timer.

"Well, I think I need some help." And Eleanor proceeded to explain the situation with Alfred. "He's used to me always going to buy his liquor, but now, I can't explain it, but it just doesn't seem like the right thing to do. But, he's an alcoholic, and well, I guess I'm afraid of what will happen if I don't come home with a bottle. Yes, afraid of what will happen to me, but also to him, I mean, I don't think people can just stop drinking without some kind of help, can they?"

"I see what you mean. Gosh, I'm not sure what to do." Carrie paused for a moment to think. "Eleanor, why don't you come over here after work? Joe can help us figure out what to do."

Eleanor was quiet for a few seconds as she considered the frame of mind Alfred would be in if she didn't come home. However, she also knew she couldn't go alone.

"Ok, I will, I should be there around 5:30. And Carrie, thank you." Eleanor felt a great burden lifted from her shoulders.

****

Alice rubbed some arnica gel onto Liz's bruises and some antibiotic ointment on her cheek.

"Liz, I'm so sorry. I'm very ashamed of my son – we didn't raise him to be like this." Alice said.

Liz was desperately fighting back tears. Yesterday had seemed a wonderful day, filled with the promise of new things. Today was the same as every other day. And here was Alice, treating her wounds, and soothing her as if Liz were her own daughter. The changes were overwhelming and Liz fought to keep her hard shell closed.

"Oh my gosh!" Alice jumped up. "I nearly forgot!! Liz, your mom sent you a box!" And Alice ran out to get it from the car.

A box? Liz wondered what in the world her mother would care to send to her.

Alice plunked down the box from Laura on the floor, near Liz's couch. "Now, you just go through that, and take as much time as you want to. I'm going to spend some time with these sweet babies." Alice gave Liz a warm smile.

For a time, Liz simply stared at the box. She hadn't spoken with her mother in years, and Liz was absolutely positive her mother, by now, wanted nothing to do with her. With all the trouble she had caused over the years, Liz was sure that her mother had given up a long time ago. Maybe this was just some of her things that she had left behind, and Mom no longer wanted around the house.

Finally, she peeked in. She pulled out pretty blouses, cosmetics, lotions, why these things were brand new. It wasn't any of her old stuff. What in the world? And a note taped on a box of cookies, "for my darling grandchildren, who I love so much." Tears ran down her cheeks. The gifts spoke to her heart, as though her mother had been right there in the room with her. They had broken through her hard shell, and in truth, where was that hard shell? Where was that protective comfort that had shielded her from all these feelings? It was gone. And feelings of warmth and love flowed through Liz. Her mother still loved her, she hadn't been forgotten, her mother wasn't mad at her. Liz could barely see the box and its contents now, for the blinding tears. And an envelope, what? Liz opened it. She gasped at what she saw. Two hundred dollars? To Liz, it might as well have been two million dollars. Quickly she put it in her jeans pocket, looking around to see if anyone had noticed. If Dennis found that, he'd drink it down in about five minutes.

Alice watched from the corner of her eye, as Liz went through the box. Her heart ached for this precious child of God, who had strayed so far away. "Oh Father, heal her heart, and draw her back to You." She prayed silently.

****

Gert stood in her yard, hands on her hips, staring at her garden. She could recognize corn stalks now, coming up in every row. Some things that might be squash, and those little things might be carrots. It was too soon to tell. She couldn't even tell which green things were weeds, because the rows were gone. There was no order to this garden at all. She had an uneasy feeling she was looking at some kind of truth here but had no clue what it was. Some kind of picture, that for just a moment revealed Gert's own life, but it was gone in a flash.

Gert gave a loud harrumph! And turned to give that mangy dog next door a glaring he would never forget. He simply jumped up and down on his chain, wagging his tail and giving her that funny doggy smile. Gert stomped into the house, tripping over the too big rubber boots she wore when gardening.

****

Eleanor knocked on Carrie's door. Funny how she felt out of place, when she had been on this porch as an invited guest once a week for nearly 20 years. It was just that it wasn't Thursday, it was Friday.

"Oh Eleanor! You never have to knock!" Carrie opened the door and gave Eleanor a hug. "You've been coming to my house far too long to be a knocker! Come on, let's go sit in the kitchen."

Carrie's kitchen was large and old fashioned, and she loved it. The white tile countertops, the honey colored pine cupboards, and the old stove with a warming oven in it, well, you just couldn't find a kitchen like this anymore. They sat at the chrome kitchen table, covered in red formica, holding a set of salt and pepper shakers, a napkin holder and a little log toothpick holder Joe and Carrie had picked up on a trip to Yellowstone. It had a walnut on it painted to look like a little man and it had a saying printed on it "Tis very plain to see, toothpicks are made for nuts like me." Joe still grinned when he pulled out a toothpick.

Eleanor gratefully sat down, setting her purse on the floor next to her chair. Her feet hurt like crazy.

"Joe ought to be home any minute. I'm heating some water for tea, do you want a cup?" Carrie was bustling around the kitchen, getting down cups and tea from the cupboard. "Are you ok?"

"I'm just so nervous, Carrie. I've never not gone home before. I'm sure by now Alfred is so angry, and climbing the walls with no more whiskey." Her voice trailed off, "Maybe I better just go home." Her eyes flickered with fear and uncertainty.

Carrie was silent for a moment while she thought about what to say. She certainly couldn't hold Eleanor here against her will.

At that moment, whistling was heard as Joe came up the walk. Carrie breathed a sigh of relief. She hadn't been happy at the thought of Eleanor going home alone.

"Hello ladies! What's up?" Joe set down his lunchbox, kissed his wife and sat down at the kitchen table with them.

"Joe, Eleanor needs some help." Carrie looked at Eleanor, not sure how much she should say, how much did Eleanor want to say?

"Carrie suggested I come over here after work. I need some help with my husband."

Joe nodded, in a way that said, Go on.

"Well, the truth is, he's an alcoholic. And all these years I've been buying him whiskey whenever he wants me to. A couple weeks ago, well, the Lord showed me that I was wrong to be doing that. And now, well, now he's out of whiskey and expecting me to bring some home for him tonight. And I just won't. But at the same time, I don't know what to do about him, I mean, he's addicted to alcohol, he can't just quit cold turkey, especially when he doesn't want to." Eleanor paused to take a breath, this had been a long speech for her. "Carrie thought you might be able to help me … somehow." She ended uncertainly.

Joe nodded again. He thought quietly for a few minutes and prayed a quick prayer of guidance.

"You know, Eleanor, I think I can help you. Just last week a guy came in for a load of gravel and can you guess who he was?" Joe smiled.

Carrie and Eleanor wondered what he was talking about.

"He's the head of Evergreen!!" he smiled triumphantly, as if single handedly he had solved the whole problem.

Carrie and Eleanor looked at each other, Carrie with one eyebrow raised, Eleanor eyes saying, What?

"Honey, can you guess that we don't have a clue what you're talking about?" Carrie patted Joe's hand, in a nice way.

Joe laughed, "Evergreen Rehabilitation Center. You know that new place out on the highway. You've seen it!" He seemed to be enjoying himself hugely for the moment. "Ok, I'm sorry Eleanor, I know this is serious. How about if I give him a call? He gave me his card; he seemed to be a really nice guy. They have a 24-hour number."

Joe scraped his chair back as he headed for the phone in the other room.

Carrie rolled her eyes, "Men!" she said as she shook her head.

Carrie and Eleanor drank their tea, feeling nervous. Especially Eleanor. She had never done anything like this in her life. But now she was stepping out on faith, changing the status quo, and it was nerve wracking. And even a tiny bit exciting, she thought, her heart fluttering.

"Ok, it's all set." Joe came back into the kitchen. "Eleanor, don't worry about anything. He's going to meet me, and we'll go together to talk to your husband, what's his name, I can't remember?"

"Oh my, well, his name is Alfred, but he's not going to like it that I told anybody, and that you're going to talk to him, he won't like that, he'll be so mad!" Eleanor was alarmed, now her heart racing.

"Eleanor, don't worry! This is something you can't take care of, it's got to be taken care of by other men, who know what to do, ok?" Joe looked at her kindly. "I want you to stay here, with Carrie, until I get back. You'll never be in any danger, I promise!"

Joe grabbed his ball cap off the coat rack on the wall and started out.

"Joe! Don't you want to eat first?" Carrie called.

"I'll eat when I get home!" came Joe's voice as he went out the front door.

Chapter 14

Bud and Alice left Dennis' house, and rented a motel room not far away. They brought in their suitcases, setting them on the hotel racks provided for that purpose. Alice began to unpack the overnight case, setting out their own soap and shampoo for the morning. She hung up the few changes of clothes they brought, on hangars that wouldn't come out of the closet.

"Good grief! You've got to be pretty desperate to steal hangers." She struggled with her blue print dress.

"Hey, the clock radio is glued to the table!" Bud laughed.

"Yeah, well, clock radios are not cheap, but hangers. They're a dollar a dozen." Alice shook her head.

"Bud, what in the world did you say to Dennis? He looked like a whole new man when you two came back." Alice asked him, wonderingly.

"Well, now, perhaps that's better left unsaid. It was man talk ... would you like to tell me all about your *women talk*, and think that I understood?" Bud grinned.

"Oh Bud," Alice laughed. "You know you wouldn't understand women talk if it bit you in the nose!" She went into the bathroom and took the pins out of her hair.

He came over and hugged her tight. "Then let's just say that God is working in his life, and leave it at that, ok?" He ran his big hands over her hair, now let out of its daily bun, hanging down her back in smooth ripples.

They sat down on the hard motel bed, with its garish, multicolored bedspread.

"Bud, do you remember the night Dennis asked Jesus into his heart?" Alice asked tenderly.

"Oh yes, that's a night I'll never forget as long as I live. Even if I get old enough to get senile, I'll remember that night. It was Sunday and we were putting the boys to bed. Doug was snickering in the dark, but Dennis was brave when he told me he had invited Jesus into his heart in Sunday School that morning. He wanted to know how Jesus fit in his heart." Bud smiled at the memory. "And I told him that Jesus had created his heart just exactly the right size."

"I wish we knew the same about Doug." Alice said.

"I know, me too. But whether we know if he's saved or not, God knows, and He knows how to direct our prayers. Until we know different, we'll never stop praying, and speaking of which, we'd better get to it." They held hands tenderly and went to their Heavenly Father for their two sons.

****

The children had been in bed for two hours now and were sound asleep. Bud and Alice had left half an hour ago, after Alice had fixed them macaroni and cheese with hot dogs for dinner. There had been no time to defrost the roast that was in the freezer. But now it sat on the kitchen counter, thawing, for tomorrow's dinner. Bud had washed the dishes, while Alice had read the children a story, and taught them how to sing "Jesus Loves Me" and then tucked them into bed. Dennis and Liz were in their usual positions, Dennis in the old recliner, and Liz lying on the couch. Now that they were alone, they hadn't said a word to each other. Liz had noticed a difference in Dennis when he and his father had come back from breakfast but hadn't known what to say. She hated to take a chance and say the wrong thing.

"Well, I'm going to bed. Good night." Liz sat up on the couch and struggled to her feet, grabbing for the crutches. The bruises on her arms made using the crutches almost unbearable, but she had no choice.

"Liz, here let me help you." Dennis jumped to his feet, as if suddenly becoming aware of her presence.

He put his arm around her waist and lifted her slightly to make it easier for her to walk. He nearly carried her into the bedroom, where he helped to put on her T-shirt, and lie down on the bed. Gently he covered her with the blankets, even straightening them out for her the way he knew she liked them. He was stalling. He hung up the clothes she had taken off and put her shoes in the closet. He opened the window slightly. And finally sat on the edge of the bed.

"Liz, well, see the thing is, well, I don't know quite how to say this." His head was down, and he was mumbling quite well.

She waited, not knowing what he was trying to say.

He took a deep breath, and lifted his head, looked her straight in the eyes and said, "Liz, I'm sorry for what I did to you, not just last night, but for all the terrible things I've done to you. I'm sorry, and I, well, I don't expect you to, but I hope, that is I'd like it, if … if you'd forgive me." He swallowed hard but held her eyes.

Of all the things Liz had thought he might say, this speech had never entered her head. Dennis had never apologized to her, not ever. Except for an occasional sarcastic, "I'm soooorrry!" Drawn out like that. Although the way he said it, still made it seem like her fault.

Despite the harshness of her life, Liz had a graciousness inside of her that could not be quelled. And God had been doing a work in her heart these many years, and in particular these last few days, that was finally becoming visible.

"Dennis, thank you. And yes, I do forgive you." Tears came to her eyes … would these tears never end? "Just please, don't ever do it again." She wiped her face with the back of her hand and sniffed.

"I won't, baby, I swear I won't!" he leaned over and kissed her gently. "Tomorrow, I'm going to get a job, and I'll start taking care of you and the kids like I'm supposed to. I promise!"

As he left the room, and turned out the light, Liz wondered what in the world his father had said to him. Tiredness overtook her, and she snuggled deep into the covers, feeling the cool summer breeze wash the room as she fell fast asleep.

****

"Carrie, I'm so tired. What do you think is taking so long?" Eleanor yawned. It was after 11 and she had to get up early to clean the Miller's house, and Mrs. Miller was always so picky about everything. It was her hardest house.

"I don't know! Here, take this quilt," Connie handed her a brown and cream scrappy Courthouse Steps quilt, "and lay down on the couch. Eleanor, do you remember when we made this quilt? Abby was in a playpen on the porch." Connie smiled at the memory, "I'll just snuggle down into this easy chair. There's no reason for us to stay awake. Just go to sleep, I'll wake you up when Joe gets home."

They both snuggled into warm quilts and soon Eleanor was fast asleep, her aching feet propped up on a pillow. However, for Carrie, sleep came slowly. Thoughts of a tiny baby, held in her arms for less than a minute before the nurse took him away would not leave her alone. She could see his perfect little face as clearly as if he was in the living room with her tonight. Tears ran down her cheeks as she prayed for deliverance from these torturing thoughts.

Lord, why do these thoughts come? Why won't they leave me alone?

Carrie, my sweet daughter, you know why. Why won't you trust Me? Don't you know I would never lead you to a place that I wouldn't provide for you?

Chapter 15

Tuesday morning, the ladies gathered on Carrie's porch to work on the blue and white quilt. It was nearly done. They were planning the quilt they would make for Liz, and what color it would be. Now that they knew her a little bit, they were beginning to get an idea of what she might like. They had already decided on a Jacob's Ladder block in beautiful jewel tones of ruby, violet, emerald, and a creamy background. They had seen Liz the way God sees her – as a beautiful woman, with a gracious and kind nature.

The heat of summer had set in, and Carrie had made two pitchers of iced tea. She had plenty of ice in the freezer, as well as some ice cream which she had planned for a snack later. Ice cream would feel good after sitting with their legs under the quilt frame on a hot day.

They threaded their needles and got out their scissors and thimbles. Work on the quilt began in earnest. They exchanged prayer requests, as was becoming their custom. Martha asked them to pray for her back, which had a habit of going out and was on the verge of doing so again. Esther asked for prayer for their aunt, who had cancer. Connie asked for prayer for Ron but shared very few details. Lydia told them about a lady she had met on the Internet who needed prayer for her sick child. Eleanor asked for prayer for Alfred, who had voluntarily admitted himself to the rehabilitation center. And Carrie asked for prayer for Abby.

They spent some minutes in prayer, and they shared a few Bible verses that had been important to them in the last few days. They shared a few things they had heard on the radio, and decided to pray for a little girl who had been kidnapped right from her own front yard.

"Let's also pray for the man who took her that God will move in his heart to return the little girl and that she won't be hurt or …" Esther's voice trailed off, not willing to say anything else. They all nodded in agreement.

They stitched and prayed.

Eleanor, who was becoming more and more outspoken these days, shared about life alone in the little guesthouse, without Alfred. She was not allowed to see him for at least two months. Her home was peaceful and filled with light, now that the curtains were opened, and the windows washed. Now the radio filled the air with praise and worship music rather than the constant drone of game shows. Her face was acquiring a pretty glow.

"You know, I was always so afraid of what would happen if I stood up to him that I just never did. But somehow when I gave it all to the Lord, He just worked everything out so perfectly!" Eleanor had a contented smile. "I know that we still have rough times ahead, but it's so good of God to give me this time of rest."

"Eleanor, I'm so happy for you! God is working in your life, that's for sure. And I got another letter from Abby yesterday. This one was only addressed to me. I know she did that on purpose because we never sent her any money like she asked us to. It wasn't a very nice letter and was a bit more demanding. But she'll just have to get over it. We aren't doing her any favors by financing her rebellion." Carrie said.

"That's true!" Esther said, "It's hard on you though, I know. Things like that are hard on a mother's heart."

They stitched and talked. And finally, they stopped for a short break.

"You know, these days are just not the same without Gert!" Lydia said with a sigh, taking a long drink of her iced tea. "What are we going to do about her? I mean, I think she's too proud to ask to come back, and I know she won't just come back like nothing happened!"

Martha shook her head. "I don't know what to do. I still feel bad about the whole thing."

"You know," Esther said, "Maybe we should just all walk over there and ask her to come back. All she can do is say no." She looked around the group.

Connie shrugged and said, "Why not?"

"Let's go right now!" Carrie said, standing up, "I could use a little walk anyway to stretch out some of these muscles!"

Gert's house was three houses down from Carries. "I'd kind of like to see how that jumbled garden is coming along anyway!" Lydia laughed.

As they approached Gert's house, they heard a commotion in the back yard. They left the front walk, to go around the side of the house, figuring Gert was probably working in her garden. The back yard came into view and they stopped in their tracks, unable to believe their own eyes.

The goat, which belonged to Dennis and Liz, had gotten loose and was eating choice greens from Gert's garden. She was shooing him away with her apron but having no luck. She yelled and stomped and threw an old coffee can at him, but he only looked at her and blinked.

Gert's hair was flying in all directions; her face was red with the heat and exertion. She had on a pair of plaid walking shorts with a tight T-shirt that said, "Dude, you're gettin' a Dell!"

"Git out of there you blasted ole goat!" And she went after him with her garden shovel. He stood his ground. She whacked him on the hind end with the shovel and he gave a sudden bleat, jumping in surprise. She stood back to let him leave, but he merely looked at her through narrowed eyes. This was war.

Gert had not noticed the ladies, gathered together in a tight group, so amazed they were unable to say anything.

Gert decided the shovel wouldn't do the job and went for the pitchfork. She was pulling out all the stops. She tried to wrestle the pitchfork from the tangle of garden implements but couldn't pry it loose. It was stuck in the blades of the push mower. She bent over to untangle the blades from the tines, and the goat saw his opportunity. He pawed the ground twice ... and the quilting ladies sucked in their breath, unable to speak ... and he charged–plowing right into Gert's bony behind parts. She fell over, crashing into the tangle of garden tools, knocking her head on the handles of rakes and spades.

The ladies gasped, and Martha, the consummate Home Improvement fan, murmured, "That had to hurt!"

Finally, they came to themselves and ran over to rescue their poor friend. The goat had not noticed the ladies either, but now seemed startled by the sight of five gray haired ladies running at him, flapping their hands and yelling. He figured he'd gotten all the snack he was going to get and left while the leaving was good. And off he trotted, in search of calmer snacks.

"Gert! Oh my gosh! Are you ok?" They all tried to help her up at once. There was a nasty goose egg growing on Gert's forehead. "Come on, let's get some ice for that bump. Oh, you poor dear."

Dazed and docile, Gert let them lead her into the kitchen, and treat her with ice and kindness. She sat at her kitchen table, with an ice bag held to her head, her spindly legs sprawled, and her hands shaking.

"I think we should take her to the hospital, don't you?" Carrie asked worriedly. "That's a bad goose egg and look, her hands are shaking ... she can barely sit up in this chair."

At the mention of *hospital* Gert became alert. "Oh no! No way are you takin' me to any hospital. People die there, you know. I'm not ready to go yet, no thank you." She eyed them suspiciously, "What are you doin' here anyway?"

Suddenly the ladies were very self-conscious. This wasn't the way they had planned to drop in and visit with Gert. They had been caught peeping into her backyard without so much as a Hello! to let Gert know they had arrived.

Eleanor patted Gert's shoulder and said, "Gert, we came by to ask you to come back to quilting. We really miss you."

Gert looked up in surprise at the outspoken Eleanor. When had Eleanor ever said more than three words in a row?

Eleanor was developing a gift for words, and all the ladies nodded in agreement.

Gert's face turned even redder, and she blustered, "Oh well, I don't know, I'm pretty busy you know. I, uh ... well, I ..." and her voice trailed off. She wanted back in the group more than she could say, but would her pride allow it? Gert was silent for about ten seconds and in the end she simply could not bring herself to say *Yes, I'll come back.*

"I'll haveta think about it and let you know." Gert mumbled, "I think I better go lie down, you guys don't have to stay." Gert wobbled over to the couch, where she lay down with a thump, wincing as she hit the couch. And she closed her eyes.

The ladies could do nothing but leave, and so they did.

Chapter 16

Bud and Alice were both sitting in the front seat, every now and then turning to check on the three children in the back seat. The Impala had a large back seat, so everyone was comfortable with their car seats, and blanky's and favorite stuffed animals. The visit with Dennis and Liz had gone better than they had ever expected, and then they berated themselves for their lack of faith. Hadn't they been praying for this very thing?

When they realized they would need two car seats, they had gone right down to K-Mart to purchase them, only to be astonished at their cost. They were mighty expensive! The clerk, who was about their age told them about a program the hospital sponsored where they could get what they needed for $10 each. So, off they drove to the hospital, where in about a half an hour, a car seat and a toddler seat were installed. Twenty dollars was paid and they were in business.

They had packed up what clothes the children had, strapped them into their new seats, hugged and cried with Dennis and Liz and they were headed home. To a completely new and different life. And how hard it had been to leave the two new grandchildren, Danny and Katie. Alice could hardly bear to leave them. They had taken lots of pictures for themselves, and to share with their other Grandma and Grandpa.

They had to plan the trip with plenty of stops. Trevor and Cindy had to go potty often, and they all needed to get wiggles out fairly regularly. The trip home would take much longer than the trip out. They had tried buying coloring books with crayons, but Dougie ate the crayons, so that was quickly ruled out. At one gas station, there had been an aisle with lots of cheap toys. After Bud strapped in the babies, Alice had run in and bought one of nearly everything. Whenever they would get bored, she'd reach in her bag of tricks and pull out a new toy, and they were thrilled for another twenty miles.

****

The day had come. Dennis was off to find a job. The house was different with three less children, and even though it was a relief, it was hard to get used to. They didn't dare think about what Doug would do if he came back.

Dennis was fairly certain he would come home that night employed, and for good money too. He was still young, and strong. He could work with the best of them, he believed.

Liz's ankle was nearly healed and she only limped slightly. She was looking forward to Dennis being out of the house for the day. Maybe today her dream of cleaning and cooking and minding children would come true. She would even fix up the house a little.

It seemed to be a new beginning in their household.

Liz dressed in her new blouse, and used all her new cosmetics. She felt like a woman and a mother. The day was new and filled with promise. She kissed Dennis good-bye and he was out the door.

She started by opening all the curtains, and then the windows. The fresh air came in and chased away the cigarette smoke and stale odors. She picked up toys, and books and all manner of clutter that didn't belong anywhere. What was this stuff anyway? Paper clips, old envelopes with names and numbers written on them, an empty jam jar, an expired advertisement for two medium pizza's, rubber bands, an empty aspirin bottle, the ice bag which was full of water, the little plastic end wrappers from countless packs of cigarettes that had just been tossed on the floor, and the list went on and on.

She dumped them all in the ever-growing mound in the trash can. She got a bucket of hot soapy water and a sponge and started scrubbing. Walls, woodwork, tables ... if she saw it, she scrubbed it. For a while the children played happily. They ran in and out of the house, chasing each other and taking turns riding on the big plastic fire truck. She swept and vacuumed. She took down the curtains and put them in the washing machine. She emptied her bucket of dirty soapy water and traded it for a bucket of hot water and vinegar, and a stack of newspapers to wash windows.

Then the children began to get bored, they were used to playing with three other children. They whined for something new to do. Liz began to get tired. Her muscles ached and the romance of housekeeping was wearing off.

Liz fixed them a sandwich and sent them to their room to eat it, and she lay down on the couch. This was normal and she felt comfortable with it. And besides, her new blouse was all wet and dirty from cleaning. She was sweaty, and tired. What was so wonderful about this? How did those women do this?

"Hello?" Carrie's voice came through the screen.

Liz sighed to herself. Now why couldn't Carrie have come when she was in the middle of cleaning, so it didn't look like all she did was lay on the couch?

"Hi Carrie, come on in." Liz opened the screen door.

"Oh my, you've been cleaning!" Carrie said immediately, looking around the room. "How's your foot doing?"

"It's doing good, I'm not limping much anymore." They sat down on the couch. The children were fighting over the last cookie in the bedroom.

"You must have had an energy burst! My goodness, you've torn this place apart." Carrie said.

"Well, I tried. I've never been much of a housekeeper, but you know? All of sudden I felt like I wanted to be a ... well, a real woman. You know, keep my house, cook, take care of my children ... the kind of thing you must do every day. But I guess I don't have what it takes, it's only a little after noon and I'm pooped." Liz sighed in disgust. In so many ways, Carrie reminded Liz of her own mom. And what she needed now was a mom who could instruct her, encourage her and help her on this new way of life.

"Liz, I know what you mean, but I don't do this every day." Carrie patted her hand.

Liz looked at her questioningly, "What do you mean? I'm sure your house is clean, what do you do every day?"

"Yes, it's clean. But I don't do all the heavy cleaning in one day. No one has the energy or the muscles for that. Every day I pick up and vacuum if it needs it, do the dishes, cook the meals. Then about once a week I pick what I call a *heavy job*. Doing laundry, changing beds, and all that. And some of those things aren't even weekly jobs. Gosh, washing walls and curtains is something I do maybe once a year!"

"Really?" Liz crinkled her brow.

"Really!" Carrie laughed.

"Then … I can do this, do you think?" Liz asked, looking hopeful.

"Oh honey, you're not a failure! You just took on too much at once. You've just recovered from a sprained ankle, your body has been busy healing itself. You probably don't have all the energy you normally do."

Liz refrained commenting on that, because she never had any energy, or maybe it was simply laziness. This was the most housework she had done in years.

"Well, I'm so glad. What a relief. The thought of doing all this hard work every day was making me feel sick to my stomach!" Liz smiled, happy with everything Carrie told her..

"It would make me sick to my stomach too. Well, I just wanted to stop by and ask if you wanted to come to church with me. It's nothing fancy, you don't have to get dressed up or anything." Carrie smiled.

"Church?" Liz was startled, church was the last thing on her mind. "Uh, well ….I don't know. I'll let you know." Liz looked down at her feet.

"Ok! I also wanted to make sure you were all right. I saw you had company for a few days, so I didn't come over." Carrie got up to leave.

"That was Dennis' parents. They came to get Doug's kids, he's taken off and we don't know where he is. We just have the two, Danny and Katie. You can hear them in the bedroom." Liz nodded towards the kitchen, where sounds of fighting over a stuffed Elmo could be heard.

"Oh I'm so sorry to hear that. How sad! We'll pray for him at our quilting times." Carrie gave Liz a hug and left for home.

****

Dennis got off the bus at the end of the street. He was tired and discouraged. No one had wanted to hire him. He had applied for more jobs today than he had in his entire life. He had filled out so many forms he had writer's cramp.

He shuffled slowly down the street, reluctant to face Liz. The nearer he came to his house, the more he wanted a drink. He had promised his father and Liz that he would get a job. And now it seemed impossible. No one wanted him, why should he put himself out there just to be rejected at every turn? He had better things to do than to spend another day like this. And who did Liz think she was anyway, expecting him to support her? She was perfectly healthy; she could go out and get a job.

Very quickly he talked himself out of all his good intentions and rationalized all his feelings.

"Hello Dennis!" Came Joe's voice from the yard, where he was inspecting his candytuft, which was taking over the flowerbed. "How are you today?" Joe came down to the sidewalk.

"Oh, hi." Dennis muttered. The last thing he wanted to do was get into a conversation with this old geezer. He tried to hurry on by, but Joe kept talking.

"So, you've been to town? Did you just get off work?"

Dennis sighed. "No, I just got back from looking for work. And I didn't find any either." Damn! How did that slip out?

"So, what can you do?" Joe asked him, brushing the dirt off his hands, tipping back the brim of his ball cap.

"I don't know. I guess I can do just about anything. I don't know, just work I guess. I never went to college or anything. It's not like I'm a doctor you know!" Dennis gave a halfhearted laugh.

"Well, I might give you a job." Joe cocked his head, looking at Dennis, sizing him up. "Can you drive a dump truck?"

Dennis whipped his head up. This old guy could give him a job? "I did drive a dump truck once, a couple years ago, yeah, I can drive a dump truck!" Could this be real?

"Ok." Joe scratched his chin. "Now for the big question. Can you pass a drug test?"

Dennis sighed again, his shoulders slumped and he ran his fingers through his hair. "No, I guess I probably couldn't."

"I'll tell you what. You wait thirty days, and if you can pass a drug test, I'll give you a job. I need a driver to haul loads of sand and gravel. Deal?" Joe held out his hand.

Dennis stared at him. And considered this offer. He had to admit it was the best offer he'd had all day, okay, it was the only offer he'd had all day. Dennis reached for his hand, and they shook. "I'll be back to see you in a month."

"And in the meantime, if you want work," Joe continued, "Go down to 3rd and Main about 7am. The farm trucks come by every morning and pick up day laborers. Moving pipe and all that. They pay at the end of the day, and they don't drug test. It's hard work, but it'll keep you going."

"Ok! Hey, thanks!" Dennis actually smiled. "See ya!"

Chapter 17

The alarm clock rang loudly, jarring Dennis out of a sound sleep. He sat up like a shot, wondering what the heck that noise was, and why wasn't anybody turning it off? Groggily he looked around, and then realization hit him. He had to go to work today. Well, to be precise, he had to go to the corner of 3rd and Main, and hope some truck picked him up.

He reached over and turned off the alarm, sitting on the side of the bed with his head in his hands, trying to wake up. He normally went to bed at this time, not got up while it was still dark. What was he thinking? He reached over and shook Liz who had not moved and shook her again.

"Hey! If I've got to get up, so can you. You can at least make me some coffee." Dennis said, croaking out his morning voice.

Liz opened one eye, and shook her head, burrowing back under the pillow.

"Come on!" Dennis repeated, "Get up – if you want me to work," he spat the word out, "the least you can do is fix me some coffee and food."

Liz groaned, and got up, stumbling out to the kitchen. Who in the world got up at this time of night? Running water into the coffee pot, she peered out the window, and was surprised to see lights on in many of the houses. It seemed almost everybody got up at this time.

She put a few slices of bacon in the frying pan, and got out some eggs, which she scrambled in a bowl. She put some bread slices in the toaster and poured the coffee.

Dennis came out of the bedroom, dressed and hair combed. It was a miracle, Liz thought, they were like any other couple on the street. The husband getting ready for work, the wife making breakfast for him … it was almost as if they were normal people. She began to wake up and gave up the idea of going back to bed as soon as he left. There were things she could do, house things. Maybe today she could continue cleaning and start fixing up, and even plan a dinner. Ideas began to buzz around in her mind, and for the first time in a long while, she was looking forward to the day. This was another beginning to their new start.

Dennis opened the front door to leave, "Liz! What's this?" he asked, as he nearly tripped over a brown bag on the front step.

"I don't know, what is it?" Liz peered out the door.

"Here, take it, I've got to go. See ya tonight." And Dennis was gone.

Liz brought the brown bag into the kitchen where she set it on the table. She looked in, why, it was full of groceries! Hadn't those ladies brought enough groceries? Now they were dropping them on the porch in the middle of the night? She brought out a bag of popcorn, a box of cereal, a bag of celery and a bag of carrots. There was a bottle of dish soap and two boxes of cookies. It was nearly a repeat of what they had brought before, what were they thinking? She sighed and put the groceries away. Once was fine, but Liz didn't want her neighbors feeling obligated to keep them in groceries.

****

Eleanor no longer needed an alarm clock. She had been waking up at 6:30 every day for more years than she could count. Her eyes automatically opened. But these days it was different. She was alone. Wonderfully alone! She experienced some guilt feelings about being so happy at being alone, but life with Alfred had been so awful, she couldn't help it. And it was also comforting to know he was getting help. It would still be at least five or six weeks before she could see him, and that didn't bother her. She needed that time to get strong.

After she showered and dressed, she sat at the kitchen table with her Bible, which by now was not dusty anymore. She loved these early morning minutes with her Lord, who was still whispering words of love into her heart, every time she opened His Word.

It was Thursday and there was no need to rush off to work today. It was her day off, and quilting day. Yesterday Carrie and Connie had gone to buy the fabric for Liz's quilt, and Eleanor couldn't wait to see it. Starting a new quilt was always an exciting thing.

Eleanor made a pot of coffee, hazelnut coffee. Her favorite kind, but something she had never purchased when Alfred had been here. She was finding all kinds of things she enjoyed – hazelnut coffee, butterscotch lifesavers, lilac scented candles, and most fun of all was the fresh flowers she picked from the yard. Not that much had been done to take care of the yard, but some flowers had survived out of sheer orneryness. Some tall marigolds seemed to thrive no matter what, there were some Shasta daisies that nothing would kill, and in the shade of the willow tree, she had found a bleeding heart with its last bloom of the spring on it. She had gathered them and put them in a mason jar, not having any vases. But they were beautiful and brightened up the room.

And that was another thing, Eleanor thought, as she looked around her house. It was not large, it was small and cozy. But oh so shabby. Her house needed some fresh ideas, and no time to lose! The curtains were thin and had holes. The furniture was dull and scratched and broken down. Alfred's chair was missing a leg and had been held level by a stack of Reader's Digests for years. The slipcovers were old and threadbare. The rug had holes that could no longer be covered by furniture. She had to do something. And this morning would be the start. She had five hours before she had to be at Carrie's for Quilting Day, and she was going to make some new curtains!

The fragrance of hazelnut filled the little house, as she searched her closet for suitable fabric. She set up her sewing machine on the kitchen table and began measuring and marking her fabric. Just as she was beginning to sew, the phone rang.

****

Bud and Alice pulled into the driveway. They were tired beyond belief, and it was only midafternoon. The children had been cooped up in the car, and in their car seats far too long. They needed a good long play in the backyard.

Alice unstrapped them all from their seats and tried to herd them into the house. They stood in an uncertain little group, looking around at the strange house.

There was a tugging on Alice's skirt. "Grandma, I got to pee." Trevor said.

"Of course you do! It's right down here." Alice led the way to the hall bathroom. Trevor went in and shut the door.

Little Dougie had already found the glass candy dish on the coffee table and was about ready to throw it on the floor, when suddenly there was a yell from the bathroom.

"GRANDMA!" Trevor yelled.

Alice grabbed the candy dish and ran down the hall to the bathroom to see what the matter was. She opened the bathroom door, and there was Trevor, leaning against the bathtub, his legs crossed, and pointing into the toilet.

"What's the matter?" Alice was breathing heavy, her heart pounding. "Are you hurt?"

"Grandma, what's wrong with your toilet?" Trevor pointed inside the bowl.

Alice looked, then smiled, "It's just blue water, honey, it has cleaners in it, it keeps the toilet clean. It's ok. Go ahead and go."

He eyed her uncertainly.

Alice made it out to the living room in time to see Little Dougie pushing buttons on the remote control. Amazingly enough, he had turned on the TV and was changing channels!

Bud came in with the luggage, and the bags of toys. "Alice, where are we going to put these kiddo's? Don't we need a crib?"

"Yes, we need a crib for Dougie. We'll put Trevor and Cindy in Doug's old room, it still has two twin beds, so we're ok there. You'll have to get the old crib out of the attic, and we'll just have to put that in the guest room.

A crash came from the kitchen, and Bud and Alice looked at each other, eyes wide. "You keep going, Bud, I'll find out what crashed!" as Alice ran into the kitchen. There was Cindy, chin quivering.

"I'm sorry, Grandma, I thought there were cookies in this jar." Tears puddled in her big brown eyes.

"It's ok, darling, don't worry about it. You're not in trouble." Alice scooped her up in a hug, just as Little Dougie found the volume control on the remote. "Let's go get Dougie!" They laughed and ran back to the living room.

****

Around 11 or so, Esther decided to run into town for a few errands. She had library books to return, a bank deposit to make, and a package to mail to her niece.

"Martha, I'll be back before its time to go to Carries, ok?" Esther grabbed the car keys off the hook by the back door. Martha was in the kitchen doing up the dishes.

"Ok! Bye!" Martha called, as Esther headed for the garage.

Martha's hands were plunged deep into soapy water, scrubbing pots and pans she had left soaking from the night before. Ralph was winding around her ankles like some kind of furry snake. She kept pushing him away with her foot. Every time she moved so much as two inches, she stepped on Ralph, who seemed to delight in lying right there in front of the sink, at the precise moment she took a step.

"What do you think this is? Some kind of game?" Martha said exasperated. "Get out of here!" And she gave him a good shove in the direction of the living room. Within five seconds, he was back, laying and rolling at her feet, his green eyes gleaming.

Martha sighed, loudly. She'd had enough of this. She grabbed the sprayer from the back of the sink and gave Ralph a soaking. He jumped up quicker than a wink and streaked into the living room, yowling his indignation as he went.

"Martha!" Esther's voice came from the back door. "What on earth did you do that for? Poor Ralph!"

Martha spun around, "Esther! I, uh … I thought you were gone to do your errands!"

Esther was in search of Ralph and Martha was red-faced, caught in an aggressive act against Ralph. In a short minute, Esther came back into the kitchen, with a bedraggled Ralph in her arms, and a towel which she was using to dry him off. He gave a hateful look in Martha's direction.

"Esther, I'm sorry. He just wouldn't get out from under my feet, and I kept stepping on him." Martha's explanation seemed pretty lame. *She* kept stepping on him, so she *soaked* him? Somehow, Ralph was turning into the innocent party.

"Oh Martha, he just wants to be where you are, cats are very social, they like to be with their people."

It seemed hopeless to Martha to try to explain to Esther that Ralph just didn't like her, in fact he hated her, and the feeling was mutual. Esther wouldn't understand, she believed Ralph loved everybody. But Martha and Ralph knew different.

"What are you doing here anyway? I thought you left?" Martha asked.

"I forgot the library books!" Esther said, a little coolly.

"Oh." Martha said, quietly. Any more words at this point seemed moot.

****

Connie fixed herself some lunch, took it out to the backyard and sat down at the redwood picnic table. Things had changed drastically in her home. At first there had just been little things, like Ron was grumpy, or he was more annoyed than usual. He watched more and more TV all the time, escaping it seemed to her. From who or what, she didn't know.

She munched on her peanut butter sandwich, trying to figure out his behavior. He was very cool towards her, and the boys. He didn't call her anymore during the day. In fact, he was barely even talking to her. All the attempts she made to talk with him were met with stony silence. Or as was becoming more and more frequent, anger.

She glanced at herself. Had she let herself go? Was she putting on too much weight? Granted, she weighed more than the day they married, but she'd had two kids. Ron wasn't exactly the same svelte figure of a man he'd been on their wedding day. She reached a hand up to her hair – it was combed. She touched her face – she had makeup on. Her clothes seemed ordinary, but they were clean and colorful. Had she been too tired for him? No, that didn't seem right; he wasn't interested in even coming to bed. Was she ignoring him? She thought over that one for a while, had she been too interested in the kids, had she put the children before him, making him draw away?

She continued in this train of thought for some minutes, before giving up. She was coming up with nothing. She had no explanation for his recent behavior, and he wasn't talking. She got up, brushed the crumbs off her shirt and headed into the house to get ready for quilting day. Yesterday she and Carrie had gone to the quilt store and bought the fabric for Liz's quilt, which they were starting today. Carrie had taken half of it home, and she had the other half. They each had washed and dried their fabrics, so they would be ready for cutting. Connie needed to get fabric out of the dryer, fold it and get her quilting bag ready to go.

Ron and his problems would have to wait, she couldn't solve them today.

Chapter 18

As each lady arrived at Carrie's house, the first thing they wanted to do was see the new fabric. When it was all unfolded and arranged in layers over each other, they oohed and awed ... this was probably going to be the most beautiful quilt they had ever done. The jewel tones sparkled in the sunlight and lit up the air.

"Ok, here's the pattern." Carrie brought it out. "Let's get cutting." And they divided up the fabric, each lady cutting out the requisite number of the piece she was assigned. Rotary cutters flashing, they very quickly had all the pieces cut, and were ready to settle down to stitching.

"Guess who called me today?" Eleanor was near to bursting with her news. "My daughter, Emma! She hasn't called me in such a long time. I was so happy to hear from her, and of course I told her all about her dad and where he was. She was so relieved that things were changing at home." She had a great big smile.

"Eleanor, that's wonderful! How is she doing anyway?" Connie asked. "She's married, isn't she?"

"Yes, she's married, and they have two little girls – Ashley and Brenda. I have pictures of them at home, but I would dearly love to see them. But they live so far away, I doubt they can afford to come and visit." Eleanor became quiet.

"Eleanor, why don't you go visit them?" Lydia asked. "You could get a bus ticket pretty cheap and spend a few days with them."

Eleanor stopped what she was doing. "Me? Go on a trip? By myself?" she squeaked. Her eyes were wide, as she considered the impossible. "No, I couldn't go by myself, and I'm sure Alfred would never want to go. He never wants to go anywhere. And besides, I doubt I could afford it." She shook her head quickly, no it was impossible.

"Ok, just a suggestion." Lydia smiled.

The ladies sewed quietly for a few minutes and then Carrie asked for prayer requests.

Connie sighed and then decided to go for it. "I wish ya'll would pray for my husband. I don't know what's wrong with him, but he just hasn't been himself lately. Getting kind of hard to live with."

Martha suggested they continue praying for Gert and for Liz.

Esther said quietly, "I have an unspoken request."

Martha looked at her quizzically. Esther had never mentioned this to her. Was she still mad about Ralph? Surely not. Well, Esther would tell her tonight. They didn't have any secrets.

"Pray for my internet friend, Laura, I just met her a few days ago. She seems like a lovely woman, she's a quilter too, but she is having a really hard time with her daughter. Hasn't seen her in years. And I guess the daughter is in some kind of trouble, bad boyfriend and all that. She didn't really say too much. But we could pray for her," Lydia requested.

"Ok, and I'd also like to pray for Abby, as usual." Carrie said. *And my broken heart and my big fat secret.* She stifled a sigh.

As needles flashed and scissors snipped, requests were brought before the King, and praises offered, and thanksgiving repeated for the many blessings they enjoyed.

They prayed for Liz and Dennis, and the quilt they were now making would be the blessing they intended. Prayers wafted upward on a gentle breeze, a sweet fragrance to the Father.

"Hello?" came Liz's voice as she came up the porch steps.

"OH! Hi Liz!!" Carrie, startled, stood up, and all her quilt pieces fluttered to the porch floor.

The other ladies looked up, guilty, and seemed at a loss for words. They had never counted on Liz coming to their quilting meeting. What would they say about the quilt? It seemed as if every piece of fabric had LIZ'S QUILT stamped in golden ink on it.

"I'm sorry; I didn't mean to startle you!" Liz was a bit uncomfortable. It was the first time she had ventured to a neighbor's house. She had told Danny and Katie to stay in the yard and wait for her, as she would only be a minute.

"Oh, I guess you did startle me!" Carrie laughed, musically. "I'm sorry to be so rude, please come in and sit down." Carrie dragged another chair over – Gert's chair to be exact. "We were praying, and I guess we just didn't hear you coming up the walk!"

"Well, I can only stay a minute, I really only wanted to say thank you for the groceries." Liz said, with one eye on her children in the yard.

"Oh Liz," Martha said, "You already did! You don't have to keep on thanking us." She reached over and patted

Liz's hand. The ladies were regaining their composure, and realizing what an answer to prayer this was – Liz dropping over this way.

"Why don't you ask the kids to come up here for a cookie? Connie brought some oatmeal raisin cookies today, I'm sure they'd love 'em." Carrie said.

"Well, no … I mean, what do you mean keep on thanking you?" Liz said, puzzled. But the ladies were busy looking at the two children and asking them to come up for cookies and didn't hear her question.

Danny and Katie ran up the steps, eagerly looking for cookies. What more fun could there be than five grandma's waiting to hand out cookies? Danny and Katie were beginning to develop some rosy little cheeks, and filling out a little, now that they were having some decent meals. Their clothes were clean, and their hair was brushed. The ladies silently and covertly inspected them, with an eye only a Grandma has. Connie was the best grandma-in-training there ever was.

Cookies were munched, and the ladies chatted on about everything and nothing. Trying to draw Liz out of herself and make her feel comfortable. They chatted about children and recipes, and some favorite verses were mentioned.

Then it seemed as if Liz finally noticed what they were doing. "What are you all making?" she asked. "Those colors are beautiful!" She ran her fingers over the piece nearest her, with a loving touch.

"Oh, we're just making a quilt." Carrie said casually.

"A quilt?" Liz said, her head tilted to the side and a faraway look came into her eyes, "My mother is a quilter."

Startled eyes flicked up and then down. That couldn't possibly be true. They had convinced themselves that Liz probably had no mother or at the very least a mother who lived the same way she did – in squalor and immorality. A quilter? They quickly hid away their thoughts, so they wouldn't show on their faces. But they wondered.

"Is she really? That's wonderful! So, you must have grown up with quilts. Do you sew or quilt?" Carrie had gathered her composure more quickly than the others.

"Yeah, there were always a lot of quilts at home. Mom was always working on one. She did it for money, I mean, people would send her quilt tops and she would hand quilt them. She never had much time to make her own quilts." Liz said. "Oh, no, I never learned. But now I kinda wish I had, this is so beautiful!" Again, she looked longingly at the fabrics.

"Well ..." Lydia stopped, looking to the others. It hardly seemed right to ignore this opening and not invite her to quilting. "Why don't you come and learn here? We'll teach you. Would you like to?"

And suddenly it seemed like the most wonderful idea in the whole world. The other ladies nodded their heads, and cries of "Oh, Liz, that would be so much fun! Would you?" were heard. Who knew who was saying what?

Liz's mouth fell open at the invitation. "Are you kidding?" She looked wonderingly at each lady, but only saw open, smiling faces.

"Now, Liz, I think that is a wonderful idea!" Eleanor said, "You know, all of us, well we're not getting any younger, and some new young quilters seem to be just the thing we need around here. It would be so nice to spend some time with your children too." Eleanor looked over at the cookie munching children.

"Well, I guess I could. I mean, I really don't know anything at all, maybe I'd just be a terrible drag on you." Liz said.

"Not at all!" Carrie was already gathering up some scraps and collecting needles and thread. "We'll show you what to do, and then you take these home and practice on them."

Liz laughed. What a lovely laugh! "Ok! I will." Her face was glowing from the acceptance, the free-flowing love and way in the back of her mind was a tiny thought of how surprised her mother would be.

The next several minutes were spent in instruction and helping Liz's unaccustomed hand and fingers to conform to the proper position. The stitches were at first, clumsy and uneven – as was to be expected. But quicker than anyone thought, she grasped the idea and began to take some lovely, even stitches.

"Liz! I think you have a natural talent for this! Look at those stitches." Martha crowed, and passed around her first seam. They all agreed that Liz was a natural.

"You just keep practicing, and next week, oh we meet here every Thursday afternoon, 'bout one o'clock, we'll start you on a quilt block." Carrie told her. "I'm so glad you're going to come." And she leaned over and gave her a little hug.

"Me too!" Liz looked up from her stitching and smiled at them all. "And it's ok if I bring the kids? They won't be any trouble?"

"Are you kidding? We were just sitting here talking about how much Eleanor misses her grandchildren, so this will be just perfect. We're just a bunch of Grandma's who go goofy over little ones, sorry Connie, I know you're not a Grandma yet." Martha laughed.

"No offense taken, I'm not ready to be a Grandma yet." Connie laughed along with her.

Esther had smiled along with the others and been very warm to Liz and welcoming, but she said very little.

Amidst all the activity, Liz forgot about the brown bag of groceries that had been on her porch early this morning.

The afternoon hours were over, and it was time to go home and start dinners for husbands and children. They gathered up their belongings and made sure Liz had everything she needed for practice.

"Dennis will be so surprised to see me sewing." Liz laughed, as she went down the steps. "Come on kids, let's go home."

"Mommy, we want to stay! Why do we have to go home?" Danny whined.

"Now, don't start that. We'll come back. We have to go start dinner for Daddy, who will be hungry as a bear when he gets home. Come on!" Liz took their hands, and off they went.

Everyone else went along down the street, as no one wanted to be seen by Liz in a cluster of whispering women, but they all knew the phone lines would be buzzing tonight. How was this going to work out? Liz working on her own quilt? Maybe it had been the Master Plan all along.

****

It did not escape notice that Liz attended a quilting afternoon, or that she sat in Gert's chair. The nerve!

Chapter 19

Liz was working in the kitchen, preparing dinner. It had been such a fun day, more fun than she'd had in such a long time. In the midst of these happy and contented thoughts, was the realization that Dennis would be home soon. This was a little scary. He'd been gone all day; she assumed he was working somewhere, on one of those farms. Would he be happy at the money he earned? Or would he be angry that he'd had to work at all? She was uncertain and more than a little nervous.

She shooed the kids to play in the bedroom, trying to make things as quiet and nice as possible for when he came home. She had a large hamburger casserole in the oven, which was covered in bubbling cheese. The aroma of cooking dinner filled the house. Every house should smell this good when a man came home from a long hard day's work. Liz found an old jar candle in a box, and had cleaned it up. Now the glass sparkled as the flame was lit, and she set in the middle of the table.

"Danny? Katie? Come here, I want to talk to you." Liz called, eyeing the front door. "Now, listen to Mommy. I want you to be quiet tonight, and mind your manners at the dinner table. Daddy is tired, he's worked hard all day, and I don't want you guys fussing at the table, ok?" She held their eyes with her own.

"Ok, Mommy. We'll be good." Danny said, and Katie solemnly nodded.

The front door opened, and Dennis was home. Liz looked carefully, trying to ascertain his mood. He was dirty, and dusty, and sunburned. She could only surmise that he was in a bad mood. But she bravely put a smile on her face and went toward him.

"Hi honey. How was your day?" she reached up to give him a kiss. "Dinner's just about ready." Liz was tense and ready for anything.

He looked at her and muttered, "Hi" and he immediately sank into the recliner. He leaned his head back and closed his eyes. Clearly this day had been hard on him.

Liz left well enough alone and went back into the kitchen to finish up dinner.

Several minutes later, she looked into the living room and it looked like Dennis was asleep in the chair. Should she wake him to eat or let him sleep? If she woke him, he would probably get mad. If she didn't wake him, he would be mad because he was hungry, he had to be hungry, he hadn't eaten all day. She sighed. It was a no-win situation, she might as well toss a coin. In the end, she decided to wake him to eat, and let the chips fall where they may.

"Dennis!" She shook his shoulder. "Come and eat dinner, then you can go to bed. It's all ready, come on."

He roused, obviously too tired to exert angry energy. "Yeah, ok." He stumbled to the table and watched as she dished up his plate.

They ate dinner in relative silence; the children were as good as their word and ate quietly. They cast furtive glances in Daddy's direction. Why was he so quiet?

After dinner, Dennis reached in his pocket and took out fifty dollars in cash. "There. That's what I earned today. Fifty lousy bucks."

"Dennis, that's wonderful." Liz smiled, and reached for his hand.

"Wonderful?" he yelled. "Wonderful? You don't understand at all what I had to do today. All day long, bend over, pick up a pipe, walk it twenty feet, lay it down. Walk back, and pick up the next pipe, walk it twenty feet, lay it down. Over and over and over again." He crashed his fist into the table, and the dishes jumped. The children's eyes opened wide and they gasped. In their hurry to get out of the kitchen, Katie knocked over her glass, and milk spilled on the table and dripped down onto the floor. "Damn it! Can't you kids be careful at all?" He yelled after her. "All for a lousy fifty bucks. If you think I'm goin' back there, you're crazy!" He stood up, knocking his chair to the floor, and went into the bathroom. A minute later the shower came on.

Liz let her breath out.

****

Martha hurried into her nightie and found it too warm for a robe. She wanted to have a few minutes to talk to Esther, but ever since they came home from quilting, Esther had busied herself with many tasks. Martha felt so bad about Ralph – not for Ralph's sake, of course, but for Esther's sake. She never meant to hurt Esther's feelings.

"Esther? Are you ready for devotions?" Martha called outside Esther's bedroom door. She felt it would be a good thing if she took the initiative tonight.

Esther opened her bedroom door. "Oh, thank you Martha, but you know, I'm just going to go to bed. I'm really very tired and I have a small headache. But thank you." Esther smiled, and started to close the door.

"Esther, wait! What's wrong? Is it Ralph? I'm so sorry for doing that, I never meant to hurt your feelings. It was just downright mean of me." Martha said, pleading for Esther's understanding.

"Oh Martha! I'm not upset about Ralph. I accepted your apology; I'm not holding it against you! I … well, I just have some things on my mind, and I need to work and pray through them, that's all. It's really nothing you've done." Esther reached out and gave Martha's hand a squeeze. "Good night, dear." And Esther shut the door.

Martha stood in the hallway. Alone and confused. They had always talked about everything, she had never known a time when Esther had shut her out like this. She didn't know what to do, but she went downstairs. And faced a dilemma. She knew in her heart that she should continue with the devotions and spend the time reading her Bible. She vaguely remembered how exciting it was when God had spoken to her heart. But in her flesh, she wanted nothing more than to sit back in the comfortable overstuffed chair and watch TV. She glanced at her watch, and found it was nearly time for I Love Lucy.

She plopped into the chair and pushed the button on the remote. All the while feeling the tug of the Holy Spirit on her heart, and all the while ignoring it. Ralph twined around her ankles, causing static electricity in her long cotton nightgown. Martha seethed.

****

The week passed slowly. The days were beginning to get downright hot. They had had no rain for some time, and the city was dusty, and the air was still and thick.

Every night, for five days in a row, Dennis came home, throwing his lousy fifty bucks on the table, and declaring he'd never go back. But for some unknown reason, every morning that week he went back to the corner of 3rd and Main.

Every day, while Dennis was working, Liz cleaned little parts of her house, and practiced her sewing. She was enjoying it and couldn't wait until it was time to go to quilting again. She often felt small thoughts flitting around her heart about God, but knew not what to make of them. The children were settling down and getting into a routine. They were getting used to things without their cousins.

Carrie stopped by Liz's house one hot morning to see how her sewing was coming along. She also brought some more scraps of fabric, and Liz felt like she was in heaven.

Connie asked Ron to leave Saturday night open so they could plan a night out, just for the two of them. He had grudgingly agreed. She wanted to try to get things worked out. It could be a chance to rekindle their love.

Lydia and Carl left the city to go on a two-week vacation. Their daughter and family lived in the nice cool mountains, and they were looking forward to seeing their grandchildren and swimming in the lake.

Gert had been nursing her bumps and bruises, while at the same time trying to keep her yard green. This wasn't easy, with the heat and the way the bruises slowed her down. She swore retribution on that dang goat, practically daring him to come into her yard again.

****

Alice perched on the edge of the couch, changing Dougie's diaper for the third time this morning. As he lay on the couch, he played with a toy duck, and spoke his own gurgling version of Chinese. The children were settling into the routine here ... if it could be called a routine. In Alice's eyes, things were chaos. She and Bud never stopped running, or picking up, or cooking, or doing laundry. It seemed the children never slept longer than fifteen minutes.

A knock sounded at the door. Alice called out "Come in!" It was a crucial time in the changing ritual, and it wouldn't be a good time to leave him on the couch, unattended and uncovered.

"Alice! Hi!" Laura MacKenzie walked in the door. "How are you?"

"Oh Laura! How do I look?" Alice laughed, and held out her hands to survey the living room with toys here and there, and a stack of folded small shirts and shorts, the breakfast dishes still on the table. "I don't know how I'm going to do this. Bud and I are too old for this." she fastened the last diaper tape. Dougie ran off into the bedroom, to find his brother and sister.

"Alice, dear ... you look so tired." Laura came over and gave her a hug. "How can I help you?"

"Want to move in?" Alice, laughed, half serious. "Actually, I don't know how you could help. I barely know what I'm doing. Bud's gone to the grocery store, and I'm trying to get the laundry done. But honestly, I just can't keep up with them." She sank back into the couch, leaning her head back.

"Have you heard from Doug, at all? No news from Dennis either?" Laura asked, noticing a basket of laundry waiting to be folded. Her hands just naturally began folding the little clothes as she talked.

"No, nothing from Doug. I can't give up these children to a foster home, Laura, you know I can't. But we also are at the point, where we realize we just can't do this. I don't know what to do." Alice sighed.

"Alice, let's just pray." Laura went over to the couch and sat down next to Alice, took her hands, and began to pray. Tears slid down Alice's cheeks as she felt the burden lifted, and shared, as her friend interceded for her before the Lord.

****

The same morning, Liz kissed Dennis goodbye, only to find another brown bag of groceries on the front porch. He nearly tripped over it on his way out, swearing a blue streak about her thoughtlessness in leaving a bag of junk right in front of the door.

Liz brought the bag into the kitchen and took out two packages of hamburger, a jar of mayonnaise, a bottle of shampoo, a small box of toothpicks, a package of hamburger buns (squished because they were on the bottom), a bag of BBQ potato chips, and a white cake mix. She sat in the chair and stared at the groceries, trying to figure this out. These ladies had to stop bringing food It was kind and all that, but for crying out loud, enough was enough already. She'd just have to tell them tomorrow at quilting. And that would be hard, considering how kind they were being to her.

****

Thursday dawned hot, even at nine o'clock in the morning. The air was stifling. Liz opened all the windows in the small house, hoping to catch any kind of breeze that might appear. The children were fussy, and complaining, not accepting any comfort from their mother. She was looking forward to going to Carrie's this afternoon for quilting. Even though it would be hotter than it was now, they would be hot together.

****

Gert left her house early Thursday morning, walking to the market, hoping to get her shopping done while it was still cool. No, cool wouldn't be the word, the word would be *less hot*. She carried her own cloth shopping bags in one hand, and her old brown faux leather handbag in the other hand. She wore a bright pink sleeveless dress, dotted with orange sprigged flowers. Her skinny arms poked out like bristles. She wore a pair of yellow socks with her black and white oxfords.

She clomped along the sidewalk, periodically wiping the sweat dripping from her face with a kitchen towel, brought along for that purpose. Clomping and thinking. Gert had never in her life heard the voice of God. Not in church, not in her own home, not outside in the twilight, never. Until last night. She had been out in the jumbled garden, poking through the growth, identifying plants, and trying to make some semblance of an order. It was an impossible task. The plants were growing where they were, they had set down roots. They couldn't be moved without killing them.

Finally, she had simply plopped down in the grass, at a loss as to what to do.

Gert, I can make your rows straight.

She had jerked her head around, hard enough to pull a muscle. Who had sneaked into the backyard? There was no one. Who said that? She looked both ways, searching for her intruder. No one was here. Was she over the edge now? Hearing voices in her head?

Gert, I am the One who can make your rows straight.

A tear slipped down her rusty cheek, as she recognized the speaker. It was God! Speaking to her! She swallowed hard. Make **her** rows straight? There was nothing wrong with **her** rows, it was the garden …it was the pesky dog's fault! As she sat on the grass, she remembered that day, so long ago, when as a little girl, she had sat in Sunday School class, and repeated the Sinner's Prayer. My goodness, she hadn't thought of that day in decades.

And suddenly in a flash that was crystal clear, she realized that the garden was a picture of her life. Her own rows were not straight; they were willy nilly, just like the garden. She had been like the pesky dog next door, wallowing through her life as she pleased, not paying any attention to the neatness of the rows that God had laid out for her.

A few more tears slipped down those wrinkled old cheeks, as she felt a moving in her heart, and was sure God was straightening rows this very minute. Some plants in her heart had set down deep roots, and she knew instinctively that straightening them would be no easy matter. But at the same time, she felt that God had come alongside her or maybe He had been there the whole time, and she had never paid attention.

As she continued her trek to the market, she whispered a few words to the patient and loving God who had entered her backyard last night and then knew what she had to do. It was Thursday morning and it was time to make mud cookies.

Chapter 20

The ladies sat on Carrie's front porch, in their regular chairs. The heat was oppresive, and the air was not moving. Not a leaf stirred, not a flower nodded her head. Katie and Danny sat quietly in a corner of the porch which was shaded; sucking on popsicle's that Carrie had brought out. Sweat trickled down their faces annoyingly.

"It's hotter than blue blazes out here!" Esther wiped her face with a handkerchief. "There is not one breath of air!"

Hands were sweaty as they tried to push needle through cloth.

"Well, it's no cooler in the house," Carrie said, "We haven't got that air conditioner, and as you can see … Joe never got the ceiling fans up."

The ladies had noticed the boxes still sitting on the porch but had been too polite to say anything. It would have been nice if Joe had put up the ceiling fans, today would have been bearable.

"Oh my gosh!" Martha gasped, "Look!" She pointed discreetly at Gert coming slowly up the walk, carrying a plate of cookies covered in Saran Wrap.

They all followed Martha's finger. "Gert!" they jumped up, mindless of the heat, and ran to greet her before she reached the steps. Liz was left at the table, with not a clue as to what was going on. Who was Gert?

"Gert, come on up … here's a chair. Do you need a pillow for your back?" They fussed over her as if she were the prodigal daughter, come home at long last. And wasn't she? They smiled and each found something to do for her. A frosty glass of iced tea, with little rivers of water running down the outside of the glass. A small paper plate for her piece of coffee chocolate cake, a napkin here … a fork there.

"I uh … well, I brought cookies." Gert thumped the plate down on the table. She almost smiled, and all the ladies knew she had just apologized. Gert glanced at Liz.

"Gert, I'm afraid you don't know our newest member." Carrie laid her hand on Liz's shoulder. "This is Liz MacKenzie, she lives down the street, very nearly across the street from you."

Liz smiled warmly at the funny little lady, and Gert nodded curtly. "How do."

Gladly, they each reached for a mud cookie. How they had missed these tasteless concoctions! Politely Liz reached for one as well, although it was so hot, how anyone could have an appetite, she didn't know. Even more politely she chewed her bite of cookie and washed it down with a long drink of tea. She glanced at the other ladies – why they were enjoying them! What in the world was going on?

"Liz, Gert has been part of our quilting group since day one. She's just been unable to come for a while." Eleanor explained tactfully. "We're so glad to have her back."

Gert looked at Eleanor suspiciously. There was Eleanor, talking again. Since when had she started that?

"And Gert, Liz just learned to sew a couple weeks ago, and already she sews a seam as fine as anyone here. We're so proud of her." Eleanor said, smiling.

"Oh." Gert said. It was plain that Gert still felt somewhat uncomfortable, and clearly was not at ease.

"Why don't we go ahead with our prayer requests?" Carrie said, to take the attention off Gert, and help her to adjust to the group that included Liz.

"Well, I have one." Liz said, and shifted in her chair. She had never given a prayer request before, but this was the only way she could think of to get the ladies to stop bringing her food. As she spoke, they all looked at her in happy surprise. "While I do very much appreciate the food you're bringing, I just want you all to know that we don't need it anymore. Dennis is working and bringing home money every day, and so … well, I don't want to sound rude … but you can stop now. But I am very thankful." She said awkwardly.

"What food?" Martha asked, puzzled.

They all looked at her, puzzled as well, and Gert ducked her head.

"The grocery bags of food, on the porch. One last week, and yesterday morning." Now it was Liz's turn to look puzzled. "Didn't you bring them?"

They all looked at each other, to see if someone had, "No, we didn't."

"Well, I don't understand. Where did they come from?" Liz asked, now a little worried.

They were clearly at a loss for an explanation.

"You must have an angel, Liz!" Carrie laughed. "I don't know where they came from, but we'll thank the Lord for them anyway."

They continued their sewing and praying. This part was new to Gert as well, and she was at a loss for words. Although her heart was newly tender, she was of no mind to share her experience with anybody. You didn't change more than fifty years of personality in one evening. She mopped her face with her kitchen towel and had a long drink of iced tea and burped.

Carrie turned on the sprinkler for Danny and Katie, and after receiving permission from their mother to get wet in their clothes, they ran through the cool droplets in delight.

"You know, that looks like a pretty good idea to me!" Connie laughed. "It's just way too hot."

"Oh my! Look over there." Carrie pointed to the horizon. Dark, black clouds were rolling and billowing in angry movements. "We're going to get a storm."

"Good. It'll clear the air." Martha said. "Maybe we should pack this up and go home. I don't want to walk home in a gale."

They agreed, and hastily packed up the fabric, and all their sewing supplies. The clouds were racing closer by the second. Leaves began to move on the trees as a very slight breeze began to blow. The air was thicker and hotter than it was five minutes ago.

"Maybe we should just go inside and wait it out there; this is coming up faster than I've ever seen before." Carrie hurriedly picked up paper plates and used napkins.

Now a gust of wind caught that last napkin and she was unable to reach it in time. Rumbles of thunder could be heard in the distance, and faint flashes of light in the clouds could be seen. Suddenly, the branches were bending in the wind, and leaves were flying through the air. A wicker chair went tumbling across the porch.

"Come on! Hurry, get inside!" Carrie called above the wind.

Liz gathered her children to her, who were now shivering in the wind and the drastically dropped temperature.

The other ladies busily grabbed their belongings and tried to reach anything that wasn't nailed down. Arms full, they quickly went into the house.

The wooden screen door slammed against the house as it was snatched from Carrie's hands, and then slammed right back at her, hitting her on the forehead. She had no time to even put up her hands for defense.

"Oh!" Carrie staggered against the doorway, the wind blowing her hair in her eyes, and a trickle of blood running down the side of her face. Gert grabbed her with strength that was surprising for the size of her skinny self and pulled her inside. Connie shut the door. And the storm was outside.

"Oh my gosh, Carrie!" Esther helped Carrie to the couch. "Martha, get some ice, and a wet cloth."

Carrie sank down onto the couch gratefully; her legs were wobbly as she realized what happened to her. She reached up and gingerly touched her head. Blood was flowing freely and dripping onto her clothes.

"Carrie, lay down. Here's a towel so we don't get blood on the couch." Esther gently helped Carrie lay down.

Danny and Katie stood silently, eyes wide, watching the scene unfold. Liz stayed out of the way, unsure of what to do or how to help. Lydia quickly brought two quilts for them to wrap around their shoulders, stopping their shivers.

Martha filled the ice bag, and brought it along with a wet cloth.

Esther pressed the wet cloth against Carrie's forehead, keeping pressure on it, trying to stop the bleeding.

"Carrie, how are you feeling?" Esther looked into her eyes.

"Um ...well, kinda ..." Carrie mumbled, half closing her eyes.

"Martha, we've got to get her to a hospital. I think she needs stitches, and she may have a concussion."

They both looked out the window, at the rivers of water running down the glass, so heavy you could not see outside. At that moment, a crack of thunder and a flash of lightening crashed outside. Static electricity could be felt in the air.

Katie began to cry, "Mommy, I'm scared!" she reached up for Liz. Liz picked her up and held her close. "It's ok, honey, just a storm. It's just clouds bumping their heads together, that's all." Danny stood stoic, although he moved a little closer to Liz. She put her arm around him and drew him closer. Liz sat on the loveseat with Katie on her lap, and Danny standing as close as he could get without actually sitting on her lap.

"We can't drive to the hospital in this. You can't even see a foot in front of you." Martha said, her voice quavering. "Maybe it will be over soon. You think?" She wrinkled her brow.

Thunder rolled and rumbled, and lightening flashed brilliantly. The house shook with the noise. Eleanor came over to sit on the loveseat near Liz. She smoothed Danny's hair and smiled at him reassuringly.

"I think we better pray." Eleanor said quietly. "This situation is out of our hands."

Nodding in agreement, the ladies drew close to Carrie's couch, in a small circle around her.

Gert followed, hesitantly. Pray? Quietly, they all joined hands, and a reverent silence followed.

"Father, we are at a loss as to what to do here. Please give us wisdom, and please help our friend Carrie, Lord we don't know what to do." Connie prayed out loud.

"Oh Lord, please watch over Carrie, and don't let any serious harm come to her, show us what to do." Martha prayed.

Thunder cracked overhead and the violent wind shook the corners of the house. They tightened their grip on each other's hands.

"Lord, please help us." Liz whispered.

Gert realized, with a pounding heart, they were praying in turn. In a few minutes, it would be her turn. She had never prayed out loud in her life, aside from that morning in Sunday School. What would she say? She barely knew how to pray silently, it hadn't been a practice of hers. She let the minister pray, that was his job. Blood rushed to her face, and the pounding of her heart grew louder till she was afraid everyone could hear it, even over the wildness of the storm.

"Uh ... Lord, well ... help Carrie." Gert let out a rush of air, in relief that she had done it, and it was over. What had she been thinking coming here today?

"Father, we need You here right now. Please show us what to do, how to help our sweet friend. You said if we needed wisdom, we had only to ask, and we're asking. We don't know what to do. We can't drive in this, but Carrie needs medical attention. Please provide for us. We ask in Jesus name, Amen." Esther finished the prayer and wiped her eyes of a tear. A few sniffles were heard.

"What about calling an ambulance?" Martha asked. "I don't know if they could get through the storm either, but we could at least call and ask them what to do."

"Good idea!" Connie went for the cordless phone. "Don't use the phone wired into the wall, not while lightening is going on. Here." She handed the cordless to Martha.

Martha pushed the Talk button. And nothing happened. No dial tone. "Oh great, the phone's dead." Martha groaned.

"Oh! Here, use my cell phone!" Connie reached for her purse.

A huge crash was heard outside, and they rushed to the window. A large branch of the maple tree in the front yard had blown over, into the street.

"Give me the phone, Connie, Thank God that branch didn't hit any electric lines." Martha dialed 911 on the cell phone.

Esther continued keeping pressure on the gash on Carrie's forehead. Esther was shaking her and speaking to her, and Carrie was mumbling back at her. The bleeding had slowed, and maybe even stopped. But Esther was taking no chances and kept the pressure on.

Gert sat quietly, not sure what to do. She was feeling a strange sensation. It was almost like pleasure, but what from? She hated to think she felt pleasure over Carrie's unfortunate bump on the head. The more she thought, the more it seemed like the pleasure she felt came from a smiling Heavenly Father, smiling down on her. But why? Just cause she muttered a small prayer? It would take more than that to impress God Almighty. Wouldn't it?

"Ok, 911 said to do just what you're doing. And they are sending an ambulance. They said it might take longer because of the storm, but they will come. They said to keep pressure on the cut and keep her awake! I'm going to call Joe at work. Where's the phone book, does anybody know?"

"Carrie! Carrie!" Esther shook her again, as she was appearing sleepy.

"Wha ...?" Carrie mumbled.

"Carrie, you have to stay awake. You can't go to sleep, not now. Talk to me! Tell me about one of the babies at the hospital. Are there any new ones?" Esther shook Carrie's shoulders.

"Babies ...? Um, my little Teddy ... he ..." and her voice trailed off.

Esther looked up helplessly. "How do I keep her awake? I don't think we should make her sit up or walk around."

Connie sat on the other end of the couch. "Let's just keep talking to her. We'll take turns." And the two of them took turns talking and shaking her shoulders.

Eleanor sat quietly, her eyes closed, her lips moving slightly. Liz, sitting next to her, could feel her communion with God as clearly as she could feel Eleanor sitting next to her on the loveseat. The whole room seemed alive with the presence of the Holy Spirit. The storm, although raging wildly and violently outside, seemed to have taken a backseat to the work of God going on in this room. As Liz was drawn into His presence, she felt such a longing in her heart for Him as she had never had before. She closed her eyes, and the voices of Esther and Connie faded to the background as she reached back into her memory. To places she had long ago forgotten and pushed out of her mind.

"Mommy? I want Jesus to live in my heart, like my friend Lisa said. Does He want to live in my heart too?" A little tomboy, 7-year-old Elizabeth looked up into her mother's eyes.

"Oh yes, honey, Jesus wants to live in everyone's heart. He is only waiting for us to ask Him. Do you want to ask Him?" Laura smoothed back her daughter's hair, her heart near to bursting at this momentous occasion.

"Yes, Mommy, I do." Elizabeth nodded her head vigorously. "I want to belong to Him."

"Then let's pray. Do you want me to pray with you?" Laura took Elizabeth's small hands in hers.

"No, I want to pray by myself." Elizabeth stated. "I know what to say."

Laura bowed her head and waited for Elizabeth to pray.

"Dear Jesus, I want you to live in my heart, just like you do my friend Lisa. Please help me to be a good girl. I love you, Jesus. Thank you for coming into my heart. Amen."

Tears filled Laura's eyes, and she hugged Elizabeth tight. "Honey, I'm so happy for you. Now you belong to Him forever, and He will never leave you."

"The ambulance is here!" Martha ran towards the door, ready to open it as soon as the paramedics reached it.

Liz opened her eyes quickly, startled back into the present. Eleanor went over to help Martha hold the door, as they wanted no more injuries due to flying doors today. In their busyness, they had not noticed the storm had begun to calm. The thunder was farther away, and the rain was lightly falling.

The paramedics quickly assessed the situation, praised Esther for her treatment of the wound and loaded Carrie onto the gurney for a trip to the hospital.

"Anyone coming with her?" one of the paramedics asked.

"I'll go with her." Esther grabbed her purse, and Carrie's so she would have insurance information. "Martha, call Joe back and tell him we're on our way to the hospital, ok?" And they were out the door.

Chapter 21

Lydia and Carl sat on the wooden deck of their daughter's house in the mountains. Birds sang, and dust motes floated on the sunlit air.

"Carl, I almost don't want to go home!" Lydia said, closing her eyes and breathing in the pure mountain air. "It's so beautiful here."

"It sure is, sweetie. I can't remember when I've been so relaxed." Carl stretched out on the lounge chair, his arms over his head, hands clasped behind his neck. "You know, I could retire, and we could move up here." He glanced at her out of the corner of his eye. "Be close to Gwen and the little ones …" his voice trailed off.

****

Eleanor finished preparing her simple supper of broiled trout and steamed broccoli. She had set the table with a pretty cloth, and placemat, and fresh flowers of course. The radio was tuned to an all Christian music station, and the notes floated around the house, blessing every corner.

She sat quietly, offering thanks for her food, and savored each bite. What a blessing to eat at the table, in serenity, instead of in front of the television watching game shows with Alfred. She felt ashamed to admit that she didn't miss him at all, and hoped it wasn't a sin to feel this way.

****

Connie stood in front of the mirror, adjusting her dress. It didn't seem to fit as well as it did the last time she wore it, but it was black and hid a multitude of sins. She fluffed her hair and sprayed a little more hairspray. She opened her makeup bag, reached in for her new lipliner and lipstick. She hurried, wanting to make a good impression on Ron, as she came down the stairs. Maybe she would even take his breath away, and he would see her as beautiful once again.

Downstairs, Ron sat in front of the television, dressed in a suit and tie. He grumbled, and squirmed in his chair, waiting for Connie to come down. He ran his finger around his collar and tried to loosen his tie. There was a baseball game on television tonight, and he wanted to watch it. Why Connie insisted on going out to dinner was beyond him. And why was she always harping on their *relationship*? He leaned his head back against the upholstery of his recliner, closing his eyes, but listening for the start of the game.

"Honey?" Connie touched his shoulder. "Are you ready to go?" She smiled invitingly.

He opened his eyes, "Yeah, I'm ready. Let's go and get this over with." He huffed and puffed his way out the door, not even holding it open for Connie.

Connie stood in the entry way, tears threatening, yet determined to give this evening her best shot. Once they had had such a lovely marriage, talking and loving, working towards the same goals. Somewhere along the way, they had lost each other. And Connie wanted to find their way back.

****

Dinner sat on the kitchen table, cold and unappetizing. It was past nine o'clock, and there was no sign of Dennis. Demons of Saturday night's past haunted Liz, they tapped on her head, telling her she was in for it tonight.

She knew he had gone drinking with the fifty dollars he had earned today.

But Liz was fresh from remembering her experience with the Lord and seeing how the Lord had taken care of Carrie after they prayed. She quickly cleaned up the kitchen and put the children to bed, praying with them for the first time. They smiled innocently, and prayed to Jesus, thanking Him for their food and toys. The demons retreated to the outside walls of the house, not quite comfortable going any closer with that *Name* being spoken.

Liz went into her bedroom and searched for her Bible. She couldn't find it anywhere and couldn't remember what she had done with it. She knelt before her bed and prayed, haltingly.

"Father, I'm sorry I've done such terrible things. I really want to be a good mom, like Carrie is, and the other ladies. I … I want You to forgive me, if You would. Lord, I'm awfully tired of doing all this on my own. Would You please help me? And Lord, I'm really scared tonight. I know Dennis is out drinking and when he comes home … well, I'm not sure what he will do. Um … well, I just really need You tonight, please take care of me. Amen." She stayed on her knees a few minutes longer and felt the peace of God flow over her. Suddenly she felt protected, and relaxed. What was that verse her mom had told her once? Something about a weapon that was formed couldn't hurt her. Well, she'd hang on to that thought. She slipped into bed, and quickly went to sleep.

Some hours later, the front door slammed open. Liz startled awake, and in seconds realized that Dennis was home. She heard things falling in the living room, as if they were thrown, she heard cursing and mumbling. She clutched the covers to her chin, and her heart pounded as she listened, and waited.

"Lord? Are You still there?" she mouthed, barely making a sound.

The demons trembled.

Suddenly, the bedroom door flew open, and Dennis stumbled in, crashing against the door post. He cursed the name of God and the demons danced in delight.

In the dark, he hit his shin on the bed frame and roared in pain.

Liz trembled. She thought of her children, alone in their bed, hearing their Daddy roar and curse, maybe crying in their fright. "Lord, please comfort my children. Watch over them, please Jesus. Help them not to be scared." She whispered.

At the name of Jesus, the demons fled. It was too much for them. There were other, friendly places that would welcome their mischief. Dennis sat on the edge of the bed and said nothing. A few minutes later, he sniffed, as though he were crying.

Crying? Liz thought, *Lord, what's going on here?*

"Liz? Are you awake?" he said, his words only slightly slurred.

"Yes, I am. Anyone would be with the noise you're making." She replied in a strong voice, no trembling here!

"Oh man, I screwed up, huh? I mean, I promised you I wouldn't drink no more and look at me. I'm a mess just a big ole drunk mess." He sniffed again. "The guys kep' askin' me and askin' me, and I kep' tellin' them I wouldn't go but then ..." He leaned over the bed, his head in his hands. "I'm just a loser, that's all I am, just a loser, I don't deserve you or the kids, how can you stand me?" he cried.

"You're right Dennis. I don't deserve this, and the kids sure could use a Dad who doesn't drink and cry and feel sorry for himself." The strength in Liz's voice was amazing, it was God–sent.

"Huh?" he sat up, and trying to focus, looked her right in the eye. He ran his fingers through his hair.

"I'm not kidding Dennis. You straighten up and fly right, or I'll take these kids and go home to my mother. Don't think I won't!" and Liz turned over, and closed her eyes. While she pretended to be asleep, her heart pounded and every second seemed to last an eternity. She expected to feel the back side of his hand any minute, but it never came. She felt Dennis get off the bed, so she peeked under her eyelashes and saw him go into the bathroom, where she heard him throw up. Minutes later, he came, and got into bed, and went to sleep.

"Oh Lord, thank You!" she smiled, and slept peacefully, in the arms of her Lord.

Chapter 22

Esther sat in the overstuffed chair, near the picture window overlooking the front yard. Her chin rested on her hand, as she stared out the window. Ralph jumped on her lap and rubbed his head against her arm. Absentmindedly, she reached down to pet him. He touched his little cold nose to her face as if to say, "Pay attention to me! I'm here!"

"Oh Ralph. How's my sweet kitty?" Esther scratched his ears, and he purred loudly.

Martha watched from the doorway and wondered once again what was bothering Esther. It had been a few days since the spraying incident, and Esther insisted she wasn't mad about it. So, what was wrong with her? Esther sat and stared and said little. It was almost as if she were depressed. Martha decided to barge right in and take the bull by the horns.

"Esther, mind if I sit down? Can we have a little talk?" Martha sat in the rocking chair.

"Of course, Martha, come in and sit down. I was really just about to go upstairs anyway." Esther started to get up.

"No, Esther please don't go. I wish you'd tell me what's wrong. You seem ... well, almost depressed. What's wrong?" Martha asked, reaching over to touch Esther's arm.

Esther sighed, and was silent for a few seconds, "I guess I've been acting kind of silly huh?"

"No, not silly. But I'm really concerned about you. Getting worried about you would be more accurate." Martha blurted out.

Tears welled up in Esther's eyes, and she struggled to find her voice.

"Martha, it's been two years since Glen died." Esther paused, trying to compose herself. "I just, well, I still miss him so much. And I'm lonely, I want… I don't know what I want." Martha handed her a tissue, and Esther dabbed her eyes.

"Esther, I know how you feel. I've been through this, remember?" Martha came over and hugged her sister. "I know how hard it is, I remember, but it will get easier every day."

Esther cried quietly for a minute. "I almost feel ashamed to say this. I'm not sure I can say this." Esther was quiet. "It's only been two years … I would be unfaithful if I …"

"If you what?" Martha asked gently and waited.

"If I wanted to get married again." Esther whispered.

Martha sat back, shocked at what she had heard. *Get married again?* Thoughts raced through her head. *If Esther married again, I would be alone – again.*

"Esther," Martha swallowed hard, "There is nothing wrong with wanting to be married again. You and Glen had a wonderful marriage, why wouldn't you want that again?"

Esther raised her tear-filled eyes, searching Martha's eyes. "Really? Did you ever want to get married again?"

This was getting far too personal for Martha's tastes. Again, Martha swallowed hard, her mouth suddenly dry.

"Well, no, I didn't." Martha said, hoping Esther would leave it at that. "But don't you think Glen would want you to be happy, and remarried, if that's what you wanted? Do you think he'd be upset with you?"

Esther thought for a minute. "No, I guess I don't think he'd be mad. He'd want me to be taken care of and loved. He always wanted good things for me." Esther smiled through tears.

Esther sat and thought for a minute. "Well, I do feel better now that I've talked to you. I don't know why I didn't want to, I guess I was just kind of embarrassed ... to have these feelings I mean." She smiled a watery smile. "I'll just have to think about this for a while."

A thought suddenly hit Martha, "Have you met someone?" she furrowed her brow, looking at her suspiciously.

"Met someone? Oh my, no!" Esther laughed. "Oh no, I don't know anyone I'd want to date, let alone ... oh my!" Esther blushed slightly.

Martha breathed a sigh of relief. Things wouldn't change much, at least in the near future.

"How about if I fix us a cup of tea?"

So Martha and Esther sat in the living room, watching the sun set and drinking a cup of tea, and talking. Ralph fell off the windowsill, ripping a hole in the lace curtains.

Chapter 23

Carrie lay on her bed, covered by the Log Cabin quilt, quietly thinking. Her head throbbed and that nasty little cut had been closed by five nice neat stitches. The doctor in the emergency room had told her to go home and rest for a few days.

Joe was downstairs making a cup of tea for her.

She didn't remember much about what happened that Thursday afternoon, except it had seemed as if little Teddy had been with her. She had named him Teddy, just in her own heart, the day after he had gone to live with his adopted parents. There wasn't a day that went by that she didn't wonder about him and how he was doing. Her heart beat faster as she realized the time had come. If she was ever going to be free, she had to tell Joe. And she was scared. *Oh Lord, help me!*

Joe came smiling into the bedroom and set her tea down on the nightstand. "It's still kind of hot." He took her hand in his. "Your hands are so cold!" He rubbed both her little hands with his large warm ones.

Tears formed in Carrie's eyes. "Joe, I'm so scared."

"Why, honey? The doctor said you'd be all right. Just need a little resting time that's all. You're getting better every day." He smiled reassuringly. "Nothing to be scared of."

"No, that's not it. I, well, I ..." And her voice trailed off, as she was so unsure of what to say. How do you tell your husband of more than twenty-five years that you once had an illegitimate child and gave him up for adoption and never told him? There were no words for a time like this.

Joe saw the fear in her eyes. "Honey, what's wrong?"

"I thought that if I did enough good things …" Her voice cracked. Her throat was hot and dry, feeling like it would close off her air any minute.

Joe wisely realized he had to listen, as Carrie was talking in a way he didn't understand.

"Oh Joe, I've been so wicked, and dishonest." The tears flowed freely now, and Carrie was unable to talk.

Joe waited.

"I … oh how do I say this? We were so brokenhearted when we couldn't have any more children after Abby. How could I ever tell you?"

Joe looked at her quizzically. His heart was beginning to pound, and he was cold and hot at the same time. Suddenly he didn't want to hear any more.

Carrie blew her nose. And in quiet whispers began to tell her story. Of the child she had given birth too, out of wedlock, and quickly given up for adoption. It had been the seventies, there had certainly been no shame in having a child out of wedlock, but she had been more interested in pursuing her college education than in being a mother at that time. She was young, she would have more children, later, when she wanted them. She had felt virtuous that she had given birth rather than had an abortion.

As she talked, Joe felt his forehead break out in a sweat. His heart pounded even harder, if that was possible. Could she just be delirious from the bump on her head? She couldn't possibly be serious! They had never kept secrets from each other. Well, at least he hadn't.

Finally, Carrie stopped talking.

Joe was silent.

"Joe? Honey, I'm so sorry. I've carried this horrible secret for thirty years now. The Lord has been telling me I need to confess, I need to be honest, but I was scared. I'm so sorry, can you ever think about forgiving me?" She tightened her grip on his warm strong hands.

Joe looked at her, not knowing what to think, or even say. He coughed, covering his nervousness and his thoughts that were suddenly a blur.

"I, well … I have to think about this Carrie. I'm … I don't even know what to say." Joe patted her hand. "I think I need some time alone." And he gently left her bedside.

Carrie watched him go. *Oh Lord, he's so hurt. And why wouldn't he be? Please help him to understand. Comfort his heart.* Her own heart was lonely, wishing Joe would come back, and knowing he wouldn't.

Carrie turned over and buried her head in the pillow and cried, which only made her head hurt more than it already did.

Chapter 24

Laura and Dale smiled conspiratorially at each other, as they got out of their car in front of Bud and Alice's house. They couldn't wait to spring the surprise on them and hurried to the front door.

It was a few minutes before Alice answered the door, and her sweet face was so tired.

"Surprise!" Laura said, smiled, and reached out to hug Alice. Dale followed, making sure the door was shut.

"Surprise? What are you talking about?" Alice laughed. There was a crash in the bedroom. "You know, I used to go running at the sound of a crash, but now … unless there's crying …" she shrugged her shoulders, "these kids are pretty tough. Now, what surprise are you talking about?"

"Dale and I are here to babysit – for the whole day! We're giving you a gift, a gift of time with each other." Laura came in, setting her purse on the coffee table.

"Oh I wouldn't put that there. Not unless you want it emptied in about four seconds and flushed down the toilet." Alice laughed and moved Laura's purse to the top shelf of the coat closet.

"Alice, I'm sure you make them sound worse than they are!" Laura laughed. "Flushed down the toilet!"

Dale looked nervous.

"Now, you just go on and get Bud, wash your face, and then get out of here!!!" Laura said, "We're here to relieve you for the day. Go out to lunch with your husband, go to the park and sit on the bench, take a walk, go shopping, I don't care, but we're kicking you out of your house for the day! Go on now!"

"Laura, you are just one of the best, I mean, do you have any idea what a blessing this is?" Alice hugged her quickly, and then turned to yell down the hallway, "Bud! Come here!"

He ran out, "What's wrong? Hey, hi you guys! Dale, good to see you." They shook hands.

"We've been sprung for the day! Come on, let's get out of here before they change their mind!" Alice laughed, a girlish laugh that Bud hadn't heard around the house for many days now.

"Well, I don't know what you're talking about, but I trust ya, and you can explain it to me later." Bud laughed with Alice, his big belly laugh overpowering her girlish one. It was music, a symphony!

Bud and Alice prepared to go out for the day. "Laura, listen, the diapers are in the top drawer of the dresser, and the wipes are on top of the dresser. Now, Trevor doesn't like peanut butter, he eats cheese on his sandwich. And Cindy is real particular about her food not touching on the plate," Alice whispered, "I give her a bigger plate so she has more room," and then returning to a normal voice, she continued with instructions, "Dougie needs to take a nap at 1:00, and make sure he has his blankie and the blue stuffed dog, he won't sleep without them …"

"Alice! Go, shoo … go on! We can do this, we've raised children before." Laura gently pushed them out the door, as if she were herding chickens. "Bye! See you tonight." and she closed the door. "My goodness, they must think we're teenager's."

"Ok, now what do we do?" Dale asked, looking around.

"Well, they seem to be playing quietly in the bedroom, let's just sit down. It may be the only chance we get today."

They sat on the couch, and then leaned back, relaxing as no sound came from their rooms.

"You know, Laura, as I recall … this quietness, is not usually a good sign." He frowned.

Laura gasped, "You're right! We better check on them."

They hurried down the hall, and peeked in the first bedroom, to find Cindy with a plastic container of Vaseline, smearing it on her little brother, and on the walls and in her hair.

"Oh my gosh!" Laura measured her words. "Where is Trevor?" she ran to the next room and found him sitting on his bed, quietly looking through a dinosaur picture book. "Oh, good, Trevor, you're a good boy!" she smiled at him.

Dale was leaning over the tub, filling it with warm water. "How are we going to get all that Vaseline out of their hair? Let alone the walls!" he groaned. "What were we thinkin' Laura?" and then he grinned at her, loving her giving spirit and loving that they were giving this gift to Bud and Alice.

****

Gert sat at her kitchen table, making a list. If she was going to get her rows in order, she'd have to have a list. She drummed her fingers on the plastic tablecloth, wondering what to write. The paper was empty. How could she get her rows straight if she couldn't even make a list? Why had God spoken to her about this if He wouldn't even tell her what she needed to do? She wasn't naïve enough to think He was going to do it all by Himself. Didn't the Bible say, "The Lord helps those who help themselves?" She sighed and glanced outside.

"Hey!" She jumped up, and ran out the back door, tripping over the garden boots she had left on the stoop. "You dirty rotten goat! Get out of here you stupid ole thing!" She flapped her apron at him.

He looked up at her, blinked and seemed to remember the old lady who had whacked him with a shovel, and he thought twice about the snack he was about to munch. But he thought too long, and suddenly Gert's hand was a vice grip on his rope, and he was trapped.

"Come on, you blasted goat! I'm taking you home. Get going!" She yanked on the rope as he dug his feet into the ground. "I don't care if I have to drag you the whole way and choke you to death. In fact, it'd give me great pleasure. Go ahead, dig your heels in the dirt, I dare you!" Gert narrowed her eyes and shot the goat her meanest look. She pulled and tugged at the rope, and finally he began to move. All that exertion was beginning to show, and Gert's face was red with anger and the heat of the day. Her bright yellow T-shirt was damp with sweat, and her loose-fitting gray walking shorts were beginning to inch down just a tad too low for comfort.

She hitched up her shorts with one hand and managed to keep hold of the goat with the other.

Across the street she clomped, striding into Liz's yard, goat in hand. She let go of her shorts long enough to knock loudly on the front door.

"Hi! Um … its Gert, isn't it?" Liz smiled and opened the screen door. Before Gert could even say a word, Liz noticed the goat, "Oh, my gosh! Was he in your yard? I'm so sorry." Liz took the rope from Gert's hand, "Just let me tie him up, wait just a sec, ok?" And Liz ran the goat to the other side of the yard and tied him to the fence.

Gert stood still, she had not expected to be treated so graciously, she was loaded for bear and fizzling fast. "Please, Gert, come in, and let me apologize." Liz smiled and held the door open for her.

Curiosity overcame Gert, and she went inside. Clearly surprised at the warm and inviting room she found herself in, she looked around, taking in everything from the warm red floral tablecloth on the kitchen table, to the mason jar of flowers on the coffee table.

"Please, sit down. Would you like some iced tea?" Liz gestured toward the couch.

"Um, ok." Gert mumbled, and sat down. She was determined to find fault with this house, this woman, these children who were surprisingly clean. Her sharp little eyes continued around the room taking in the sewing basket filled with jewel toned fabric, and small quilt pieces. The clean curtains blowing in a small breeze. The scent of something baking in the kitchen. Every theory she had about these people was being destroyed, one by one. She decided they were simply more deceptive than most, and it would take more work on her part. She was ready for the task.

"Here you go, I put sugar in, I hope you don't mind." Liz handed a frosty glass of iced tea to Gert. "I really am sorry about the goat, he's a real pain in the neck, isn't he?"

Gert snorted. "More like a pain in the rear end, if you ask me."

"Oh, he didn't!" Liz gasped.

"Not much he didn't! I fell over and hit my head on the fence, had a goose egg for weeks." Gert narrowed her eyes and took a cautious sip of iced tea; it may have marijuana in it for all she knew. What was the plant in the windowsill anyway?

"Gert, I am so sorry. That goat drives me crazy. I wish we didn't even have him, and for the life of me, I'm not sure why we have a goat. Dennis brought him home one day. Could I offer you some cookies? I just made them this afternoon." Liz hurried into the kitchen and loaded some freshly baked oatmeal raisin cookies on a plate.

"So, how long have you been quilting with the ladies? I've only just learned a few weeks ago, although my mother is a quilter." Liz asked, eagerness in her face to learn more about this strange member of the group.

"I've been quilting from day one. We all started together 'bout twenty or so years ago. We've never invited new people, well, except for Connie that is." Gert pointed out. "Your mother is a quilter?" It suddenly dawned on Gert what Liz had said, and her eyebrows lifted in surprise.

"Oh yes, she's been quilting ever since I was a little girl. Well, she doesn't piece the quilts, she hand quilts what other people send her." Liz tried to explain.

"Really?" Gert said dryly. She would bet money this was a lie. "How come you never learned to quilt?"

"Oh, I was too busy playing, and then when I got older, well, I was too busy running around with boys and getting in trouble." Liz surprised herself at the honesty with which she spoke. It seemed the Lord had stripped away all pretense. She had barely admitted those things to herself, how come she was telling Gert? A strange old lady, who eyed her as if she might whip out an ax from behind her back and come at her with it at any minute.

"Hmmph! No good ever came of any of that did it?" Gert eyed her warily.

"No, it didn't." Liz admitted.

Gert's eyes opened wide in surprise, and suddenly she wished she'd brought her kitchen towel. She was hot and uncomfortable with Liz's honesty and openness, and she could feel the sweat dripping down her back. It had to be a trick.

"So, do you work or what?" Gert saw no reason to try to be tactful.

"No, I take care of our children, and Dennis works at some of the farms, moving pipe." Liz said.

"You don't think taking care of children is work?" Gert barked out.

"Oh yes, it's certainly work. I just meant, I don't get paid for it of course." Liz was feeling a bit flustered. What was wrong with Gert? She sure wasn't as friendly as the other ladies. It almost seemed as if she had a grudge against Liz, but what could there be? Other than the goat of course.

Gert ate the last bite of cookie, wondering if it was cookies they put marijuana in, and stood up. "Thanks for the cookie, I better get going. 'Preciate it if you'd keep the goat tied up." And she made her way to the door.

"I will, and again, I'm really sorry. But I'm glad we got to visit." Liz said and smiled her gracious smile

"Yeah, see ya."

Liz stared at the funny little woman who walked across her yard and out the gate, holding onto her shorts with one hand. Well, everyday seemed to bring something new didn't it? She smiled and went inside.

Chapter 25

Eleanor smiled excitedly. Had she lost her mind? She nearly giggled. She snapped the suitcase shut and picked up her hat and purse. Yesterday she had called all the ladies she cleaned house for and arranged to be away for a week to visit her daughter. She had bought her bus ticket and was about to venture four hundred miles – on her own. This was no complacent woman standing here with a packed suitcase; this was Eleanor Beecham, woman of the world, on her very own trip across country. She lifted her chin a bit higher and could not stop the grin from spreading foolishly over her glowing face. *Oh, thank you Lord!*

She had to stop at Carrie's before heading for the bus station, and then she was on her way. One week with her daughter and her granddaughters. There was a spring in her step and a definite bounce going on as she walked down the street.

Eleanor knocked on Carrie's front door. She remembered Carrie telling her she didn't need to be a *knocker* that she could come in any time. But it still didn't feel comfortable. And she knew Joe was home while Carrie was recuperating from her tangle with the screen door. She waited, and hearing no one, knocked again, a little louder. Surely Joe was here, he wouldn't have left Carrie alone.

Eleanor walked over to the window and peered in. There was no sign of anybody. She began to be worried, maybe Joe had to take Carrie back to the Doctor? Eleanor turned to go back down the steps, when the door opened, and there stood Joe.

He didn't look himself, his hair was messed up as if he had been sleeping, and there was a sadness in his eyes.

"Hi Joe, is everything ok?" Eleanor said quietly, sensing the need for quiet.

"Eleanor, Carrie's sleeping right now. Maybe you could come back tomorrow?" Joe was polite but was already stepping back inside the house.

"I'm going to visit my daughter for a week. Just let her know when she wakes up, ok?" Eleanor looked at him deeply, "Are you ok?"

Joe blinked. "Ok? Oh, yeah, I'm fine. I'll give her the message." He nodded curtly and Eleanor knew he had already forgotten her.

My, my, I wonder what's going on with him. I better spend this bus trip praying rather than watching scenery. Eleanor shook her head as she headed down the walk.

****

The boys had finally quieted down, the dishes were done, and Connie was tired and ready for bed. It was late, but Ron was in his usual place, doing his usual thing – watching TV.

She was still smarting from their romantic night out which had fizzled big time. Ron had said very few words, even though Connie had turned on all the charm she possessed. When they got home, she had practically thrown herself at him, only to have him politely but firmly remove her hands from him, and then remove himself to the family room, where he spent the night watching television. She had been hurt beyond belief.

Tonight, the room was dark except for the blue glow of the television, and Ron was simply staring at it. He had been here all evening, ever since he got home from work.

He had even eaten dinner in here, although Connie had set the table like she usually did. He dished up his plate and brought it into the family room, to eat alone. This had gone about as far as Connie was going to go.

"Ron, it's late. Please come to bed with me, come on, let's go, please?" Connie nearly pleaded. She stopped by his chair and took his hand. "Please come to bed with me."

"Yeah, I'll be there in a minute." He never took his eyes off the set.

Connie sighed.

"That's what you always say, but you never come!" Connie said, exasperated.

"Fine!" Ron turned off the TV and threw down the remote. "Fine! Let's go to bed."

"Ron, why are you so angry? I don't understand!"

"Look, do you want to go to bed or not? I'm doing what you want and you're still arguing with me." Ron yelled.

"Ron, I want you to *want* to go to bed with me, not just do it because I say so. Don't you miss being in bed together, talking and cuddling? Spending time together?" Connie had tears choking her voice.

"Look, just tell me what you me to do. If you want to go to bed, let's go to bed. If you want to argue, I'd just as soon watch TV. I was watching a movie, I'd like to finish it, if that's ok with you!" he ended sarcastically.

Tears ran down Connie's face, "Never mind, just watch your stupid old TV. See how warm it keeps you tonight!" And she ran upstairs, crying. She heard the TV come back on, and Ron sat back down in his chair.

Oh God, what is going on? Why is this happening? Connie fell onto her bed, crying tears that would not stop. The hurt in her heart was the same as if a knife had been stuck there. It was actual physical pain, how could that be? She cried and prayed and prayed and cried. And finally, with her tears spent, she lay on the bed, simply focusing on Jesus. He surrounded her with His presence and filled her heart with peace. She got out her Bible and began to read in the Psalms. She needed the bread of life now, to nourish her, to sustain her through the darkness of this valley. "The Lord is my Shepherd, I shall not want …" and on she read of His very sweet and careful love for her.

And Ron sat alone in his family room and nurtured the anger in his heart. Where it had come from, he didn't know, and didn't ask. He was tired of this day to day struggle to bring home the bacon, with no appreciation from anybody. The very least they could do for him was to allow him some time to relax in the evening. Instead, everybody wanted something from him. The boys needed help with homework, they wanted to practice catching, Connie wanted him to go to bed, she wanted him to talk, she wanted him to listen. And he wanted nothing more than peace and quiet. Why couldn't they leave him alone? Why couldn't Connie be like Peggy? He relaxed as he thought of her pretty face, her long brown hair, her trim figure, and the way she always smiled at him when he had reason to come into the office. Lately, he'd had more reason to be in the office than ever before. His conscience pricked him, but he turned up the volume on the television, and squirmed in the recliner until he was comfortable.

Chapter 26

"I know Carrie has to rest and recover, but I sure do miss quilting today," Martha said, sighing, drumming her fingers on the table. She was restless, not used to being home on a Thursday afternoon. She got up and paced back and forth in the living room.

"Esther, what are we going to do today?" Martha was such a routine person, to have a twenty year *date* altered was more than she could take!

"Well, I have an idea. If you're game." Esther watched her out of the corner of her eye.

"What?" Martha was suspicious.

"I've thought about buying one of those new CD players." Esther smiled, waiting for Martha to take the bait.

"A what?" Martha cried, "What's a CD player? And why do we want to play a CD anyway?"

"It plays music, like a record player, or the cassette tape machine. Except they … the CD's … don't wear out, they last forever. We could go down to the store and look at one this afternoon." Esther smiled.

Martha crinkled her forehead. "How do you know about this? I've never heard of it."

Esther laughed. "When I was at the library, they have lots of them to check out. The librarian was telling me about them, and the CD player. She said they have a good one on sale this week at Rigby's Department Store. Come on, it can't hurt to look." Esther got up and grabbed her purse. "It'll be fun!"

Martha wasn't so sure, but she went along cautiously. "So, then we have to check out these CD's from the library all the time?" They got into the car.

"Yes, we can do that. They also have clubs that you can join. Like, when you join," Esther was looking over her shoulder as they pulled out of the driveway. "you get something like 12 CD's for a penny!"

Martha was even more suspicious. "Twelve for a penny! How much do they normally cost?"

"Oh, I don't know for sure, around twenty dollars or so." Esther said nonchalantly, as she pulled into traffic.

"Twenty dollars?" Martha's voice rose an octave. "A piece?" her voice cracked.

"Hush Martha let's just go look. Can't hurt anything to look." Esther said, exasperated. Martha was such a penny pincher.

****

Alice leaned against the kitchen counter, more tired than she ever remembered being. The day out with Bud had been such a blessing and they'd had a wonderful time. They had been too tired to do much more than sit in the park and watch the birds. It had been a beautiful summer day. They sat on a bench, in the shade talking and enjoying each other's company. They ate lunch in a little Italian restaurant near the park. They had returned home rested, and refreshed, and ready to carry on. But the next day, they were just as tired as if they'd had no holiday, and now they just lived on the memory of the wonderful day out together, alone. *Oh Lord, this is simply not going to work. I'm old and I've already raised my children, I can't do this,* she prayed.

She spread peanut butter over slices of white bread, added a layer of homemade strawberry jam, and cut the sandwiches into quarters. Dougie sat in his high chair, waiting for lunch, and the other two sat quietly at the kitchen table. She fixed a cheese sandwich for Trevor and made sure Cindy's food didn't touch.

"Grandma, when's our daddy coming home?" Cindy asked matter of factly, chewing.

"Oh, honey, I just don't know." Alice smoothed Cindy's hair tenderly.

"Well, I wish he would come and get us. I think we make you tired." Cindy took another bite of her sandwich.

Tears leapt to Alice's eyes. She swallowed hard, and suddenly she felt blessed, instead of worked beyond her measure. *Oh Lord, thank you for these precious children. I am glad they're here, and not in a foster home. I'm sorry for complaining, and not being thankful for these dear children. Thank you, Lord, for Your supply of grace and strength that always comes just when I need it.*

She wiped off the kitchen counter, and went to sit at the table, while they ate.

"Well, I'm not too tired to go to the park! Anybody interested?" Alice smiled at their shouts of glee. "Maybe we can get Grandpa to come, too. But you have to eat your lunch first. Hurry up now."

Sandwiches were quickly eaten, and milk cups were drained. "Ok, Grandma, we're ready, let's go!" Cindy and Trevor scampered down from their chairs, jumping up and down, and waiting for Alice to get Dougie out of the high chair.

"Go get Grandpa and tell him we're going to the park." Alice wiped Dougie's face and hands with a washcloth. They ran out of the room, racing for the couch where Bud lay taking a nap.

"Grandpa, Grandpa, we're going to the park!! Get up and come with us." Trevor pulled on Bud's arm. "Come on Grandpa!"

"Grandma, come here. Grandpa won't get up." Trevor called.

"Oh, he's just playing with you. He'll get up." Alice turned to call back to Trevor, and saw Cindy and Trevor in the doorway, tears running down her cheeks.

"Honey, what's the matter?" Alice hugged her close.

"Grandpa. He's not getting up." Cindy cried harder. Trevor's face was white, his eyes wide.

There was a sudden chill in the room, and an iron hand gripped Alice's heart. She was frozen to the spot on the kitchen floor and could not move. Instantly she knew Bud had gone home to be with the Lord. She could feel that he was gone, she could feel the kiss he had brushed against her wrinkled cheek as he had gone up, with his angelic escort.

"Trevor, come here." Alice said.

Oh God, no. Alice screamed inside her soul. *No, I can't live without him. Please don't do this to me. Wake him up, Lord, Wake him up.*

For the second time in minutes, her eyes filled with tears. Mindful of the children, she carefully went to the phone to call Laura. Then she sat in the kitchen and waited for her to arrive. The children huddled around her, patting her arm, and telling her they loved her. She sat staring at the wall, unseeing, and trying to keep hold of her mind so that she wouldn't scare the children. She couldn't go in and see Bud. She knew he was gone, the children knew he was gone. But she couldn't look at him until she was alone. This was unthinkable; this had to be a dirty trick. But the silence in the house told her it was no trick.

Laura's car could be heard coming up the driveway. The closer Laura got, the harder it was to hold on to her emotions. Tears began spilling down her cheeks.

Laura quickly came in, and took Alice in her arms, and Alice began to cry.

"Ok, honey, keep hold of yourself for just a second more. Let me call Sarah next door to take the children ok?"

Alice sat on the kitchen chair, crossing her arms in front of herself, in a sort of a hug. Laura quickly found the number on the wall beside the phone and dialed. She spoke quietly and hung up.

"Come on, you guys. How about if you spend some time with Aunt Sarah next door? I think your Grandma needs a little bit of time." Laura gathered a few diapers for Dougie, and quickly whisked the children out the door.

Suddenly Alice was alone – and scared. She knew as soon as she went into the living room, everything was final. There would be no turning back. But she couldn't stay away, and she ran in, and threw herself on Bud's chest, his strong barrel chest that moved no more.

She laid her head on his shoulder, watering him with her tears. *Oh Bud, you can't do this to me. Come back, please come back! You can't go without me. We agreed to walk this life together, that we would never leave each other. You lied to me, you left me, how do you expect me to do this alone? Oh Bud, I love you so much, please don't go ...*

Sometime later, Alice felt Laura's hands on her back, and heard her voice, softly praying and then singing, then praying again. So softly sometimes she couldn't be heard, but praying down comfort on Alice, and praising Jesus because He inhabits the praises of His people, and they needed Jesus now. Alice reached for Laura's hand, silently thanking her for her quiet presence.

"Alice, honey, I've called the funeral home. They'll be here pretty soon to pick him up." Laura smoothed Alice's hair as she talked, in her soothing quiet voice laced with mercy and grace.

"I can't let him go, Laura, I can't let him go out of this house. Once I do that," Alice's voice was raw and cracked, "he'll never come back. I can't do it."

Laura sang quietly, *Turn your eyes upon Jesus, look full in His wonderful face, and the things of earth will grow strangely dim, in the light of His glory and grace ...* Laura's tears mixed with Alice's tears, and her voice cracked often in her singing, but she didn't stop.

Soon, a quiet knock came at the front door. Humming the tune of the worship song, Laura answered the door. There were two men in dark suits, with a gurney, quiet and somber, respectful in their silence. They nodded at her, and she let them in.

"Alice, come with me. It's time." Laura gently held her shoulders and guided her to a chair. She held Alice's face against her own shoulder, so she wouldn't have to see the two men perform their jobs. She made soothing sounds, continuing to sing and pray, smoothing Alice's gray hair at the same time.

"Come in, and lay down, Alice. Just for a minute." Laura led her into the bedroom and laid her down, covering her with a quilt. She got a cool washcloth from the bathroom and laid it on Alice's forehead.

Laura!" Alice suddenly sat up. "Dennis! I've got to tell him. Oh, he doesn't have a phone, how will I tell him? I need him Laura, I need my son!"

"It's ok, I have the address, I'll send a telegram. Don't worry, I'll take care of it. Lay down, now and try to rest. I'll let you know as soon as I hear anything."

"I want Dennis to come, for the service. I'll have to send him money to come, and Liz too." Alice's voice faded away, as she lay down again.

Laura's heart skipped a beat as she realized this meant, Dennis, Liz and the children would come. *Oh Lord, how strange are Your answers to our prayers sometimes.*

Chapter 27

Esther and Martha carried their new CD player into the house. They had been overwhelmed by all the different models available, and the salesman had been no help. He couldn't have been more than sixteen, pimply faced and wearing big baggy pants that threatened to fall any second. Martha had been so embarrassed she didn't dare look, yet at the same time wondered, how do they keep those pants up? She annoyed herself by surreptitiously peeking from time to time.

"Ok, let's see what we do. Open it up, Martha!" Esther was so excited.

"Well, it better only have to be plugged in. I don't know how to do anything else." Martha grumbled. This seemed a huge waste of money to her.

They got the box open, and removed Styrofoam and booklets and cords, and finally came to the CD player itself.

It took both of them to tug it out of the tight-fitting box. But finally, it stood there, in all its glory. Black, with silver dials, and little windows ready to display cryptic messages. They pushed buttons, and turned dials, and finally plugged it in to the wall.

"I think that's all we have to do, Esther, is plug it in. Do you have a CD?" Martha stood up, rubbing the small of her back.

Esther was quiet. "A CD?"

"Yes, a CD. Isn't that what we put in here, to play music?"

"Oh, uh, well ... I think I forgot to get a CD." Esther made a face, at her own absentmindedness.

Martha stared at her as though she had lost her mind. "We went through all this, spent well over a hundred dollars, and now we can't even play a darn CD?"

Esther nodded her head, laughing at her own absentmindedness. "Yup, I guess so. Hey, let's go back to the store and buy some!"

"Back to the store?" Martha cried, "We've already been there once!"

"Ok, tomorrow I'll go to the library and check out some CD's." Esther sighed. Sometimes Martha could be a real wet blanket. No spontaneous trips to the store with Martha.

Slowly, they cleaned up the box, and Styrofoam fillers. Somehow the excitement of the afternoon had worn off.

****

Liz thought again of the two hundred dollars she had stashed away, hidden from Dennis. What was she going to do with it? In her mind, she had spent it a hundred times, but something always held her back, and she kept the money. There was the letter from her mother which had arrived soon after the box, and Liz had never answered it. What could she say to her mother, after not speaking to her for so many years? Even though the letter had assured Liz she was still the love of her mother's life, Liz was uncertain. And so, the letter and the money remained just as they were. Hidden.

There was a knock at the door.

Chapter 28

Carrie and Joe sat across the kitchen table. Carrie had cooked them breakfast, and now they sat without touching their food. It had been two days since she talked to Joe and he had been silent ever since.

"Joe, you're going to have to talk to me sooner or later." Carrie said quietly.

He looked at her for a few seconds. "I know."

"Well, then, what? Say something! Tell me you hate me, tell me you're leaving me, just say something. I can't stand this silent treatment anymore." Carrie spoke loudly, tears welling up in her eyes. "I know I was wrong, I've admitted that from the start. I know I was a liar, I know. I know!" She laid her head down on her arms, on top of the table and cried. "I'm sorry! I can't say it enough." She muffled from under her arms.

Joe got up from the table and went to Carrie's side. "Come here," he reached for her, and gathered her into his arms. Carrie sobbed as she felt her husband's arms around her once again. "Joe, I'm so sorry. If I could do it again, another way, I would."

"Shhh ..." he smoothed her hair. "I know you're sorry. I'm sorry to. I should have talked to you, instead of keeping quiet."

"Joe, please say you forgive me. I need to be forgiven." She looked into his eyes, almost fearing what she would see.

"Carrie, I love you. I always have, ever since the day I first saw you. I can't live my life without you, and so I have to forgive you. Even if I don't feel like it. Hey," he said, as Carrie jerked out his arms, "You got to be honest, I get to be honest." He said firmly, and continued, "It's not so much what you did that hurts me, it happened before we met. It's the way you didn't trust me to know the truth. It tears at the trust I have in you, because, now that I know you lied to me, how do I know it's the only thing you've lied about? You see what it does?" He smoothed her hair away from her healing cut. "It's not as easy as this cut here on your forehead. It will heal, the stitches will be taken out, and you'll have a little scar on your head that you can cover with your hair." He paused, taking a deep breath. "But, it doesn't work that way on a person's heart. It will heal, but it can't be covered up with hair or anything else. It will always be there."

They returned to their respective chairs, each quiet, and contemplating.

"Well, I do understand that Joe, I really do. I know I can tell you I've never lied about anything else, but how can you know? You can't." Carrie blew her nose. "What are we going to do?"

"We're going to do what we should have done in the beginning." Joe said, taking her hand and leading her to the couch. "We're taking this problem to our Heavenly Father."

And quietly they knelt down before the old couch and took the matter to a higher authority. And once again, peace entered their household.

****

Liz stared at the man in her doorway. "Telegram?" she said. "I didn't know people got telegrams anymore."

Liz held the envelope in her hand, intuitively realizing it would not be good news. Suddenly, she just wanted to throw it away and not open it. Life was getting good, and she didn't want any changes. This envelope represented change. Should she open it? She pondered the question. It was addressed to both her and Dennis, she could very well open it.

Eventually, curiosity won out, and she opened it, reading it quickly.

She gasped, and sat down, shaking. *Oh, God, this couldn't possibly be true.* Tears flooded her eyes, and she could no longer see the words. It was signed by her mother and there was a check included. Her mother said to pack, and reserve plane tickets and come home for the service. Reserve plane tickets? How in the world do you do that? Oh, God, who cares about plane tickets, Bud is dead! Her thoughts raced around quickly, and she felt dizzy. Dennis wouldn't be home for hours yet. She wondered if Carrie was up to visitors.

"Kids! Come on, hurry up!" Liz yelled.

****

Carl and Lydia pulled into the driveway. It was so good to see their house again. As wonderful as it was to get away, it was even better to come home.

"Carl, looks like we had quite a storm!" Lydia said, "Look at those branches that came off the tree, and good grief, two of our shutters are missing!"

"Yeah, looks like a little bit of clean up! Sure you don't want to turn right around, go back and retire, disappearing from all this?" he grinned at her.

"It's a wonderful idea, Carl, but I need time to adjust to that kind of thing. I can't just drop everything …" she stopped talking when she noticed the mischievous glint in his eye. "Carl!" she laughed. "Come on, let's get this stuff in the house, I wanna check my email."

****

Eleanor had a wonderful seat next to the window. She looked out at the countryside, enjoying every minute of her new freedom. Sometimes she felt a little bit scared, and panicky. Then she would pray and relax again. Before she left, she had stopped by to see Alfred. She was allowed to spend about an hour a week with him. He was quiet, clean and sober. But he never said much, just looked at her in a way she couldn't understand. She didn't know what to talk to him about. What could she say? They cancelled his favorite game show? But she felt it would be wrong to go on a trip without talking to him, and so she went to the center and told him. He was sitting in the recreation room, at a table, playing solitaire. When she told him about her plans, he just nodded, as if to say ok, whatever. And he went back to playing cards.

Quickly, she left the center. She had done what was required of her, and now she felt free to enjoy her trip.

She looked out her window again, marveling at the scenery and how it changed all the time. Thank you, Lord,! she breathed.

Chapter 29

Liz knocked on the door, impatiently waiting for Carrie to answer. *Carrie, please be home! I need you.* She knocked again, just as Joe opened the door.

"Oh Joe, I'm sorry! How is Carrie? Is she up to seeing visitors? I'm sorry, this must be a bad time but …" tears slipped down her cheeks. Annoyed, she brushed them away with the back of her hand.

"Come in, honey, come in. Now, what's the matter?" Joe led her into the living room and sat her in the armchair.

"It's Dennis' father, he … he passed away." Now it was real, now that she had spoken it out loud. The tears fell faster.

Joe handed her a tissue box. "Oh, my. I'm so sorry. How's he taking it?"

"He's still at work, he doesn't know." Liz blew her nose.

Joe shook his head. "It's a hard thing when a man's father dies. I remember when my father died, seems like I've never really gotten over it. I'll get Carrie for you." And he went upstairs.

Liz sat quietly with Danny and Katie. She noticed a few magazines on the end table and whispered to them to look at it and let her visit with Carrie. They were unusually quiet, and when Liz looked closer, she could see little white faces, and droopy bottom lips.

"Hey, what's wrong with you guys?" she asked, tilting Katie's head up with her finger.

"Did ... what happened to Grandpa Bud?" her little chin quivered.

Oh my. I didn't even think. They saw him only a few weeks ago, playing games and climbing on his back. I should have told them, what's wrong with me? Can't I do anything right?

"Honey, come here." She pulled them both close. "Well, Grandpa Bud, he um ..." What in the world did she say? How do you tell your children their Grandpa is dead? You can't say a word like *dead* to children.

"I think your Grandpa Bud went home to be with Jesus." Carrie's voice came from the stairs.

"Oh Carrie!" Liz looked up in appreciation, "Are you ok? Is it ok that I visit you? I'm so sorry to run over here with my problems when you have your own." She looked at Katie and Danny, and seeing their tears, pulled them close to her. "Oh honey's, it's all right. I'm sorry I didn't tell you." They climbed up on her lap and cuddled against her shoulder.

Carrie waited patiently, smiling to herself while watching Liz mother her children. So different from the first day.

Liz smoothed their hair, and they seemed content to simply sit on her lap. Liz looked up at Carrie, the tears visible.

"I'm perfectly fine, healing every day." Carrie smiled. "The question is, are you ok?" She rubbed Danny and Katie's heads and leaned over to give Liz a hug. "I'm sorry about Bud, honey." Liz nodded, and sniffed again, and then blew her nose again. Katie and Danny slipped off her lap and sat on the floor near her feet.

"Dennis is still at work. He doesn't know." Liz's eyes reflected a depth of pain she had never known before. It wasn't pain for herself, but pain for Dennis. He might act like he was tough, and didn't need his father, but Liz knew the truth. Dennis respected his father more than anyone else, and he loved him deeply. This would be a very hard for him, devastating in fact.

"Oh honey, Joe and I will be praying. Is there anything we can do?" Carrie held Liz's hand.

"Well, yes there is. I have this telegram and this money from my mother. She said to book airline tickets." Liz's tear-filled eyes locked onto Carries. "I miss my mother so much. You're so like her." And Liz threw her arms around Carrie, giving her a hug and sobbed into her shoulder.

Carrie was startled, she had never seen this kind of emotion from Liz. But she returned the hug and held Liz as she cried.

"It's ok, there now." Carrie uttered soothing sounds and rocked Liz as if she had been a baby. Silently, she prayed.

After a few moments, Liz drew back, and wiped her face with both hands. "I'm sorry. I don't even know what brought that on. I was going to say *I don't know how to book airline tickets* but out came *I miss my mother*." Liz's voice broke. "I don't know what's wrong with me!" she gave a small self-conscious laugh.

"Don't even give it another thought. What a stressful time for you, and you were right to come here. I'm so glad you did." Carrie smiled – a clear smile, unmotivated by good works – just a smile of pleasure that was true and good. "And besides, I know how to book airline tickets! Joe, could you call …"

"I'm all over it!" Joe grinned. He had heard one of the young guys at work use that phrase and had been dying to use it. "Ok, what dates, and where are you going?"

Liz gave him the particulars, and he trotted off to the kitchen phone.

"Carrie, really, how are you?"

"Honey, I'm doing better than I was before the accident."

"What do you mean?" Liz crinkled her forehead.

"Well, without going into a lot of details, there was something I had to get right with God, and with Joe. This little accident was the means to that end."

"And everything is all right? With Joe, and … God … and your head?" Liz asked.

"Yes, it is. God always leads us in the right direction, and He provides what we need when we get there, at the time we need it and not a moment before."

Haltingly, Liz began to tell of the other night, her simple prayer, Dennis coming home drunk, and how God had taken care of her. "Kinda like that?" Liz said shyly.

"Yes, dear, exactly like that. I'm so happy for you." Carrie leaned over and hugged her. Liz smiled, and the Holy

Spirit deepened the bond between these two women He had brought together, each one for the other.

"Ok, here ya go." Joe came out of the kitchen, holding papers. "You'll leave tonight at 7:45 – I'll drive ya to the airport – and here is the flight schedule. Now, with the layovers and transfers, you better try to sleep on the plane. You won't get there until tomorrow morning. Now, they aren't the cheapest flights, last minute ones never are. But I think I got you the best deal I could."

Liz, full of gratitude and thanksgiving, gave Joe a kiss on the cheek. "Thank you, Joe. I never could have done that myself." She turned on her glowing smile and threw it in his direction.

"Well," Joe sputtered, and blushed. "Gosh…"

Carrie laughed. "Liz, you're going to turn his head! Hey, I just thought of something, oh please don't be offended, but do you have luggage?"

"Luggage! Oh my gosh, no we don't. Never had use for luggage." Liz realized there was a lot more to traveling than she ever realized.

"Not to worry." Carrie turned to Joe, "Honey, would you …"

He was already halfway up the stairs, "I'm all over it." Came drifting down.

The two ladies giggled.

"I feel guilty laughing. I probably shouldn't be laughing, huh?" Liz said.

"Now, there will be plenty of time for tears and sadness. Yes, this is a sad time, but you do have the comfort of knowing Bud is with Jesus. It's Alice who needs you now; she's the one whose sadness will seem never-ending. I can't even imagine what she must be going through." Carrie shook her head. "You go on home now and start getting things ready. Joe will bring over the luggage."

They walked to the door and hugged one more time. "We'll all be praying for you and looking forward to the day you come home. Call us, and we'll pick you up at the airport, ok?"

Liz nodded, and held Katie and Danny's hands, as they left. *What a blessing, Lord, to have a friend like Carrie.* Liz didn't realize it, but she was acquiring the habit of her mother – holding an ongoing conversation with the Lord.

Chapter 30

It was just slightly past mid-summer, and the temperature was climbing higher every day. Carrie had asked Joe once more to put up the ceiling fans on the porch, and he did. Trees were fully leafed, shrubs and flowers were at their peak of glory, the roses were blooming to beat the band, and all in all, summer was in full throttle.

Everyone was looking forward to quilting day again; it seemed like forever since the last one. Esther spent time in a hot kitchen to make her chocolate cake with coffee, and Gert slaved in her kitchen over a smaller than usual batch of mud cookies. Lydia was bursting with news of her vacation and couldn't sit still long enough to bake, so hurried to the bakery where she bought a box of chocolate éclairs. Connie was feeling too depressed to cook anything, and besides, what she cooked, she ate. So, she also opted for the bakery, buying a dozen maple bars, and ate four of them on the way home. Before leaving for Carrie's house, she changed her clothes into an elastic waistband pair of shorts and a looser fitting tank top. Carrie brewed a gallon of iced tea, adding some lemonade to it for a kick.

Finally, it was nearing one o'clock and one by one the ladies began arriving.

"Hi Carrie! You look so good, running around pouring iced tea, and fluffing pillows!" Lydia gave her a hug. "I sure wish I had been here to help you."

"Oh, honey, I'm just glad you're back. I had plenty of help, really, I did. Could you grab the rest of the glasses off the kitchen table?" Carrie began to sweep off the porch of any debris left from the storm, and Joe's day of putting up ceiling fans.

"Carrie! How are ya doin'?" Connie was breathing heavily in the heat, and the exertion of the walk from her house, lugging her quilting bag and the box of doughnuts. She had eaten two more on the way over, this way she could say she bought half a dozen, although she was slightly sick to her stomach. Whether over the six doughnuts in her tummy or her trouble with Ron, she couldn't say.

"Hi, Connie, I'm doing great. You all took such good care of me." Carrie smiled, again, that clear smile. She was resting in the arms of her Heavenly Father, and not working for His approval.

"Come on, you guys, let's sit down. It's so nice to be having quilting again, I missed it a lot." Carrie smiled, again. The smile seemed to be such a part of her face, that it couldn't possibly go anywhere. "Hi Gert!" Carrie waved as Gert lumbered up the walk, carrying her plate of mud cookies, and her kitchen towel.

"Anybody know where Eleanor is?" Lydia asked. "I don't even see her coming down the sidewalk."

They all shook their heads; no one had talked to her. "Well, that's not like her, she's never missed a day!" Connie said. "This makes me a little worried. And I don't see Liz coming either." She peered down the street, both ways. Gert looked smug on hearing this; it simply proved her original claim, that Liz and her family were shiftless. She mopped her face with her kitchen towel.

They settled into their respective chairs, the two empty ones practically shouting the absence of their occupants.

"Oh, I haven't had a chance to tell you yet. Liz had to go back home, Dennis' father passed away." Carrie said quietly.

"Oh my!" Esther said, as she walked up on the porch. "What happened? That's so sad." She and Martha sat down quickly.

"He just died in his sleep, right there on the couch. His wife, Alice is her name, was in the kitchen with their three grandchildren – they are raising them you know – and they were going to go to the park, and he was … well he had gone home to be with the Lord." Carrie told the story as Liz had told it to her.

"We will certainly be praying for them." Connie said.

Lydia wrinkled her forehead. "You know, it's so weird. When I got home from vacation, I checked my email and there was another one from my quilter friend Laura, remember her, with the daughter who had the wild boyfriend?" They nodded as they recalled the prayer request. "Well, she asked me to pray for her friend Alice, whose husband had just passed away. She told me he and Alice – oh Bud was his name – were raising their three grandchildren!" Lydia looked around, "Could it possibly be the same person? Did Liz say what her mother's name was?"

Carrie thought for a minute, "No, I don't think she ever did. Wow, what a coincidence. I wonder if this is all the same people? Dennis' father's name is Bud, she did say that. Grandpa Bud!"

Gert narrowed her eyes. "What does this mean? Your friend Laura," she looked at Lydia, "is really Liz's mother? And friends with Dennis' parents, Alice and Bud?"

Gert may have been cantankerous, but she could put facts together faster than anyone.

They were silent for a minute as they thought it all over. "Lydia, where does Laura live? I know where Liz and Dennis flew." Carrie asked.

"Hmmm, let me think, if she ever said." Lydia closed her eyes, furrowed her brow. Her eyes suddenly popped open, "Georgetown!"

"Oh Lord." Carrie said, quietly and reverently.

Nobody said a word. They simply stared at each other, at a loss, to even know what to think.

"You know," Carrie started, "I think God is so good. How else could all of this happen? I mean, we already know He intended for us to meet her and minister to her and look how wonderful that has turned out. She told me before she left that she had prayed and made things right with the Lord. And now, we know her mother too. Lydia, tell us more about her." Carrie turned to Lydia, eyes aglow.

"Well, I met her on a quilting bulletin board. She had an ad on there for hand quilting, and I wrote to her, not really because I wanted hand quilting, but I just told her, I was a hand quilter too, and a Christian. She said in her ad she was a Christian, and we struck up a friendship. She's married and they live in an old farmhouse they renovated. She's one of the best hand quilters' available. If you can call a year's waiting list, available!"

"Really?" breathed Esther. "How exciting that must be!"

"Sounds like a lot of pressure to me." Martha said, clamping her lips closed.

"What else, Lydia? I'm dying to know." Carrie prodded her for more details.

"Well, she has wanted grandchildren, but because she wasn't in touch with her daughter, didn't even know if she had grandkids ... OH!" Lydia broke into a big smile, "We know she has grandchildren!"

They all laughed, except Gert, although she did manage a sort of a small smile that never reached her eyes. She would never understand all the fuss over this one girl, no matter how fast she picked up sewing a seam. She was still living in sin. Gert suddenly felt slightly uncomfortable thinking these thoughts about Liz. Man, if she only knew what she was getting into when she'd said Yes to God. It was downright hard, being charitable to the undesirable. Gert sighed loudly and began to unpack her quilting bag. Grudgingly she was working on this quilt for Liz, but only so she could be back with her friends.

"Isn't this exciting?" Esther was laughing, "To look back and see how God has moved all along? And now He's given us this opportunity to know Laura, and well, really we'll never have to lose touch with Liz at all!"

They all looked at her. "What do you mean, lose touch?" Lydia asked.

"Well, they are in a rental. They are getting their lives back together and making something of themselves. You don't think they'll live in that shack forever do you?" Esther asked.

Realizing the inevitable, they felt deflated all of a sudden. "I kind of thought she'd be part of our group forever. You know, the next generation. I never thought about her going away ..." Martha's voice trailed off.

Carrie sighed. "Neither did I. She's become like my own daughter to me. Why, they may not even come back from the services, they might stay there to help Dennis' mom."

What had started out as a happy afternoon, quickly dwindled to an unhappy group of ladies.

Except for Gert, of course. "I don't know what you're getting all upset about. We gave her a taste of the good life, now she's moving on. Those kinds of people are like that. Never grateful, never appreciate anything you do for them." She squinted as she threaded her needle. "I told you from the beginning."

"Gert!" Carrie stood up, her chair skittering backward. "I will not have you speak of Liz that way, in my house." Her face was serious and deadly calm.

"What? You'd choose that hussy over your friend of twenty years?" Gert's eye's opened wide. Her freckled chest was beginning to spread red blotches, as Gert became angry, rather than smug. "I suppose you'd like me to leave, is that it?" Gert began to throw things in her bag once again.

"No, I'd rather you didn't leave. I'd like you to stay. But I won't have you speaking of Liz like that. She's very important to me."

For a long second, Carrie and Gert stared at each other. Then Gert sat down, "Fine, I'll be nice." Carrie gulped in surprise, but only said "Thank you."

The other ladies stared at the drama unfolding before their eyes. Gert? Backed down? Be nice?

"Mom?" came a voice from the steps. All the ladies turned to look.

Carrie turned with the others, and then gasped. "Abby!" She ran to embrace her daughter, "Abby, I can't believe it. What are you doing here? I mean, why didn't you tell us? Oh, that's not what I mean either!" she laughed nervously. "I'm just so surprised to see you Honey." She hugged her again. "How long can you stay? Daddy will be so surprised."

"Stay? I'll be staying. I don't have anywhere else to go." Abby flicked her long blonde hair off her shoulder with one move of her head. "I brought all my things." She glanced back at the pile of luggage, sitting on the sidewalk. In the excitement on the porch, no one had heard the taxi.

"I see." Carrie took in the situation, as well as the fact that Abby looked to be approximately seven months pregnant. "Well, then we better get you settled in, hadn't we?" She smiled and started for the luggage.

"Oh no, you don't!" Martha jumped up, "You're not hauling luggage in this heat with those stitches in your head. Take Abby inside, we'll get the luggage." The other ladies agreed and jumped up to help. Gert snorted. Would the surprises of this day never end?

And where the heck was Eleanor? Not a stitch of sewing was done today. And the éclairs and the maple bars, melted in the heat.

Chapter 31

Dennis and Liz, holding tightly to the children's hands, carefully made their way through the crowd at the airport. They had to get all the way to luggage claim, before they could expect to see a familiar face. Liz knew it was her mother waiting for them, and a lump grew in her throat. She looked up at Dennis, who was not talking much. He was white under his tan, and the muscle in his jaw continually flexed as he swallowed down his feelings. When she told him about the telegram, his knees had buckled, and he suddenly sat down. He had said little but sat for a long time with his head in his hands. She had sat with him for a while, rubbing his back, holding his hand. Silently she had prayed over him. When Joe had knocked on the door, to take them to the airport, then Dennis got up and loaded the luggage in the car. He and Joe shook hands, and Joe murmured something to him, Dennis had swallowed hard and nodded.

Now, it was late, and the children were tired. Liz and Dennis were on their last nerve.

Suddenly Liz saw her mother, waving her hands. A big smile on her face. Liz's eyes filled with tears, and she grabbed Katie up in her arms and ran the last hundred feet, into the arms of her mother. Gentle hands surrounded Liz, and smoothed her hair, and touched sweet Katie's face. Eyes full of love swept every inch of her daughter, and then her granddaughter.

Dennis arrived with Danny. And Laura hugged Dennis tight, touching his face in kindness. Dennis was stoic. She knelt before Danny and looked right into his eyes, smiling, tears running down her face. Danny went into her grandmotherly hug, and Laura closed her eyes, *Oh Lord, how can I ever say Thank You enough for this?*

"I'm so happy to see you. All of you." Laura was smiling though tears, looking at each of them. "I've missed you so much, honey." She held Liz's hand, as if Liz were a little girl again, and might get lost in the crowd.

"Here, take Danny. I'll get the luggage." Dennis went off to the luggage carousel, in search of their belongings, and escaping from all the emotional display.

Liz and Laura knelt before Katie and Danny and hugged them. Laura looked her grandchildren over from head to toe, and then over Liz. Gone was the hard veneer Laura remembered so well, the last time they had *clashed*, now she was open and inviting. Her eyes were clear; her hair was bouncy and shiny. Laura knew she was looking at a miracle. "Honey, we'll have lots of time to visit later, I know you must be exhausted, and the kids are tired. Are you hungry?"

"We're starved. A few little packs of peanuts on the plane, that was it." Liz felt her stomach grumble, and a little lightheadedness, as the lack of protein made itself known.

"We'll go through the McDonalds drive-thru, I know Alice wants to see Dennis, so it's probably not a good idea to stop somewhere and eat. Is that ok?" Laura asked.

"It'll be wonderful. Thanks Mom." Liz smiled her all out smile, and Laura hugged her again, crying.

"Ok, I'm sorry. I know I've got to stop crying! This is just such a wonderful day." Then Laura caught herself, "I didn't mean ... how could I have said that?" She covered her mouth with her hand.

"Mom, I know what you meant, and I agree. I'm glad to see you, too. But Dennis is having a really hard time. I know you understand that."

Suddenly, Laura felt the roles reverse slightly. Who was this peaceful, composed, beautiful woman? She watched Liz keep an eye on her children, watchful as a hawk, and also on Dennis, very nearly protecting him with her gaze. What had happened? When had God answered her prayers? Time enough to find out later. *Oh Thank You again Lord, what a blessing this is, no matter the circumstances.*

They loaded the luggage in the car, got the children strapped in, and everybody was ready to go. Laura drove out the toll booth, paying for her short-term parking, and veered off to the right, to drive through the McDonalds, so handily nearby. McDonalds must have known most people get off the plane starving.

She ordered happy meals, and big macs and large French fries, boxes of cookies and cartons of milk.

Katie and Danny were thrilled with the takeout food, not something they received very often. Life was exciting, a plane ride, eating hamburgers in the car, and now getting to meet Grandma Laura, and going to see Grandma Alice who they remembered. What next?

Chapter 32

Alice, dressed in her best black dress, sat perched on the edge of the couch. She wanted nothing more than to crawl into her bed and pull the covers over her head. But the house was filled with people. And all the people had brought food. They stood around eating, drinking coffee, talking, and watching her as if she might explode. She tried her best to smile, and accept their well wishes, but she just wanted to go to bed. And Dennis, she wanted to see Dennis.

Cindy came and put her little arm through Alice's. An older lady from church immediately bent over, and tried to take Cindy away with a, "Hush now; let's leave your Grandma alone!"

"No," Alice said firmly, "I'd rather she stayed."

The church lady straightened up surprise. "Well! I was just trying to help!" she huffed.

"This is helping." Alice smiled, as Cindy crawled up on her lap and cuddled on her shoulder. *Where was Laura? Why was it taking so long? Oh! They probably had to eat. Too bad they don't know about the kitchen full of food here.*

The front door opened again. Alice had quit looking to see who came through. She simply sat, her eyes closed, cuddling with Cindy.

Alice felt a hand on her shoulder. "Mom?" came that gruff, deep voice that sounded so like Buds. Her eyes flew open, "Dennis!" and then the tears started again. "Oh Dennis, I'm so glad you're here. I need you." And she stood up, carefully setting Cindy on the couch. Dennis took her in his arms, swallowing hard, but held his little mother while she cried.

After a minute, Laura came over and whispered to them both. Dennis took his mother into the bedroom, where they could talk in private, without the whole world witnessing their grief.

Katie and Danny quickly discovered Cindy and Trevor, and they ran off to play in the bedroom. They were thrilled to be with their cousins again, they were too young to wonder about Grandpa Bud for long. It was only when they saw their grandma or their mama crying that they remembered. The excitement of the day and all its happenings far outweighed any sadness. Soon, they also discovered the grown-ups were far too busy to notice them, and they could sneak into the kitchen, snitching cookies and treats and no one said a word.

Laura wanted nothing more than to sit with Liz and visit. But real visiting in this place was impossible. More and more people arrived every minute. Alice and Bud were both loved very much, and he would be sorely missed. She caught Liz's eye and shrugged. "This place is a zoo! There are far too many people here."

Liz nodded. "Do you know them? Can you ask them to leave?"

"Some of them, but still, how do you say *You've worn out your welcome?*" Laura shook her head.

Liz smiled, "I know how. Put away the food."

"Elizabeth MacKenzie!" Laura gasped in mock horror, quietly, so as not to attract attention to themselves.

"Mom, trust me. It'll work. Whenever we had a party and they wouldn't go home, we'd just put away the beer, I don't see why it wouldn't work the same with food ..." Liz's voice trailed off. *Party? Beer? Now why did I bring that up? Is my brain thinking at all?*

Laura chose to ignore the slip and only said, "Well, it can't hurt to try! Will you help me?"

Liz smiled, her glowing smile, thankful for her mother's understanding. "Yes, I will."

They made their way to the kitchen, practically elbowing their way through the crowd.

Laura went to the cupboard and handed out the roll of plastic wrap to Liz, and they started covering up dishes of scalloped potatoes, and pot roast, cheeseburger casserole, and jello salads. They twist tied bags of dinner rolls.

The church ladies, who were in charge of the kitchen, and the food, were a little miffed at these two barging into their territory. They clucked together, to reach a consensus before speaking to Laura.

"What are you doing?" the bravest and largest one finally asked.

Laura smiled warmly, "It would be a good idea if we put some of this food away, for the family to eat in the next few days, don't you think? Alice doesn't want to be bothered with cooking now that her son and his family are here." Laura looked at Liz, and Liz smiled.

"Well, of course she doesn't want to be bothered with cooking!" the large one bristled, annoyed that she hadn't thought of this herself, "Let's get this food put away. You go sit down; we'll take care of this!" And Laura and

Liz were shooed out of the kitchen. They kept a dignified face on, but their eyes twinkled at each other.

"I think we should check on the kids. If we can find them!" Liz said, pushing her way through the crowd.

They did find the children, all five of them, in the back bedroom. They were sitting on the floor, amidst cookies, crackers, juice boxes, chocolate bars with coconut. Their innocent little faces told the story with crumbs and smears of chocolate.

"Hi Mommy." Katie smiled innocently. Little Dougie went right on eating, with no clue he had just been busted.

"Hi Grandma Laura." Danny said, "Want a cookie?" he handed her a well-used cookie.

"Darling, I would love a cookie. Thank you." Laura took the cookie as if it were a precious gift. She looked at Liz, "Let's just stay in here, Alice is content to be with Dennis for now, and we won't be missed for a while."

Liz nodded, "Let's!" and they sat on the floor with the children and shared in the feast.

Chapter 33

Joe sat at the kitchen table, while Carrie fixed dinner. She stood at the counter peeling potatoes and keeping an eye on the pork chops in the covered pan. He stared at the floor.

"Has she said anything? Anything at all?" Joe whispered.

"Just that she's here to stay, and she doesn't have anywhere else to go. That's all I know. The ladies helped to carry her luggage upstairs, and there she stayed. Joe! She's got to be at least seven months pregnant." Carrie was practically hissing.

Joe shook his head. *Just when they thought everything was straightened out, here comes Abby. The perpetual monkey wrench in the sink of life.* Suddenly he laughed, *where in the world had that come from? Monkey wrench in the sink of life?*

"What's so funny?" Carrie frowned.

"Oh, honey, sometimes you just gotta laugh – or you'd go crazy!" He came up behind her and swung her around in a dance.

"Joe? Have you hit your head or something?" she danced with him, smiling. As strange as it may seem, her confession and their subsequent prayers had brought a whole new freedom to their relationship. Carrie knew she was finally free of the secret that had nearly destroyed her, and their marriage.

"No, honey, no bump on the head for me." He stopped dancing and just held her close. "What are we going to do about Abby?" They both sighed.

"Do about me? Why do you have to do something about me?" Abby demanded, from the doorway.

Joe and Carrie both looked up. "Oh, I guess it's just something parents say!" Carrie went back to the stove, turning the pork chops. "These potatoes won't be ready for a bit yet, why don't we sit down and visit? Abby, tell us what happened? How did you lose your apartment?" Joe and Carrie both sat down, leaving an open chair for Abby. Reluctantly she sat down.

"Oh, I didn't lose my apartment. I moved out." Abby was not forthcoming with information.

"Why?" Joe asked, plainly.

"Well, you know, New York is so dirty, and noisy. I really just couldn't stand it there anymore, and thought I'd come home and visit you while I decided what to do."

They all knew she was lying.

"Honey, why didn't you tell us you were pregnant?" Carrie asked.

"Uh … you didn't ask?" Abby scrunched her face. "Not going to work is it? Oh, I don't know. It took me a long time to decide whether or not I was even going to have it, and then I just figured as long as I was coming home, I'd save the news to share in person."

Joe and Carrie looked at each other, questions dancing in their eyes.

"Whose baby is it?" Joe asked.

"It's mine." Abby stated clearly, looking bored.

"Abby, I may be old and doddering, but even I know it takes two. Who's the other one?" Joe asked again.

Abby was silent. "Just a guy, I never told you about him, and you wouldn't know him."

Carrie clenched her hands in frustration. This was like pulling teeth!

"I thought you wrote us about a new boyfriend ... uh, what was his name?" Carrie asked, "But ... you had to be already pregnant when you met him?" She crinkled her forehead, clearly confused.

"Oh, Rod? He wasn't that great, I only went out with him a few times. I dumped him." Abby flipped her hair back, tracing an imaginary shape on the tablecloth with her fingertip.

The pot of potato's boiled over, thankfully sending Carrie to stand at the stove, her back to the kitchen table. She took a deep breath.

"Abby, honey, you know we love you like our next breath. We'd like to know what's going on, what your plans are, how are you going to pay for this baby? Where are you going to put him?" Carrie said, from the stove.

"So, that's all that really matters isn't it? Money! That's all that mattered the whole time I was gone, you were so hung up on sending me money! Aren't you even happy you're going to have a grandchild? Did you ever stop to think about that? Are you throwing your only daughter and grandchild out on the street?" Abby stood up angrily, pushing her chair back till it nearly fell over.

"Abby!" Carrie said, coming back to the table, "That's not true! We love you very much. We just want to know what your plans are."

Joe held his hand up. "Carrie, Abby is a grown woman. She can make her own plans. She doesn't have to tell us anything. Hey, when is dinner going to be ready?" He turned his attention from Abby, to Carrie.

Abby frowned. This was new. Why weren't they pleading with her? How had she lost their attention so quickly?

"Oh, I'd say it will be another twenty minutes or so. Abby, would you get the salad things out of the fridge and put together a salad?" Carrie caught on quickly.

Abby narrowed her eyes. "Sure Mom, I'll make a salad."

Joe got up and kissed Abby on the cheek, and then gave Carrie a nice kiss on the lips. "Dinner smells great hon! I'll be back."

"So Abby, tell me about this baby. When is it due? Do you have any ideas for names? Oh! Do you know whether it's a boy or a girl?" Carrie asked the questions any mother would ask.

Abby was caught off guard. This was the time her mother should sneak her some money, while her dad was out of the room. What was going wrong?

"I didn't want to plan any names, 'cause I wasn't sure I was going to keep it." Abby said, tearing lettuce.

"Were you considering adoption?" Carrie felt a knot in her stomach.

"Adoption? Oh no, abortion is much easier and doesn't ruin your figure. But I took too long, and I started to feel the baby moving, and then I just didn't feel right about abortion."

Carrie swallowed hard to keep her words down where they belonged, and not flying around the room on little wings of anger and rebuke.

"I see, well, I'm glad you decided to keep the baby. Do you know if it's a girl or a boy?"

Abby laughed. "No Mom, I don't. I didn't want to know. I guess I'll be surprised like you were when you had me."

Carrie smiled at her, these were the first warm words she'd had since she arrived.

"You were a beautiful little surprise, dear." Carrie drained the potatoes in the sink and got out the masher.

Abby looked at her mother, not sure what to think of this new element to their relationship. The dynamic had changed, she just wasn't sure how. But she'd go with the flow for now.

And so they prepared dinner in relative peace and companionship.

Chapter 34

"Hello?" Connie picked up the phone, as she hung up her dish towel.

"Connie! Lydia here. Hey, did we ever find out what happened to Eleanor?"

"Well, darn it. No, we didn't. Where do you think she was?" Connie asked, frustrated she had forgotten Eleanor.

"I don't know. I just called her, and there was no answer. She'd never go anywhere this time of night." Lydia worried.

"Maybe something happened at the center, where her husband is, and she had to go." Connie offered.

"Maybe. I'm going to call her in the morning, and if she's not home, I'm going over there. Want to go?"

"Yeah, I do. Let me know ok?" Connie asked.

"I will. Good night, I hope I didn't call too late." Lydia hung up.

Too late? That was a laugh; it was never too late around here for some people who never went to bed. She turned off the light in the kitchen, and went straight up to bed, without stopping to say good night to Ron. The worst thing was, she didn't think he noticed.

****

Alice was finally alone in her room, facing her bed. This was where she wanted to be all day and now it was here. The bed ... and it was just her who was crawling between those sheets. *O Lord, how I can face this bed all alone? He slept on the other side of me for thirty-six years, now I have to sleep here alone?* She wrapped her robe tightly around her, looking heavenward, and then turned, and went out into the living room. She'd sleep in the big overstuffed armchair. Quietly she tiptoed through the darkened living room, being careful not to step on Dennis or Liz, who were curled up in sleeping bags, fast asleep. *They had to be exhausted!* She pulled the patchwork quilt from the back of the chair, and cuddled up in it, and closed her eyes. *O yes, Lord, this is so much better.* She began to relax, as the stresses of this hard day began to flee.

"Alice?" Liz whispered. "Are you ok?" Liz touched her shoulder, lightly.

"Liz! Yes, I'm ok. I hope I'm not disturbing you." Alice reached for Liz's hand.

"What are you doing out here?" Liz returned the squeeze of Alice's hand.

"I can't ... I can't face that big bed alone, honey." Tears threatened, as the words were spoken out loud.

"Oh!" Liz said in understanding, "You are more than welcome out here, in fact, I'm glad you're here." Liz leaned over and hugged Alice's shoulders.

"And I'm glad you're here. It means the world to me that Dennis is here." Alice smiled in the darkness. Liz eased down into a sitting position on the floor. They whispered for several minutes. Finally Alice said, her voice tinged with sleep, "Liz, thank you for being so good to my Dennis, but I've got to sleep now. I'm fading fast."

Liz reached up and kissed her cheek. "Good night, dear." And she tiptoed back to her sleeping bag.

Tomorrow was the memorial service, and they all needed their rest.

Chapter 35

Connie and Lydia walked up to Eleanor's front door.

"Lydia, how come we've never been here before?" Connie asked, as she knocked on the door.

"I was just thinking the same thing. I don't have a clue!"

They waited, no sounds coming from the little guesthouse. Lydia knocked again.

Connie leaned over and peeked through the window. There was no sign of life.

"Lydia, she's not home. The house is dark, and it just feels like no one is here. But come here, look at this."

Lydia and Connie cupped their hands around their faces, looking through the window.

"Oh my, Connie, look at those holes in the rug! And the furniture is practically falling apart!"

"Can I help you?" a loud, gruff voice came from behind them.

They jumped like two schoolgirls caught peeking on their neighbor's test paper.

"Oh!" Lydia put her hand on her heart. "You scared me to death!"

"What are you doin' here?" the man asked again.

"We're looking for Eleanor. And who are you?" Connie demanded, suddenly realizing they were not schoolgirls, but grown women on a legitimate errand.

"I'm the landlord. I own this house. I'm only gonna ask one more time – what are you doin'?" he was beginning to get louder, his face was turning red.

Lydia nearly giggled as she imagined smoke coming from his ears.

Connie elbowed her in the ribs. "Eleanor? She lives here right? Do you know where she is?"

"She left for a week, seein' her daughter, but that don't give you the right to come 'round peeking in winda's!" he finished and turned back to his own house.

Connie and Lydia giggled and laughed all the way up the driveway. "Good grief, he reminded me so much of Popeye. Oh, I'm so glad she went to see her daughter. I wonder why she didn't tell us."

Suddenly Lydia stopped, "Connie! If Eleanor is gone for a week, we could ..." She opened her eyes wide and took a deep breath.

"Could what?"

"You saw that sad old room, we could redecorate for her, while she's gone. I have stuff in the basement we're never going to use again, and its great stuff. What do you think?" Lydia was excited, the plans were buzzing around in her brain.

"That's a great idea!!! Hey, we should ask that grumpy old man if he'd let us in to do that. Let's ask now, while we're here, ok? Come on!" Connie grabbed Lydia's arm and nearly dragged her back down the driveway.

Chapter 36

"Martha! Come and look at what I got." Esther called, as she came in the back door. Ralph twined around her feet in greeting. "Martha! Where are you?"

"I'm here, what's the matter?" Martha came running into the kitchen.

"Look! I went to the library and got some CD's." Esther held up a stack of plastic containers, at the same moment Ralph decided he had waited long enough for Esther to pet him. He jumped up into Esther's arms, and the plastic CD's went skittering all over the kitchen floor, scaring Ralph to pieces so that he turned in mid-air, claws out, scratching Esther's arm, landing on the floor and its assortment of slippery CD's. His legs pedaled and pedaled, but he couldn't find a foothold, and when he finally did, he stumbled and his chin hit the floor, and then there was a streak of gray, and Ralph disappeared.

Esther gasped, and ran after him, "Ralph! Here kitty kitty! Come here, Ralph, its ok, come here sweetie." She went looking in all the corners, peering into his favorite hiding places.

Martha hid a smile and picked up the CD's. She thought she was going to enjoy this music very much. Stupid cat.

****

Alice dressed once again in her black dress. She looked at herself in the mirror. Her face was so white, and the tears so ready. She touched her face. *O Lord help me through this day.*

Dennis and Liz dressed quickly and quietly in the kitchen. Laura had taken them out yesterday during all the visiting and bought a new suit for Dennis and a black dress for Liz. Dennis was uncomfortable in the unfamiliar clothing, pulling at his tie, and shrugging his shoulders.

"Dennis, honey, are you ok? You haven't said hardly two words." Liz rubbed his shoulder.

He looked at her, with pain filled eyes. "No, not now." He shook his head, and held up his hands as if to say, 'Stay away.'

"Ok, I understand." Liz turned, and went to find the children. They were going next door to Sarah's house to stay during the service.

She met Alice in the hallway, and they hugged silently, then each continued on their way.

****

Dennis tugged at his tie for the hundredth time. It was hot and stuffy in the church, and he was sitting in the front row. The service seemed interminable, with every old man in the world getting up to tell a story about his dad. He sighed, inwardly. He wanted a beer and was dying for a cigarette. *And what I wouldn't give for a big juicy cheeseburger instead of all those casseroles the church ladies brought every day.* He sighed again, the pain inside his chest threatening to burst loose. He swallowed hard, keeping it down. When Liz showed him the telegram, he honestly thought he was having a heart attack of his very own. The pain surprised the hell out of him. He thought he was too old to love his father the way it turns out he did. He had to keep his mind on something else, anything else. He'd be damned if he broke down crying right here in front of God and everybody. Dennis, be a man. He repeated it to himself over and over, until it all seemed like one big long word.

He barely noticed the minister take the pulpit; he repeated the words to himself like a mantra. He fixed his eyes on the stained glass windows and named every color. He tapped his toe, inside his shoe. He clicked his teeth together, quietly, inside his mouth. Anything he could think of, to keep his mind off what was really going on, and who was really in that big, polished wooden box.

****

Alice sat next to Dennis, feeling the comfort of his coat sleeve against her arm. His presence was solid next to her, and she thanked God she was finally sitting in church with her son. *Lord, please open his ears to hear, and speak to his heart.* The words of her minister flowed over her like soothing oil, as she heard precious Scripture read and reverent prayers offered to her Heavenly Father. *Bud, can you hear? I know you're right there next to Him, can you see us? Can you see our son sitting here in church? Isn't this an answer to our prayers?* Alice wiped her eyes as she pictured Bud sitting at Jesus feet, talking and laughing, fellowshipping with his precious Savior.

****

Liz sat next to Alice, in church for the first time in years. The last time she was in church she had been a little girl. But it was oh so familiar, the look of it, the smell of the sanctuary, the sound of the organ. She remembered the hymns with an aching heart. Tears ran down her cheeks as she listened to the minister read the Scriptures. The words fell on her heart, like water, washing away the dirt of the world. She let it soak in, every word. She wished she could see Dennis. Surely he felt the same thing, how could he not? He had to feel the presence of the Holy Spirit, the love of the many Christian people gathered in this room. *Lord, please speak to Dennis' heart, show him how much You love him, please Lord?*

****

Laura closed her eyes, overwhelmed with feelings. Her sorrow for Alice, her joy that Bud was with his Savior, her thankfulness that she was sitting in church with her dear Elizabeth. *O Lord, how can a mind fathom all these things? How can a person bear great sadness and great joy at the same time?* She reached over and held Liz's hand. Before Liz's plane landed, Laura had decided that if Liz wanted to be called Liz, then she would be. If it was a sore point with Liz, Laura wanted to let it go. There were too many other wonderful things to concentrate on, to spoil it over a name. Laura felt Liz squeeze her hand in return, and they sat there, in that church holding hands, singing mighty old hymns and praying. *Thank You, Lord!* Laura breathed. *Father, I pray for Dennis, that You would open the eyes of his understanding, speak to his heart, and that he would hear of Your love for him.*

****

Dennis shifted in his seat, fidgetedy as a child, and hardened his heart. He tapped his toe five times in a row, and then seven times in a row. He'd get through this, he would. It was only a matter of time.

Chapter 37

Later that night, after the reception held in the fellowship hall, after smiling and accepting prayers and well wishes from everyone she knew, Alice sat in the overstuffed armchair, aching with tiredness. Laura and Dale sat on the couch, Dennis and Liz sat on the floor, with pillows at their backs. Nobody said much. Everyone was too tired. A funeral was a long day. The service at the cemetery was short but took a long time because of the cars pulling in and then out, single file.

"Well, I think we better get ourselves on home." Dale patted Laura's leg, next to him, as he hauled himself out of the couch. "Honey, you're coming to see us tomorrow, right? With the kids?" He held out a hand to Liz, to help her up off the floor.

"Yes, Dad, I am. I promise!" Liz smiled and leaned into his hug. *Oh the arms of her Daddy.* How she had missed them. Laura reached over and squeezed her shoulders. "I'll see you tomorrow honey. Bye Dennis." She reached for his hand, and he reluctantly gave it.

Dennis smiled and nodded. The sooner these people left, the sooner he could rack out on the couch and go to sleep. He was dead tired. And two more days before they could go home. Lord help! He rolled his eyes when no one was looking.

Within minutes, they were sacked out in their sleeping bags. And five minutes later, Alice came tiptoeing out into the living room, curled up in the armchair and went to sleep.

****

Lydia had called this impromptu meeting. They were sitting in her living room, drinking iced tea, and waiting for Gert. Connie and Lydia sat smiling, but not revealing their plan. Everyone was a curious as a cat.

"Can you see Gert coming yet?" Martha asked, as Esther peeked through the curtains, watching for her.

"No, not yet. What is taking her so long? Lydia, are you sure you won't give us a hint?" Esther turned from her post, smiling in anticipation.

"Nope, sorry!" Lydia made a motion of turning a key in her lips and throwing the key over her shoulder and grinning even more.

"Oh! Here she comes! I see her." Esther cried from the window. "Hurry up, Gert!" And she ran to open the door. "Come on in, we're all waiting for you!"

Gert clomped in the front door, narrowing her eyes. "What in the world is going on? I just started a new paint by number. Had to clean my brush hardly before I even started. What's the big emergency?" She fumed and plopped into a chair.

"OK! Here's our idea!" Connie stood up and Lydia grinned. "Well, first of all, we found out where Eleanor is."

"Oh my! I can't believe I forgot about Eleanor!" Esther covered her mouth with her hand.

Martha shook her head, as if she too, could not believe they had forgotten Eleanor.

"So, where is our Eleanor?" Carrie asked, sitting on the edge of her chair.

"She went to visit her daughter! Can you believe it? And not a word to us. Not one word! I don't understand that part, but anyway. Lydia and I went over to her house this morning and found that out from her landlord, and we peeked in her windows. To see if she was home." Connie defended herself as the ladies looked at her. Peeked in her windows? Whatever for? – was written all over their faces. "Ok, forget that part!" she laughed, "But we did find out, by peeking in her windows, that Eleanor is due for a redecoration, big time! And we got that grumpy old landlord to agree to let us in to do it. What do you think? Can we all put together enough things to redecorate her little cottage before she gets home?" Connie smiled, expectantly, looking around the group.

Lydia was nearly bursting at the seams. "We have some old furniture in the basement that would be perfect over there. Isn't this a great idea?" she looked around at everyone.

"You mean, redecorate her house, without her knowing, while she's gone?" Carrie wrinkled her forehead. "What if she likes her house, the way it is?"

"Trust me!" Connie said, "She doesn't! You'll see when we get there."

"Are you sure? I don't think I'd care for people sneaking in my house while I'm gone, redecorating it. I like my house the way it is." Carrie said.

"Well, at least come and look at it with us, and then we'll decide. How 'bout that?" Connie asked.

"Ok, we can do that." Carrie agreed.

Immediately, they all started thinking about the donations they could make.

"We have a braided wool rug in the basement. It's the wrong color for our house, too much blue in it." Martha said.

"Oh yes! And remember, we have that little desk and chair set in the basement?" Esther joined in.

"Good! You know, I think we should all go over there and see what needs to be done, and then make a plan for what we're going to bring and move. Sound good? Well, I mean, if we decide to do it." Lydia amended her suggestion, sheepishly looking at Carrie, but toward the door as she asked.

Carrie laughed, "Ok, let's go see Eleanor's house, and pray she speaks to us again!"

Chapter 38

Abby sat in her room, looking out the window, though not really seeing anything. She had never felt so alone. Coming home like this, a failure, nothing to show for four long years in New York. She'd had to sell nearly everything she owned, just to afford the trip home. There had been no way to keep her apartment. She'd been fired from her job, and no one wanted to hire a pregnant model, no matter how beautiful she was. With the baby coming, there had been no choice except to come home. The last place she wanted to be. She had hoped they would give her enough money to at least get her own little place, but they had changed. They no longer gave in to her hints and innuendo's; it almost seemed as if they were playing dumb.

Thoughts of Randy came flitting into her mind like so many butterflies, landing here and there, touching down lightly, yet bringing great pain. She loved him so much. Her heart ached with missing him. But her pride wouldn't let her call him, wouldn't let her tell him about the baby. He had broken up with her, because, oh this was hard to admit, because he had found her and Rod, kissing near his car. What a jerk Rod was, and what an idiot she had been to ever get involved with him, when she knew that Randy was exactly what she wanted. Randy was a good man, kind and loving, gentle with her. He had a good job, and she knew he was going to ask her to marry him. They were practically living together as it was.

Tears ran down her cheeks as she realized how badly that had scared her. So scared she had come on to the first man to look her way ... Rod. The thought of him turned her stomach. How could she have been so stupid? And most importantly of all – what was she going to do now? She leaned her head back in her chair and sighed. What was she going to do?

****

      Ron Watson sat in his pickup truck, waiting for the red light to change to green. He needed to go to the job site and deliver this last load of sheetrock. But he could stop by the office now and drop off the paperwork from the lumberyard. He went back and forth in his mind. He knew the paperwork could be dropped off at any time, that he needed to get to the job site, but thoughts of Peggy haunted him. Her laughing green eyes, her curly brown hair, her inviting smile. He was drawn like a moth to the flame, unable to help himself, or so he told himself. And he turned right, headed towards the office. He felt a warning in his spirit, but turned up the radio, drowning out that small voice. He wanted a little something to look forward to, a little bit of excitement in his life. What was so wrong in that? He worked pretty darn hard, he deserved a little something, and wasn't sixteen years of marriage more than most people were able to pull off? And besides, no one would be hurt by him stopping by the office. For all he knew, Peggy wasn't even there. And on and on, he rationalized until he pulled into the parking space, right next to Peggy's car. *Well, I'm here now, there wouldn't be much point in pulling out and heading to the job site, now is there?* And so, he got out of the truck, and headed into the office – heading for the flame.

Chapter 39

Alice waved from the door, as Liz pulled out of the driveway, kids strapped into the backseat, on her way to visit with her mom and dad.

"Dennis, I'm glad we have this time together. I have some things I need to talk to you about." Alice shut the front door, and came into the living room, sitting on the couch. Dennis was slouched in the armchair, watching reruns of M.A.S.H. Inwardly, he groaned. What did she want to talk about now? It seemed all they had done since he got here was talk talk talk. When could a man get a little peace and quiet? But he pasted a halfhearted smile on his face, and clicked off the television.

"Sure, Ma, what's up?" he focused on her.

"Have you heard anything at all from Doug? Anything?" she wrinkled her forehead, finding it hard to believe that her youngest son could have just disappeared from sight, and missing him during this hardest of times.

"Haven't heard a word, Ma, nothin' at all." Dennis stopped and then thought about his mom all alone taking care of the three kids. "What about the kids? I mean, do you want me to take them back, or …?" he let the question hang.

Alice looked startled. "Take them back? Oh my goodness, no!" She tucked a few stray strands of hair into her bun at the back of her neck. "Dennis, I can't be here completely alone. No, I can't do that." She shook her head. "I guess I need them, maybe more than they need me." She gave a little sad smile. "I have to take care of them, they're happy here, and somehow, I'll figure out how to do it."

Dennis shrugged. He'd offered.

"I want to let you know how things are financially." Alice sat up straighter and took a deep breath.

Dennis narrowed his eyes the tiniest bit but didn't say anything. Why hadn't it occurred to him to wonder if his dad had left him any money? His heart beat a little faster.

"Your dad left enough money for me to live on, until I die. The house is paid for, and I won't want for anything. When I die, whatever is left, will be split between you and Doug. You can sell the house or keep it. Whatever you boys decide. If Doug still hasn't shown up, I guess it will be up to you. I'm not sure how that will work; I'll have to speak to my attorney about it. Now there are the kids to provide for as well, if I die." Alice sighed, as the realities made themselves known.

Dennis took a look around the room, wondering if he'd ever want this house. He tucked this thought away in the back of his mind.

"But your dad did leave something for you now, and I want to give it to you. I'm glad we have a little time alone." She tucked her small hand into his big rough one, and he followed her down the hallway, to Alice's bedroom.

She brought him to sit on Bud's side of the bed and opened the drawer of his nightstand. She took out his big black Bible, smoothing the cover with loving hands.

"Dennis, the most important thing about your dad, was his faith in God. He loved the Lord from the moment he met Him, and his one prayer, every single night was that you would follow in His footsteps, loving the Lord and serving Him with your life. He prayed for Doug too, but Doug doesn't know the Lord, and his prayers for both you boys were different. He prayed for Doug's salvation, and for your sanctification." She paused.

Dennis had started listening in derision, but very slowly he came to hear what she was saying. "Sanctification? What's that?" hating himself for asking.

"It means, he prayed that you would be set apart. When God created you, He had a purpose for you. When you were a little boy, and asked Jesus into your heart,"

Dennis could feel tears starting, and he silently cursed.

"He had a plan for you, specifically for you, Dennis. Your dad prayed that God would set you apart and make you fit for that plan. And he always told me ..." Alice stopped to wipe her eyes, her voice cracking the teeniest bit, "that he wanted you to have this." She set the big Bible in Dennis' hands. "This is for you, from your Dad. You'll find the wisdom of God in there, as well as wisdom from your Dad."

Dennis fought his emotions. He didn't want any part of this, God wasn't for him, what would he do with a Bible? But he took a deep breath and only said, "Thanks Mom." He could gut it out, for his mom, this little while. Soon, they'd be back at home and things would go back to normal. She leaned over and hugged him, and then left him alone with the Bible.

It seemed hot in his hands; as if it knew it didn't belong there. His hands were far from holy, and while there had been a lot of things in these hands ... Bibles weren't one of them.

Curiosity took over, and he wondered what wisdom of his fathers would be in there. He opened the book, peeking inside, trying to see what the attraction had been. Amazed, he opened the book all the way, flipping the pages to find handwritten notes in nearly every margin. Neatly written in his father's hand, notes regarding what this verse meant to him, and a date by that verse, and prayers written in the wide margins. How could this book have inspired all this? He turned the pages, one after the other, looking for something. He didn't know what.

Then he noticed a verse highlighted in yellow, "Thus says the Lord: "Refrain your voice from weeping, And your eyes from tears; For your work shall be rewarded, says the Lord, And they shall come back from the land of the enemy. There is hope in your future, says the Lord, That your children shall come back to their own border." And neatly written in the margin were the words 'Dennis, 11-19-93' He wondered what the date signified, it meant nothing to him. But he knew his father had prayed for him to come back, and in tears. He closed the Bible. This was more than he could handle. He'd take it because it would make his mom happy, but that was it. He walked toward the door, hoping no one had come over and would see him carrying a Bible. He heard his mother in the kitchen, and the soft sounds of dishes being put away. Quickly, he tucked the Bible in his suitcase, underneath his clothes. Out of sight, out of mind, he said to himself.

Chapter 40

Lydia used the key and opened Eleanor's door. The ladies followed her inside. Quietly, they looked around, taking note of every detail.

"Oh my." Carrie said softly. Her hand came up alongside her cheek. "Oh, my goodness."

The poverty was so evident in every corner; it tolled its weary notes. They walked into the kitchen, and immediately noticed the new curtains.

"See! I can tell she just made those! They look brand new; they're clean and pressed. And pretty!" Carrie looked around at the ladies. "She is trying to make a new place for herself. I would hate to offend her, by redoing this place without her knowing. And yes, I understand now, that she doesn't like this place. I do understand." Carrie nodded her head, and then shook her head at the utter shabbiness.

They continued looking around, observing every tattered cushion, every broken chair leg, every curtain reduced to strings. After a few minutes, Connie spoke, "Well? What do we think?"

Esther had tears in her eyes, "I had no idea. How could we know her for so long, and not realize what a hard time she was having? How come we weren't better friends to her?"

"I don't know, I don't understand either." Martha agreed, "But maybe we can be good friends now, and do this for her. You know, she doesn't have to know we did it! I mean ... does she?" This new idea of doing it anonymously was more appealing. Eleanor might suspect they had done it, but they could plead ignorance. If the landlord would keep his mouth shut, maybe it could be done!

"Well, I know it might be silly, but I like the idea of doing it anonymously, and yes, I agree, we should do it." Carrie said, and looked around at everyone else. "Do you?"

They all nodded, agreeing that they should. Gert sighed loudly and said, "Yeah, I guess I got a few things I could donate. Stuff in my basement I haven't used in years. But I'd guess she'll be back in three or four days, we don't have much time."

"No, we don't. Maybe we should all go home and see what we have. Then we can start moving things out. Well, it might be a good idea to have a list of stuff we can bring over ... I don't want to move something out that we can't replace." Connie said. Eleanor had never been to any of their homes, except for Carries, so it was unlikely she would recognize anything they brought in.

"Good idea! Let's go home, make a list, and then we'll see what we can move out and what we'll have to keep." Lydia led the group towards the front door, getting her key out to lock the door. "Hope ya'll didn't have any big plans for the next few days!" She laughed.

Gert snorted. "Guess it doesn't matter now does it?" And no one could tell if that meant she was upset or glad to be doing it.

****

Liz sat in the family room with her parents, watching the kids play, in the backyard. There was a plate of homemade banana nut bread on the table, covered in a plaid tablecloth, and steaming cups of coffee. They laughed at the kids – first they sat in the sandbox, and then they ran to the swings, back and forth. They couldn't decide what to play with.

"I can't believe you put up this stuff again, after all these years!" Liz smiled at her parents.

"Honey, we put those up the same week Alice and Bud came to see you. The Lord told us we would see you again, and we learned that we had grandchildren, and we just couldn't wait. No matter when the Lord was planning for us to see each other, we wanted to be prepared." Laura held on to Liz's hand.

"Mom, I'm so sorry." Tears gathered in Liz's eyes, "I've been such a terrible daughter. I really am sorry; I didn't realize how bad I was being to you." She reached for a tissue and blew her nose.

"You're a wonderful daughter, and we love you more than anything. And now, to know and meet my grandchildren, and to see you and touch you again, well, my heart is just bursting. And to see you loving the Lord again, Liz, all my prayers have been answered. I'm sure you know we never stopped praying for you." Laura now reached for her own tissue.

Dale put his arm around Liz's shoulders. "We prayed for you every night, and many times throughout the day, when the Lord brought you to our minds. You were never far from us, honey, never. I'm just glad you're here now, sitting in this room with us, and our grandchildren playing in the backyard. It's a blessing you can't imagine." He smiled at her, touching her cheek, and then smoothing her hair. "I love you, Elizabeth."

"Oh Daddy, I love you too." The tears were flowing now, "Can you ever forgive me? I really do want to do better, and to do things right in my life."

"Already forgiven, that was never an issue." Laura told her.

"But how can you say that? After everything I've done to you? I mean, yes, I want your forgiveness, but how can you give it so easily? I don't understand." Liz wrinkled her forehead.

"Because of our Example. Our Heavenly Father loves us unconditionally, and He forgives us immediately upon our asking for it. He's our example and that's what we want to show you."

Liz sat in the chair and cried, but now they were tears of joy. Laura patted her hand and let the healing tears flow, handing her a tissue now and then.

"I'm sorry; I don't mean to blubber like a baby." Liz sniffed and wiped tears from her eyes.

"I understand, but tears can be a good thing." Laura smiled as she got up to refill their coffee cups.

"Ok! I'm done crying, really!" Liz wiped her face with another tissue and smiled. "Thanks, this is good coffee! Ok, I have some other news to tell you."

"Really? What's going on?" Laura asked. Dale sat quietly, simply watching the two women he loved visit back and forth, enjoying the feeling of being a Grandpa.

"Well, I'm learning to quilt!"

"Quilt? Oh my gosh, Liz, that's wonderful!" Laura reached over and hugged her shoulders. "Are you taking a class or what are you doing? Tell me all about it!"

"Oh, I guess you could call it a class. But really, it's just a group of ladies in my neighborhood that get together to quilt every week. They agreed to teach me to sew the quilt pieces together and even gave me some fabric to practice on." Liz reached in her purse, and pulled out a block she brought with her, hoping for a chance to show her mom.

"Liz! This is beautiful, look at your work! The stitches are tiny and even, and the points aren't cut off. This is absolutely gorgeous. Honey, I'm so proud of you!" Laura spread the quilt block on the table, smoothing it and touching it.

"Thank you." Liz smiled, the approval of her mother sinking down deep into her heart. What was it she had been running from and rebelling against all these years? *Talk about a rebel without a clue, that describes me to a 'T'!*

Chapter 41

Connie hurried downstairs to the basement, excited at the prospect of re-doing Eleanor's little cottage. She brushed away a few cobwebs and pulled the string to turn on the light bulb.

Hmmm, what was down here that Eleanor could use? Oh, there was the little bookcase they had taken out of the den when they put in built in bookshelves, that would look nice in the cottage. She moved a few cardboard boxes and found two end tables from when she and Ron were first married. She added them to her list. And what was in that box marked Fabric? How in the world had a box of fabric escaped her notice? She opened the flaps to find a bundle of blue plaid decorator fabric. Suddenly she remembered buying this to recover the couch, only to find out that Ron wanted to buy a new couch. Not being a great fan of recovering furniture, she had quickly packed it away before he could change his mind. They had gone that afternoon to buy a new couch. She smiled at the memory. It had been such a fun day. They had gone from furniture store to furniture store, looking at every couch in town. When her feet were aching with all the walking, they had stopped at that little sidewalk café and had stuffed mushrooms and a glass of white wine. It had been a wonderful day, it was a good memory. It glared in contrast to the present. The good memory faded like an old pair of blue jeans left in the sun. The Ron she was married to today was not the Ron that took her shopping for a new couch. What happened? The question nagged her endlessly but found no answer.

Maybe they could spend some time together tonight. The boys were gone to summer camp for two weeks, and maybe all they needed was some time alone. Her heart beat a little faster as she picked up the little bookcase and carried it upstairs. She would fix Ron's favorite dinner – steak on the barbeque, potato salad and some new peas from the garden. There was half gallon of his favorite ice cream in the freezer. They could eat out on the patio. She smiled, now full of plans. She'd light the mosquito candles early, so they wouldn't be bothered by bugs. They could open a bottle of wine, she'd wear her white flowing summer dress that was loose enough to not show any bulges.

She stacked the furniture for Eleanor in the corner of the living room, out of the way. She took the steaks out of the freezer and started the potato's cooking for the salad. Ron wouldn't be home for another two or three hours. She'd have time to make things nice and romantic. A shower, some perfume, a little extra makeup. She smiled, thinking about the evening, and how nice everything would be. She began to feel tingly all over as she remembered how romantic they used to be. Romance, that's what they needed, a good dose of romance.

****

Carrie came out of the shower, wrapped in her terry cloth robe. Digging around in that basement had left her dusty from head to toe. She grabbed a clean pair of denim shorts and a white T-shirt. Joe would be home soon, and she still hadn't started dinner.

"Abby!" Carrie knocked on the door that never seemed to open unless it was mealtime.

Silence.

Carrie knocked again, and a sleepy Abby opened the door a crack. "What?" she whispered, her eyes half closed.

"Abby? Are you sick?"

"No, just sleeping. What do you want?" Abby pursed her lips, irritated.

"I'd like you to help me with dinner. Why are you sleeping now? Please come downstairs and help me." Carrie called on her way down. She shook her head. She was through letting Abby do whatever she wanted. The girl was twenty-four years old for goodness sake it was high time she started to take care of herself.

"Joe!" Carrie startled as she ran into him in the hallway. "When did you get home? Gosh, you scared me!" She smiled, and went to him for a kiss with a hug.

"I'm sorry, honey. I came in and I didn't think anyone was home." He hugged her.

"I was upstairs, taking a shower. Dinner will be a little late tonight."

"That's ok, I had a late lunch." he asked as he sat at the kitchen table.

"I was with the girls, we decided to decorate Eleanor's cottage while she's gone visiting her grandchildren. Of course, we won't tell her it was us, she'll just have to believe the good fairy did it." Carrie grinned mischievously.

Joe grinned back. "Sounds tricky to me!"

"Oh yes, we are being very tricky. Joe, you should have seen her cottage, it was absolutely awful. So run down." Carrie formed hamburger patties at the kitchen counter.

"I have seen it, remember? The night I went over there to talk to Alfred about the drinking?"

"Oh that's right! I'd forgotten. Well, we decided to give her a little head start on the redecorating. We're all donating something we've had in our basements, just taking up space. I got that small table and chairs out. She could use them for a kitchen table, if you would bring them up for me." She smiled over her shoulder.

"Yup, I will, after dinner ok?"

"Ok with me! I thought it was so funny that Eleanor just left without telling anyone. That's just not like her. I hope everything is ok." Carrie frowned slightly.

"Oh my gosh!" Joe rolled his eyes. "I, uh … well, I forgot to tell you."

"Tell me what?" Carrie stopped working and turned to look at him.

"Well, she did stop by here on her way to the bus station to tell you. But it was a few days after your accident and I was kind of out of it … you know …" Joe's voice trailed off, as he looked at her and they both remembered that awful time. "I'm sorry."

"Oh honey, its ok." Carrie went to him and put her arms around him, hands out so she wouldn't get hamburger on the back of his shirt. "Are we ok?" she asked him in a small voice. "Are you still wondering about me?"

He sighed and was quiet for a few seconds. "Sometimes." She drew back and they looked at each other, communicating silently with their eyes. Carrie smiled and kissed his cheek. "That's ok, Joe. I understand." He reached out and placed his hand on her cheek, lovingly.

"What's the matter, did somebody die?" Abby said from the doorway.

This time Carrie rolled her eyes.

"Joe, honey, would you start the barbeque? Abby, would you get things ready for hamburgers and buns? Lettuce, pickles and all that stuff."

Carrie finished the hamburgers. "Abby, are you sure you're feeling all right? Why are you sleeping at this time of day?"

"Well, I'm seven months pregnant; I don't really have much else to do. I feel fine." Abby said, annoyed.

"That's true you don't have much else to do." Carrie thought for a minute, "Well, I've got something for you to do. You can help me and the girls fix up Eleanor's cottage while she's out of town."

Abby whirled around as fast as her added bulk would allow. "What?" the look on her face was incredulous.

"You heard me."

"Sorry, you can count me out. I'm not exactly in shape for moving furniture or climbing ladders to hang curtains. Good grief!" Abby slammed the head of lettuce on the table.

"Sorry, but we need you. We've got a lot of work to do in a short time. There will be lots of things you can do sitting down. And like you said, you don't have much else to do." Carrie said firmly, as she took the plate of hamburgers out to Joe in the backyard.

Abby fumed as she fished pickles out of the wide mouth jar.

Chapter 42

Connie finished up the potato salad and covered the bowl with Saran Wrap. She smiled as she wiped off the counter, poked the steaks to make sure they were thawed, and checked the peas. Ron should be home in a half an hour and she just had time to change into her white dress and fix her makeup. She ran upstairs, humming, and happier than she had felt in a long time. She just knew this was going to be a wonderful dinner and an even more wonderful night. The house to themselves, no boys to interrupt or divert their attention from each other … it would be like a second honeymoon she determined right then and there.

****

Esther came up from the basement, dust clinging to her clothes, her hair, and her eyelashes. She brushed her hands together, trying to rid herself from the awful dust.

"Martha, that basement is so dusty! We should get it clean one of these days." Esther wet a dish towel at the kitchen sink to wipe her eyes, before dust got in them, making them red.

"One of these days." Martha wasn't too enthusiastic about the idea of cleaning the basement. "Did you find the rug? And that little desk?" She was looking through the stack of mail.

"Yes, I found them. It's going to be quite a job hauling that rug up here. Anything good come today?" Esther continued wiping her face with the damp towel.

"Mostly bills and junk. Here's a letter for you though. Gosh, a real letter! Don't get many of those anymore!"

"Who's it from? I don't have my glasses."

"Um ... let's see, I can barely read the writing myself. Uh, Claire ...? No, I think its Cliff ... uh last name starts with a B, but I can't make out the rest of it. Know anybody named Cliff?" Martha set the letter down on the kitchen table and opened the electric bill. Cliff. The name suddenly brought the past into the kitchen. What in the world was he writing for now? Her heart sank.

Esther stopped washing her face at the sink. "Cliff? Oh, it couldn't be him. Let me see the letter. Oh brother, where are my glasses when I need them the most?" She hurried into the living room, looking everywhere for the wayward pair of glasses.

Martha sat for a minute, staring at the wall. Things were going along just fine; they didn't need a reappearance of Cliff. Suddenly one of the envelopes caught her eye.

"Buy 13 CD's for 1 penny!" Why, this must be one of those CD clubs Esther had been telling her about. Thirteen CD's for a penny! When they looked in the store, those darn CD's had cost about twenty dollars apiece. This was a deal! Her attention diverted, she quickly opened the envelope and started reading the pages. *Look at that list of CD's I can pick from!* Martha's eyes opened wide as she scanned the list. She sat down at the kitchen table, little slick colorful pieces of paper slithering everywhere. "Buy Two CD's and get four free!" one proclaimed. "Recommend a friend who buys five CD's and receive two CD's free!" another said. Good grief! There was free CD's floating around all over the place! They'd never have to pay for another CD again as long as they lived. Finally she found the order form, and started the hunt for her thirteen CD's.

Esther sank into her armchair, glasses firmly on her nose, and looked at the letter. Cliff Barton. Could it be the same Cliff she went to high school with? It seemed unbelievable; it had been so many years. They had met when they were both sophomores, in English class. The teacher had given them some kind of assignment, Esther couldn't even remember what it was now, but they had to do it in pairs. They had all drawn names out of a hat, and Cliff had drawn her name. They spent many evenings working on that assignment, probably more than were necessary. She smiled as she remembered their long talks, and the way he always walked her home in the evening. Soon, they were talking on the phone nearly every night, and when she turned sixteen, they began to date. They dated until they graduated high school, so in love with each other, it seemed marriage would be the logical next step. He went to his college, she went to work at City Hall in the county clerk's office, and before long, the letters didn't come and go so frequently. They quietly grew apart, and then Esther heard through a girlfriend that Cliff had gotten married. Part of her was sad, but she wasn't devastated. Before long she met Glen, they courted and then married. Her life with Glen had been good. Their marriage was happy and solid. Occasionally she had thought of Cliff and wondered how he was doing, but other than those infrequent thoughts – which usually only happened when she heard the name Cliff on the television – she rarely thought of him.

But looking at his writing now, on the face of the envelope, brought back a rush of feelings she didn't expect. Slowly she opened the letter and began to read.

Dear Esther, I hope this letter finds you well and happy. So many years have gone by that I hardly know where to start. What do I say? Somehow a simple "I'm sorry" doesn't seem to fit the bill.

I left for college, fully intending to graduate and go home, hoping to ask you to be my wife. The blood rushed to Esther's face and she was glad Martha was busy in the kitchen. *To this day, I'm not sure how it happened that I didn't. But I got caught up in the 70's scene – you know – sex, drugs and rock and roll. I never did graduate from college; I dropped out in the middle of my second year. I met a girl, her name was Hope, and we smoked pot together, and went to concerts and generally 'dropped out' of life together. I married her, and we lived in a commune for a while. We had two children, a girl and a boy. After a few years, she drifted away, off to find something more exciting than me. Unfortunately, motherhood didn't thrill her either. She left the children with me.* Esther felt her eyes fill with tears. *I'm not sure why I'm telling you all of this. I guess I want you to know what happened. Somehow, my intentions and the realities of life didn't square up. I finally did get myself together, and I'm now what you could call a respectable citizen, with a house and a job and grandchildren!* Esther smiled; Cliff always had a sense of humor.

But Esther, I do want you to know that not a day has gone by that I haven't thought of you. I know that you got married, and from the little I've heard, it seems like you were happy. I read in the paper a little over a year ago that your husband died. I'm so sorry Esther that you had to experience that loss.

It took me about two weeks to get up the courage to write this letter, and then another week to actually write it. Kind of silly for an old man, I know! I don't know if it's too soon for me to ask this, if it is, please forgive me. But I'd like to see you. Esther's heart began a pitter patter dance.

Perhaps we could get together one day for lunch? It's completely up to you, and I'll certainly understand if you never want to see me again. I'm including my phone number. Take care, dear Esther. Sincerely, Cliff

Esther slowly lowered the letter into her lap. Oh my. What had the Lord brought to her doorstep? Her recent loneliness suddenly seemed a long way off. She knew she should think about this, even pray about it. But at the same time, she knew without a doubt that she was going to call him and say yes – to lunch. She took a deep breath. Oh my. She couldn't think of anything else to say.

"Esther, look! We got one of those CD club things you were talking about. We can get thirteen CD's for a penny! I picked out six of them ..." Martha's voice trailed off. "Helloooo ....?" Esther was looking dreamily out the window.

"Oh! It was ... oh my ..." Esther smiled, "Well, remember my high school sweetheart? Cliff Barton?"

"Oh, yeah. him. What'd he want, after he practically jilted you at the altar?" Martha pursed her lips.

"Oh Martha! We were never at the altar! Don't be silly." Esther laughed. "He's invited me to lunch."

"Lunch?" Martha nearly shouted. "You don't hear a word from him for decades, and suddenly out of the blue he invites you for lunch? Well, you're not going, that's for sure!"

"Why, Martha! I do believe I will go, I just have to call him." Esther was surprised at her outburst.

"Are you out of your mind? He joined some commune and smoked pot. You certainly can't have lunch with a man like that!"

"Martha! How did you know that?"

Martha mentally groaned. How had she let that slip? Esther had asked her over and over if she knew anything about what happened during that time. Martha and Cliff's sister Maureen had been best friends. Esther had begged Martha for information, but Martha told her that Maureen wasn't talking about it, and she knew nothing. Nearly thirty years later and her little white lie had found her out.

"Oh Maureen told me, but I never told you. I'm sorry. I just didn't want you to know. Your knight in shining armor had fallen off his white horse." Martha shrugged her shoulders, disgusted with herself. "I really am sorry."

Esther was quiet for a second, "Well, it doesn't matter anyway. He may have been taking drugs and living in a commune thirty years ago, but he's not now. And really, Martha, I'm looking forward to seeing him. Remember we talked about my loneliness? Well, maybe this is an answer to my prayer." She smiled brightly. "I think I'll just go call him now, while I have some courage! You know, if I think about it too long, I might lose my nerve!" She took her letter and ran upstairs.

Martha sank into the couch. This was not good. She remembered how Esther and Cliff had been in high school. Completely and totally in love with each other. She didn't imagine it would take much to fan that flame into an inferno again. *And then where would I be? Alone. Again.* She leaned her head back and closed her eyes. Sure, Esther loved being married, and wants to be married again. It was easy for her, she had a good husband. Glen was a good man. He took care of Esther and loved her deeply. The thought of marriage gave Martha cold shivers. She wouldn't get married again, not for a million dollars. There had been a thought floating around in Martha's mind for years, one she had never even spoken to herself, but she knew it was there all the same. *I was glad when Alex died. What a relief! Lord, please don't send me to hell for that thought. You know how things were. I always kind of thought You took Alex as a way of looking out for me. Lord, what will I do if Esther leaves? I don't want to be married, absolutely not! But I don't want to live here alone either. What am I going to do?*

Chapter 43

Carl dragged the dresser up the basement stairs. "I better take this outside and blow off any spiders that might be living in here." He grinned as Lydia shuddered.

"Yes, please do! And quickly! Before one of them hops out into my house." Lydia searched the ground with her eyes.

Carl laughed. Lydia stuck her tongue out at him. He only laughed more. And Lydia couldn't help but giggle.

"Hey, I'm gettin' kind of hungry. How bout some dinner?"

"Yeah, it's coming. After you get that dresser outside, will you start the BBQ? I've got some chicken in that garlic marinade you like. And some macaroni salad!" she said, holding the back door open for him.

She went back into her kitchen, turned the chicken, stirred the salad and caught a glimpse of herself in the mirror. Good grief, she was dust from head to toe.

She poked her head out the back door, "Hey, while the BBQ's getting hot, I'm gonna run up and take a quick shower, and get rid of all this dust."

He nodded, and she ran upstairs. A nice cool shower would feel good. It had been so hot today, and all that rummaging in the basement had left her dirty and sweaty. She opened the closet door to get a clean pair of shorts when she noticed her new yellow summer dress she hadn't worn yet this year. She smiled and took it from the closet. Maybe some candles on their dinner table would be a good idea. She turned on the water and stepped in.

****

Connie looked at the kitchen clock. Ron should have been home fifteen minutes ago. Well, he'd be here any minute, she'd go ahead and turn on the BBQ, and get the steaks going. That way, when he got home, he'd smell them on the grill and it would put him in a good mood. The table on the patio was all set with a pretty cloth. The mosquito candles were lit all around, and a white candle was burning on the table. It gave the whole patio a romantic glow. In her white dress, her hair done just the way she wanted it, her makeup perfect, a bit of perfume at her wrists and neck, why, she felt like she was in one of those women's magazines. She glanced at the driveway, and finding it still empty, she picked a few flowers from the yard. She found a vase under the kitchen sink, and quickly washed it, making it sparkle. There! The table was perfect. Candles, flowers, and a pretty wife ... what more could a man want?

****

Laura pulled up to the departure curb of the airline. Dennis unpacked the luggage from the trunk, while Liz unstrapped the kids from their seats. It was a flurry of activity and Laura could feel the last moments slipping away far too quickly. Even worse was the policeman eyeing them, as if they were taking too long. There was a big sign near the door "Drivers must remain in the driver's seat". She couldn't even get out and hug her babies! Liz brought Katie and Danny around to her side, so Laura could hug and kiss their little faces.

"Bye Mom and thank you for everything. I promise to stay in touch." Liz reached inside the car and hugged her mom through the window.

"Bye, honey, I love you. Please be careful, ok?" Laura's eyes filled with tears, finally. How hard it was to say goodbye after only a few short days with them. She craned her neck to look for Dennis, but he had already loaded the luggage on a cart and was inside. She sighed and told herself to pray for him more. Liz turned at the doorway and waved again. Katie and Danny both waved, "Bye Grandma!" She sat there watching them until she could no longer see them in the crowd. Tears spilled over and down her cheeks.

"Ma'am? You'll have to leave the departure area now. You can't wait here any longer." A policeman was at her open window, his sunglasses like mirrors.

Laura sniffed and wiped her eyes with the back of her hand. "Oh, I'm sorry. I'm going now." She started the car and pushed the button to roll up her window. The policeman nodded, and she pulled out into traffic. *Oh Lord, please take care of them. Keep them safe, and Lord, please touch Dennis' heart. Take care of my Elizabeth and send her home for good soon.* She gasped. Where had that prayer come from? "Send her home for good soon?" She had hoped Elizabeth would be able to come home for a visit now and then, but never had she imagined Elizabeth coming home for good. And so she prayed her way home, pulling into the driveway of a now empty house.

Chapter 44

Esther took a deep breath, and dialed Cliff's number. What was she going to say? She was just about to hang up when she heard his voice, "Hello?" It was quiet and deep, peaceful and mature.

"Cliff? This is Esther." She was so nervous the words barely came out.

"Esther!" The joy in his voice was unmistakable. "Esther, I'm so glad you called!"

Her heart flip flopped. "I just got your letter today, I figured I better call right away before I lost my nerve!" she laughed. Oh, why had she said that? Was she so naïve that every thought spilled out of her mouth?

"I'm so glad!" he repeated. "Does this mean you'd like to have lunch with me?" She could hear the smiles in his voice.

"Yes, I would." She couldn't keep her mouth from curving into smiles.

She heard him chuckle on the other end of the line. "What a relief! First of all, I was afraid you wouldn't call. Then I was afraid, if you did call, it would be to give me a piece of your mind!"

"Cliff, it was a long time ago. I don't hold grudges. Now Martha, she's another story! She believes you jilted me at the altar!" Esther laughed. But Cliff didn't answer her laugh with one of his. "Cliff? I was just kidding."

"I know, Esther, but I look back at the time in my life and see the biggest mistake I ever made. Except for my children, I'd wish it never happened. I just can't tell you how sorry I am. Can you ever forgive me?"

"Yes, I do forgive you. Everything worked out all right, God gave me a wonderful husband, and I've had a good life. And now, we are planning lunch, right?"

There was a small silence, but then Cliff said, "Lunch! Yes, any idea where you'd like to go?"

"Well, I've always liked that little Italian place down near the big theater. Do you know the one I mean? The Spaghetti Café?"

"Yes, I know it. I eat there all the time! How come we've never ran into each other?" he laughed, incredulous.

"Oh my gosh! I have no idea! I don't eat there a lot, but I do like their food."

They chatted for a few more minutes and decided to have lunch the next day, meeting there at 12:30.

"Esther, I just can't say how wonderful it is to hear your voice. I can't wait till tomorrow, I feel like I'm seventeen again!" She could hear his familiar voice, and it sent thrills down her neck, as she remembered their long talks on the telephone. It seemed the same now.

They said their goodbyes, and Esther lay back on her bed, looking through the ceiling. Seeing them both as they had been, remembering all their dates, all the time they had spent together in school and during the summers. All the memories blurred into each other, bringing to her mind the perfect and idyllic romance they once had. She realized that her loneliness was gone, and her heart was full again. Thank you, Lord, she prayed.

She turned her head and glanced at the clock. Six o'clock! She sat up with a jerk, my goodness, she was a grown woman, and here she was lying around daydreaming like a teenager. She hurried downstairs to fix dinner and face Martha.

Chapter 45

The candles burned out, one by one, sending little smoke trails into the air. Connie sat at the patio table, and realized her husband wasn't going to be home for this romantic dinner she had planned. She moved the silverware around with her finger, trying to figure out what had gone wrong. She had called Ron's cell phone several times, but it went right to voicemail, and never rang. It was dark now and she didn't know whether to be worried or mad. It wasn't like him to be this late without calling. But good grief, he'd been so unpredictable lately, it was hard to know what he was thinking or doing. A tear spilled onto her cheek as the loneliness pressed down into her heart. She sat there, all alone at the pretty table, the cold food, the chill creeping into the air as darkness came on and the silence all served as nasty reminders that her marriage was going down the drain. And she was helpless to stop it. Where was he? Anger began to settle into her chest, causing her heart to pound for a completely different reason than it pounded this afternoon. He knew the kids were gone for two weeks, he knew she was here all alone. Then suddenly it hit her why he hadn't come home. He didn't want to be alone with her. He hated her that much. Tears flowed freely now, as the hurt twisted in her heart like a knife. She covered her face with her hands, her elbows on the table and cried. *Lord, what am I going to do?* The tears kept coming; she was helpless to stop them. The disappointment was intense. She had very different plans for this time of the evening than sitting here alone crying. Her nose dripped, and her mascara ran. She wiped her cheeks with the back of her hand, smearing the mascara to the outside of her cheeks. Her eyes were red and puffy, and her face was blotchy and empty of makeup. She sniffed and grabbed a paper napkin off the table to blow her nose, heading for the bedroom upstairs and ran smack dab into Ron.

"AAAAH!" she yelled, her heart thumping and blood racing. "Where in the world did you come from? You scared me to death!" She put her hand over her heart, breathing hard.

When she jumped, he jumped. They scared each other.

"Good grief!" he yelled, then looked at her more closely. "What happened to you?"

She looked at him, "Yeah you'd like to know wouldn't you? Where have you been? It's almost eleven o'clock!" She looked at him, her eyes defiant, and her chin trembling.

He had the grace to look sheepish. "I'm sorry, well; I had a flat tire on the truck. The tow truck was busy tonight, I guess, cause I had to wait almost two hours. Then, well ..." He looked away, "I stopped by Hank's to have a beer, I saw a coupla guys there I work with, and time just got away from me. I am sorry." He managed to look somewhat sorry.

She eyed him suspiciously. "Ron, you knew the boys were at summer camp. You knew I'd be here all alone, waiting for you. Did you break your dialing finger while you were drinking beer?"

"I tried to call you while I was waiting for the tow truck, but I lost my battery on the phone while I was calling the truck. There is no phone hooked up at the job site yet ... then, well, I just forgot. Hey, I said I was sorry! What do you want? Blood?" his voice rose as her eyes rolled.

"I worked hard today and fixed this nice dinner for us. I dressed up so I would look nice for you. I wanted us to have a romantic dinner." And the tears began again, which only made her angrier. "Thanks a lot! I had a great evening here, all by myself. Really! A great time!" The sarcasm rolled off her tongue, as she headed back into the house. "Enjoy your dinner, dear! I made it just the way you like it ... cold!" She slammed the kitchen door.

Ron stood by the patio table and sighed. What in the world was wrong with her? He was a little late coming home, and he gets this? Thoughts of Peggy floated through his mind. He couldn't help but contrast Peggy's calm cool beauty with Connie's smeared and disheveled appearance. Look nice for him? Good grief, she looked like she'd been through a world war. He began to wish he had taken Peggy up on her offer for dinner and drinks tonight; it would have been a lot more enjoyable than this. But no, he tried to be the good husband and turn down a pretty girl, and this was the thanks he got? He shook his head in disgust, and thought maybe the next time Peggy offered, he'd just say yes. He started to go in the house, when the patio table caught his eye. The tablecloth, the flowers, the few candles still burning, the wine glasses. He remembered the white dress Connie was wearing and the flower in her hair – askew as it was. And even though her mascara was all over her face, it told him she had put on makeup. He groaned. The realization that she had tried to prepare a romantic night for the two of them was like a cold splash of water on his face. And he didn't like it. He wanted to be right; he wanted to be the one wronged. He wanted to nurse his grudges and make everything Connie's fault. But here was plain evidence that she tried. Now he would have to admit he was wrong. He cringed as he thought about this. Swallow his pride; go to his wife, crawling on his hands and knees? He shook his head as he walked back into the house.

Chapter 46

"Esther, come and pick out the CD's you want ok?" Martha had cleared the table and brought out the CD club paperwork. She was anxious to get this in the mail and receive all her free CD's.

"Martha!" Esther laughed, her cheeks blooming roses. "You'd think this CD idea was yours!" Esther sat down at the kitchen table. "Oh shoot, where are my glasses?" She got back up again and went to look to for them.

Martha sighed loudly. Ralph took this as a sign that Martha needed a good twining around the ankles, and so he happily twined. Martha gave him a gentle shove, peeking out of the corner of her eye to see where Esther was. Nowhere in sight. Ralph wasn't discouraged, he returned for more twining. Martha rolled her eyes, and gave Ralph a little harder shove, still keeping an eye out for Esther. Ralph sat on the kitchen floor, looking at Martha with one eye. He turned his head slightly as if to say 'Fine! Be that way!' Then, Martha could swear he chuckled to himself, and returned to Martha's ankles. With a firm hand, Martha reached down, picked up Ralph and deposited him in the laundry room, shutting the door. She smiled to herself. *We'll see who gets the last laugh!*

"Here they are! They were in the bathroom." Esther sat down at the table. "Ok, what do I do?"

"Well, look on this list here, and pick out the CD's you want. Then write the number in these little boxes here." Martha pointed to lists and forms.

And for the next half hour or so, they busily read lists, and marked boxes, erasing and then writing, deciding which CD's they wanted to own … for a penny! The print was so small it took them some time to decipher the titles, but they persevered and finally had thirteen CD's picked out and written neatly in their little boxes.

Suddenly an eerie sound pierced the kitchen quietness. They both looked up and then at each other, hearts beating faster.

"What in the world was that?" Esther whispered.

Martha's eyes opened wide. "I have no idea. Grab the phone, in case we need to call the police." They quietly got up, slowly looking around the kitchen.

"There it is again! It sounds like something is dying." Esther and Martha clasped hands as they began a search of the house, peering out windows, and into corners. Quickly opening doors and looking inside.

The noise sounded again. "I think we're moving away from it, it's not so loud. It must be in the kitchen! I wonder if a wild animal crawled into the basement." Esther shuddered, remembering her foraging down there this afternoon. "Maybe we should call the police to come and look for it? We don't know how to deal with a wild animal?" She looked questioningly at Martha.

"Wild animal? We live in the city, how could a wild animal get into our basement? I think we'll look pretty foolish if we call the police." Martha shook her head.

"Martha! There is something in this house!" Esther whispered loudly. The clutched each other's arms.

"Let's just listen for a minute and think. Maybe we can figure out what it is. Maybe it's just a couple of kids outside."

They listened and were rewarded with a long, piercing yowl.

"Martha! I think it's in the laundry room. I'm going to peek through the window in the door and see if I can see anything." Esther tiptoed towards the laundry room door.

The laundry room! Martha suddenly remembered Ralph. Oh brother, she was in trouble now!

"Esther." Martha said out loud, in a normal voice. "It's all right. It's just Ralph. I, uh, well I put him in the laundry room earlier."

"What?" Esther whispered, then realizing there was no longer any need to whisper repeated out loud, "What? Why in the world did you put Ralph in the laundry room?" She opened the laundry room door to find Ralph sitting on the washer, washing his paws, and wiping his face. He looked up to see her, gave her a dirty look and ran out into the living room. "Ralph! Come here little kitty. It's ok. Here kitty kitty."

"Martha, sometimes I can't figure you out." And Esther ran out of the kitchen in search of Ralph, trying to calm his ruffled feathers.

"Geesh!" Martha said under her breath. "That cat scared me out of my own nine lives. How can you love an animal that makes a sound like that?"

Martha went back to the CD list and completed the address portion of the card. She fixed a stamp on the right side and put it on the counter near the back door, ready to go into the mailbox. Their CD's would be arriving any day now! She smiled in satisfaction.

Chapter 47

Joe pulled up in front of Dennis and Liz's house, the car full to bursting with passengers and luggage. They were all tired and hungry, and eager to get home again, back into their own beds, their own shower, and some privacy.

"Joe, thank you so much for picking us up. I know it's a long trip to the airport." Liz hugged him.

"Aw, it wasn't anything." Joe blushed.

"Still, we appreciate it." Liz smiled.

"Yeah, Joe, thanks." Dennis said, clearly anxious to get the car unloaded. "I'll just get all the stuff out of your car, so you can get going."

They worked together and finally got everything in the house. Joe drove back to his own house and Dennis and Liz were left alone for the first time in a week.

Immediately Dennis sank into the recliner and turned on the TV. Liz stared at him for a minute, and then shrugged. Oh well, she'd packed the suitcases, she might as well unpack them. She took the kids suitcase into their room.

Dennis flipped through channels, not even really seeing what was playing. Scenes from the previous week replayed through his mind in a loop. His mother, the coffin in the church, the Bible, the stained-glass windows, the kitchen table full of food from the church. If he died, how many people would bring food to put on their kitchen table? If they did, it would be for Liz, not for him. He turned up the TV, determined to drown out the thoughts. He flipped to MTV, turning it up even louder, trying to lose himself in the weird and bizarre images flashing on the screen and the loud screaming music.

Liz looked out of the kid's doorway, wondering what was going on. She saw Dennis sink further into the chair, lighting a cigarette and squinting his eyes as the smoke wafted past, and pushing the remote button to turn the music up louder. *O Lord, what is happening?* Quickly she finished with the kid's clothes and belongings, making a laundry pile as she unpacked.

"Honey, could you turn that down a bit? It's really too loud!" She yelled to be heard.

He continued staring at the screen. She sighed and took their suitcase into the bedroom.

Carefully, she hung up her new dress, bought for the funeral. And Dennis' new suit on its suit hangar. Most of the clothes went into a laundry pile. She carefully loaded her arms with things from the bathroom and put them away. A glance at Dennis from the hallway showed he was on his second cigarette since she'd gone into the bedroom. She took the last stack of clothing from the suitcase and noticed for the first time, a large Bible. Now, that was puzzling. It wasn't hers. Maybe Alice put it there for them. She opened it, and found Bud Oster written on the flyleaf. Oh! This was Bud's Bible, and Alice must have given it to them. Tears filled her eyes as she leafed through the pages.

"Dennis! Did you see this? Your mom gave us your dad's Bible." Liz came into the living room, with the Bible in her hands, holding it out to Dennis.

He looked up, saw her, and then the Bible, and he scowled. "Did you put this in our suitcase, or did your mom?" Liz asked again, handing the Bible down to him.

After a few seconds, he took the Bible from her, still scowling. "Aw, she gave it to me." He didn't open it.

"That's a treasure Dennis, to have something like that from your dad." Liz smiled.

He held the book for a minute, as if he was not sure what to do with it. Just looking at the book made him mad. He didn't want to hold it in his hands, but where would he put it? His end table was filled with magazines and an ashtray, there was no room for a Bible, especially one as big as this one was. And he didn't want it staring him in the face anyway.

Finally, he handed it back to Liz. "Here, put it away. I don't have anywhere to put it."

"No, it's your Bible. You put it away." And she turned to leave the room, only to hear something go flying by her head and hit the wall with a thump. She jumped out of the way, looking to see what Dennis had thrown. Tears again filled her eyes as she saw the Bible lying on the floor, all the pages folded and crinkled from the landing.

"Dennis! What ..." she cried, only to find him coming towards her in a blur. She backed up, against the wall.

"I told you to put it away. If you would only do what I tell you, this wouldn't happen!" he yelled, rage pouring out of his voice. He pinned her against the wall, his large strong hands on her shoulders. Tears ran down her face, her hair was in her eyes, but she couldn't get her hands up to clear her vision.

"Dennis, please. Stop it." She cried, totally unprepared for the outburst.

He snarled at her, mimicking her, "Dennis, please stop it. I'm so sick of you and your holier than thou attitude, I'm so sick of the whole damned thing, my mother, that church, all those damn church people, your sickening mother ... I hate you all!" And he raised his arm, hitting her face with the back of his hand. Her head spun around, hitting the wall. She screamed and he lost all self-control, and hit her over and over again, until she finally slumped onto the floor, unconscious. When she hit the floor, he stepped back, cold reason returning to him in a rush.

Oh my God, what I have done? He turned to see Katie and Danny in their doorway, faces white, eyes wide with terror, tears running down their faces, but not uttering a sound. He backed up into the middle of the room, turning this way and that. Not knowing where to go or what to do. He saw Liz, lying on the floor, bleeding and broken. He saw his children frightened to death of him. He saw his father looking at him, disapproval and disappointment etched on every line of his face. He saw his mother watching him, big slow tears running down her face. He turned the other way and saw ... he gasped. He rubbed his eyes with his hands, clearing them of their film. He looked again, and He was still there. It was Jesus, looking at him with eyes of love and holding out His hands to him. His face was pure love and light and He beckoned Dennis with His scarred hands and Dennis heard Him say *Come to me all you are heavy laden and I will give you rest. Come to me.* Dennis felt tears running down his face; he continued to back up until his back hit a wall. He turned, but he was in a corner, there was nowhere left to turn. And he sank to his knees, crying. *Oh God, I'm so sorry. Please forgive me, I don't want to treat my family like this, Oh God, help me!* He held his head in his hands, crying, still on his knees and slowly began to feel peace come over him, peace that healed his wounded and broken heart, peace that filled him like a warm light, peace that he couldn't understand. He looked back to the place where Jesus was, but He was gone. And then he understood. Jesus had left the corner, and taken up residence in his heart once again. *Oh my God*, he breathed in awe, and this time it was a prayer.

He could have stayed there forever, basking in that peace. Slowly, he remembered what just happened. He looked over at Katie and Danny who were still watching him. Liz! He jumped up and ran to her. Afraid to move her, he backed away. He couldn't see her face; it had turned toward the wall when she fell. Her body was crumpled and in a weird position. *God, help me!* He quickly prayed.

Suddenly there was a pounding on the door. And a shrill voice yelling.

"Open this door right now! I've called the po-lice, you better open this door!" He ran to the door to find a skinny gray-haired old woman, standing on the porch, a shovel in her hands, held across her body like a sword. Her face was fierce, and red, dripping with sweat from the exertion of running across the street in the heat, and in her haste, she had forgotten her kitchen towel.

She held out her shovel towards him, "Don't you dare touch me!" she glared at him. "Where is Liz? I knew you were home by the screamin'. I'm telling' you, I've taken a liking to that sweet gal, and she might be willin' to put up with your crap, but I'm not!" Gert's eyes swept the room and landed on Liz.

"Oh Lord God, help us." She prayed, unknowingly. "Don't just stand there you old goat, call an ambulance! Can't you do anything right?"

Dennis ran to the phone, reason returning. He called the ambulance. Katie and Danny trembled from the doorway, too scared to even go hide in the closet. Slowly he walked over to them.

"It's ok. I'm not going to hurt you." He knelt in front of them, not touching them. "Daddy's sorry, I'm sorry I hurt Mommy, I'm sorry I scared you. I promise I won't do it again." He looked at them little trembling lips, and the tears running down their little red cheeks. "Can I give you a hug?" he waited.

They both turned and ran into the bedroom, crawling under the covers, and holding onto each other.

Dennis slumped a bit, but he got up and went over to be with Liz. As he approached, that old lady stood up, standing guard over Liz and held out her shovel again.

"Don't you come near her!" she glared at him again.

He held up his hands, "It's ok, I'm not going to hurt her, I promise."

Gert narrowed her eyes and turned her head a bit. "Yeah, whatever." She let go of the shovel with one hand to reach down and pull up her green plaid shorts which were too big, and dangerously close to falling down around her ankles. She felt she would lose credibility with this big guy if she stood there in her knickers. She turned her head and raised her shoulder to wipe sweat off her face with her red, white and blue t-shirt emblazoned with the words 'We Will Never Forget'.

Off in the distance, a siren could be heard. Dennis breathed a sigh of relief, knowing help was on the way. He also knew he would probably be arrested and taken to jail. But he still felt the peace and going to jail didn't concern him near as much as Liz. He ran out to the street to flag down the ambulance. It wasn't the ambulance, it was a police car. Still, he waved his arm to signal them *This is the house where I beat up the love of my life.* Tears filled his eyes as he remembered what he'd done. But the peace remained.

Chapter 48

It was nearly noon, and Esther was checking her clothes in the mirror. Her heart was beating fast, and her cheeks were blooming like roses. After thirty years, she was going to see her high school sweetheart. It seemed unreal.

My gosh, when was the last time I bought new clothes? She turned this way and that, looking in the mirror, judging herself harshly. She'd been holed up in this house for a year now, rarely going shopping for anything more than groceries. Well, it was high time for a change, that's for sure. At least Martha wasn't here to give her the eye. She knew Martha didn't approve, but it was Esther's life. *I prayed about this Lord, remember? My loneliness and how much I wanted to be married again? I would never want to take a chance with a new man, someone I didn't know, but Cliff, well, he's someone I already love. Thank you, Lord,!*

She gave a final fluff to her hair and headed for the garage. A lunch date! Will wonders and miracles never cease? Her heart sang, and her lips couldn't help but smile. There was a small nagging feeling of being unfaithful to Glen in the back of her mind and she stopped for a minute, closing her eyes, and praying for guidance. *Lord?* And then she remembered the sound of Cliff's voice on the phone and shivers ran up and down her spine. She headed for the car.

****

Lydia and Connie stood in the middle of Eleanor's living room, satisfied with the progress they had made. Martha had borrowed Connie's car and gone to the hardware store to get staples for the staple gun.

"Lydia, just thinking about Liz gives me shivers. I almost wish we hadn't started this project. I'd much rather be at the hospital or taking care of her children." Connie sighed, feeling helpless.

"I know, I would to. Let's just hurry and get this done. I mean, let's do it nice for Eleanor, but let's hurry. I'm glad Esther will be here after lunch. A date! Hard to believe!" Lydia talked, as she pulled the blue plaid fabric over the couch. "Is that centered?"

And together they worked to recover the old couch. They had managed to fix the broken leg, so it no longer wobbled. They had laid down the red and blue woolen rug Martha had brought over, dragging the old one with holes out into the truck Joe had let them borrow for the day. The little desk and chair were perfect in the corner by the window, and Connie's end tables looked lovely on each end of the couch. It was becoming a welcoming room filled with beauty.

"Don't let me forget the time, I don't want Liz's mom waiting at the airport." Lydia called from behind the couch.

"I won't, I'm keeping my eye on the clock. It still seems so unbelievable that you know her mother." Connie said around a few pins she held in her mouth.

"Isn't it? God sure is in control of everything, isn't He?"

****

Gert sat next to Liz's hospital bed. She had never left her side from the time she arrived at the house. She saw to it that Dennis was taken away in handcuffs, and she rode in the ambulance with Liz. As far as she was concerned, she was staying until Liz went home.

"Gert? How's she doing?" Carrie whispered as she quietly entered the room.

"There's been no change. She just lies there, never making a sound." Gert shifted on the hard hospital chair.

"Has the Dr. been in yet?" Carrie carried the other chair over to sit next to Gert.

"He should be here any minute, I heard him down the hall."

Carrie took Gert's hand in hers. "Thank you for taking care of her, Gert. I'm so glad you were there, although it could have been dangerous for you to go over there."

"Well, I guess so. Though at the time it didn't occur to me. I been callin' the po-lice for months now, and I was tired of waitin' for them to show up. I figured I could do as much with a shovel. After all, I took care of one goat with it, why not another?" And they smiled at the memory.

"Joe went down to the jail with him and went down again this morning. It's hard to believe he could do such a terrible thing and then turn his life over to the Lord." Carrie paused and Gert snorted.

"Yeah, whatever. Jailhouse religion if you ask me." Gert rolled her eyes.

"Oh Gert! I'm sure that's not it. His family has been praying for him for so long, I'm sure it's just the answer to their prayers."

"You think it was the answer to their prayers this sweet little girl got beat to an inch of her life?" Gert's freckled chest was all blotchy as she became angry all over again.

"No, honey of course not. But it was an answer to prayer that he turned to God, instead of running away. Which he could have done."

Gert pursed her lips. It was clear they had different opinions.

"Let's just wait for the doctor, ok?" Carrie said, squeezing her hand.

Gert nodded her head. So, they sat quietly amidst hospital sounds and smells, quiet conversations in the hallway, the beep of machines keeping people alive, telephones and buzzers, elevator doors closing and waited for the doctor to come in. Liz lay quietly, eyes closed, her face nearly covered in bandages.

Chapter 49

Esther followed the hostess to a table near the window. She was early and now she wished she'd been late. So she wouldn't appear too eager. She sighed. Feminine wiles had never been her thing. She looked around, noticing the red tablecloths, the baskets of bread on each table, the beautiful gold yellow faux painted walls and the dark green tapestry drapes at each window. The atmosphere was warm and cozy, instantly making you feel like you never want to leave.

She asked the waitress for a cup of decaf and waited. Afraid to watch the door for Cliff. What if he had gained a hundred pounds? Or maybe he was still in the hippie thing, he might be wearing beads and sandals. She took a deep breath. *Lord, I'm sorry. I should only think the best, right? I mean, after all, You brought him back into my life. You wouldn't have done this if he wasn't the one for me, right?*

"Esther?" she started, and looked up into those deep brown eyes that could only belong to Cliff.

"Cliff!" she stood up. He was smiling, and they looked at each other for what seemed an eternity. Her heart melted, his presence was nearly overpowering. She felt her heart come alive again, and for the life of her, couldn't think of a thing to say.

He held the back of her chair, "Let's sit down ok?"

"Oh! Yes, of course." Esther laughed nervously. What in the world had she stood up for? Her cheeks felt hot as she blushed.

"Esther, you look so beautiful, so much like the girl I was in love with so many years ago." He laughed and went on, "You know on the way over here, I was suddenly filled with doubts. I thought, what if she's gained a couple hundred pounds? But you are just as beautiful as I remember."

"Cliff!" Esther laughed as she confessed, "I thought the same thing about you. I mean, what if you'd gained a hundred pounds. Well, you look good too. And you're right, you're downright respectable, I'd never have known you used to be a hippie!"

They laughed, and before she knew it, he had reached over and covered her hand with his.

"I've missed you so much. Well, you know, I thought I'd be suave and debonair and impress you with my conversation skills, but here I am spilling my guts like some lovesick teenage boy." He shook his head. "I just really feel so lucky that you even agreed to see me, after the way I treated you."

"Cliff, why wouldn't I see you? We have good memories together. I won't deny that I loved my husband very much, we had a wonderful marriage. But I know he would want me to be happy, and lately I've just been very lonely." The words were out of her mouth before she knew it. *My gosh Esther! Have you no self- respect? You don't have to tell everything, you've been here with him for five minutes!* Her hand flew up to cover her mouth.

Very diplomatically he handed her the menu and pretended not to notice. "What do you feel like having?"

And so they ordered, and leisurely ate their food. They talked and caught up on the years. The restaurant was quiet, music playing softly in the background and they never noticed the passing of time.

Chapter 50

Joe waited at the front counter in the police station. He brought Bud's Bible, like Dennis asked, and a few other Bible study books in case he was interested. It never ceased to amaze him to see how God worked. And in this case, he was the first to admit he didn't clearly see it yet, but he knew without a shadow of a doubt that Dennis had indeed given his life to the Lord. Joe came to the police station last night, hoping to be able to meet with Dennis. They hadn't let him, as Dennis was being processed and it was too soon for visitors. They told him he could come down in the morning though, and Joe had shown up on his lunch hour. He'd only had a few minutes to stay, but managed to see Dennis and realize the light in his eyes was real. Dennis asked about Liz first, and then asked Joe to go and get his dad's Bible. Joe thought over all these things as he waited. The police station was noisy and busy. Phones ringing, sudden scuffles could be heard as policemen escorted people in handcuffs, and doors slamming. The sound of crying could be heard through a closed door.

"Joe?" a tall policeman stood before him.

"Yeah, I'm Joe."

"Come with me." The policeman turned and headed down the hallway. Joe had to hurry to keep up with this long-legged arm of the law.

He passed the room where the crying was heard and briefly wondered what had happened. He stopped as the policeman opened the locked door in front of them. He stepped through the door and waited as the policeman locked it behind them. Joe felt a sudden claustrophobia. He took a deep breath and prayed for Dennis who no longer had the choice to go out the locked doors just by asking the guard to open them.

It seemed to take a lifetime to go through the maze of hallways and locked doors, through different sections of the police station, although Joe realized they had left the station and were now in the jail. Finally, he was brought to the visitor's room where the tall policeman searched him, flipping through the books he had in his hand. At the sight of the Bible, the policeman stopped and turned the pages more slowly. He nodded his head and handed them back to Joe.

"You've got half an hour." And he left the room.

Joe looked around at the large room, seeing other prisoners visiting with family or lawyers, and finally saw Dennis sitting at one of the tables. His elbows were propped on the table and he held his head in his hands. He looked the picture of dejection.

"Dennis?" Joe placed his hand on Dennis' back.

Dennis looked up; saw Joe and his face broke into a wide smile. "Joe! Hey, I'm glad to see you! Thanks for coming again, you didn't have to, you know."

"I know, but I figured it was important to have your Dad's Bible. I brought these other books too, in case you want them." Joe handed them to Dennis.

Dennis spent a minute holding his Bible, tears coming to his eyes. "Joe, how come I didn't realize how much God loved me until now? I mean, I wasted all those years away from Him, I … I was so horrible to my family, especially Liz …" his voice broke and he couldn't talk any longer.

"Well, I do know one thing for sure, Dennis, and that is ... nothing is ever wasted in God's eyes. I can't tell you, of course, exactly how. But I know that once we belong to Him, He never lets us go through anything for no reason."

Dennis raised his head, looking at Joe through tear filled eyes. "I'm sure you're right, I mean, you would know more than I would. But how in the world could it be God's will for Liz to go through all of that because of me? That I don't understand at all." He shook his head.

Joe was quiet for a moment. "Not sure I have the answer to that one Dennis."

Dennis started flipping through the Bible.

"Dennis, if you want me to, I can come down here every night, and we can study together. I'm no scholar mind you, but maybe I can help you get started in Bible study."

"Really? You'd do that for me?"

"Yeah. I figure this is kind of where God put me for now."

"I'd like that. One of the guards told me there is a Bible study on Wednesday night. I'd like to go to that." The light in his eyes was unmistakable.

"Yeah, that's a guy from our church, we've been leading jail Bible studies for a couple years now. I did 'em last year and now this year Bob Weber is doing them. He's a great guy, you'll like him."

"I called the hospital before you got here, but they wouldn't give me any information about Liz. How is she doing? Is she going to be ok?" A shadow came over Dennis' face.

"Well, last news I had from Carrie is that she's in a coma. Which is not entirely bad. It gives her body a chance to heal without having to worry about other things like talking and eating, getting up to go to the bathroom, that kind of stuff. They did a CT scan, which miraculously came back normal. You can see the hand of God right there." Joe stopped as the tears flowed down Dennis' cheeks. Joe wisely refrained from any further description of Liz's injuries.

"I never want to be like that again. I mean, it was bad enough what I did to Liz, but my own children were terrified of me, Joe. I scared them to death. I ... I can't be that man again."

"I know you see that now. But will you see that when walking with the Lord gets tough? How about when you want a drink? How about when you're tired and all you want is a joint ... just to relax? I'm tellin' you now, Dennis, walking with the Lord is not a walk in the park. You'll have peace, you'll know you're loved; you'll have security in Him. But some things He might ask of you are going to be hard. Can you love Him enough and want to change enough that you can stick that out?"

Dennis was thoughtful for a minute. "Man, Joe, I don't know. How can I know?"

Joe reached over and covered Dennis' shoulder with his hand. "Dennis, let God work in you and through you. Don't do the work yourself or you'll fail. Stay in the Word, take every worry to Him, and don't do a thing without praying. I only have a few more minutes ... why don't we pray now before I have to leave?"

And the two men bowed their heads before Almighty God, asking for renewal and direction.

Chapter 50

Martha, Connie, and Gert stood in Eleanor's doorway and surveyed the day's work. White lacy curtains hung at the living room and dining room windows, with heavier blue floral drapes over them which could be closed at night. The couch was lovely in its new blue plaid slipcover, the red and blue wool rug underneath it softening the edges of the room. Warm brown end tables stood at each end of the couch, one with a reading lamp on it wearing a lovely ivory shade, and the other table holding a vase of silk roses. A red print tablecloth covered the dining room table, and Martha had hurriedly sewn up some cushions for the four chairs, with ties around the back spindles. Gert had brought an old TV stand with shelves on either side. It now held the TV, some books, and some little knickknacks. They had placed a few doilies here and there, an open book on the coffee table and a large floor vase near the front door that could serve as an umbrella stand.

"Oh, it's just beautiful!" Connie breathed, "I just love it!"

"Yeah it looks nice. I better not catch any of you breaking into my house while I'm gone and doin' anything like this!" Gert grumbled.

"Oh Gert!" Martha laughed, "Don't worry, we wouldn't dare!"

Gert looked at her sideways.

"Come on let's go! I told Abby I'd pick up Danny and Katie at 6 and its five past now." Martha said, fishing the key out of her pocketbook. "Connie, can you give this back to the landlord for me? And remind him he's sworn to secrecy?"

"No problem!" Connie took the key. "What happened to Esther? I thought she was coming over this afternoon?"

Martha pursed her lips. "Sorry, I don't know. She went to lunch with that man, and I haven't heard from her since."

Gert and Connie looked at each other, eyes wide, but wisely refrained from making comment.

"Hey, I'll see you guys at quilting tomorrow ok?" and they each went their separate way.

****

Lydia had no trouble spotting Laura at the airport, they seemed instantly drawn to each other. They hugged and hurried to the car. Laura had only brought carry-on luggage, not wanting to wait at baggage claim. The conversation on the way to the hospital was sorrowful.

"Laura, please be prepared to see her. She doesn't look pretty, but she is mostly covered with bandages. And when I left the hospital, the doctor was still saying she was doing well. No complications and no internal injuries. They're waiting and watching, doing tests every day to keep on top of things." Lydia reached over to hold Laura's hand. It was cold as ice.

"I know, I keep telling myself that she's in the Lords hands, but it just seems so hard to believe. I mean, they were just there with us the other day. And Dennis wasn't violent or even angry at any time. How could this have happened?"

Laura turned towards Lydia, who was watching the traffic on the freeway.

"I'm not all that sure about the details, the why of it. I'm guessing he was a pretty angry man and the week just caught up with him. I really don't know though. I wish I did."

Laura shook her head, unbelieving. "How are Katie and Danny? And who has them?"

"They're doing good today, quiet as you would expect. They saw the whole thing." Lydia kept an eye on Laura who pressed her lips together to keep from crying. "We've been kind of passing them around amongst us; oh, it's not as bad as it sounds. They know all of us, from coming to quilting afternoons. Right now, I think they're at Martha's house. She and her sister Esther live together in a lovely old house, with a cat. All of their children live far away, and they rarely get to see their grandchildren, so I'm sure this is a wonderful treat for them to have children in the house again."

"And ... Dennis?" Laura asked quietly.

"Well, he's in jail. Joe, that's Carrie's husband, has been to see him a few times from what I understand. Carrie's spent quite a bit of time at the hospital with Liz, so I haven't gotten to talk to her too much. But last I heard from her, Joe went down to see him and Dennis asked him to come back that evening, with a Bible he had at home." Lydia looked over her shoulder to change lanes. "This is our exit right here. The hospital's only a few minutes from here."

Laura took a deep breath. "Good, I just want to see my daughter. Thank you Lydia, for calling me, and for coming to pick me up."

Lydia waved her hand in the air. "I think it's all a God thing. I mean, what are the chances of your daughter living near me, and you and me meeting on the Internet? Has to be a God thing."

Laura smiled, "I think you're right."

They pulled into the hospital parking lot and began the search for a parking place.

****

Laura stood outside the door to Liz's hospital room, took a deep breath and went in. The room was filled with quiet hospital sounds. An older lady sat next to the bed, holding, and rubbing Liz's hand, talking quietly. At the sound of Laura entering the room, the lady looked up and smiled.

"You must be Laura, Liz's mother …?" Carrie asked.

At her nod, Carrie continued, "I'm Carrie Barrister, her neighbor … and friend." Carrie smiled warmly. "I'll just give you this chair, and some time alone." Carrie gave her a soft but short hug and left the room.

Laura sat in the chair next to the bed and looked at her daughter. So small in that bed, no movement, tubes coming in and out of her, bandages covering much of her face.

"Oh Elizabeth , how did you end up here, like this?" she thought.

"Honey, its Mom. I'm here with you." Laura picked up her limp hand and held it in her own. "I'm going to stay with you until you're better. Dad's coming tomorrow. We both love you so much." Tears threatened, and she stopped talking. It wouldn't do for Liz to hear her crying, and Laura was convinced that coma or not, Elizabeth could hear what was going on. Laura pulled her Bible out of her purse and sat back in the hard hospital chair. She opened to the Psalms and began reading the first chapter.

Chapter 51

Eleanor stepped off the Greyhound bus, into the hot, smelly station. So many people all in a hurry to go somewhere. She was tired and wanted nothing more than a shower and her own bed. Her small suitcase seemed to weigh a hundred pounds. Suddenly she was scared and timid all over again. The reality of her adventure was finally hit her, and the thought of the long city bus ride home was more than she could take. Tears came to her eyes and she wiped them away with the back of her hand. Her feet hurt, her back was killing her from the uncomfortable seat, and she hadn't had a decent meal since leaving Emma's. Even the lovely memories of her visit didn't stop the anxiety from building in her chest. She felt alone, naked and open to any stranger passing by. The four walls of her own little house, shabby though it was, seemed a paradise now. All she could think of was the dire need to be at home. She made her way through the crowds, looking for the nearest bench. Children cried and parents who were annoyed and tired themselves gave short angry retorts. She spied a bench with one spot open and headed for it. Just as she got there, a young long-haired man with tattoo's covering much of his arms and neck slipped into the spot. She stood there, waiting for him to get up so she could sit down. He never looked at her. She sighed and continued standing on her poor tired feet and waited for the city bus that would take her home.

****

Esther came home walking on air. She hadn't felt this way in a long time. As happy as she had been with her dear Glen, they had been comfortable. This *in love* feeling was new and oh so welcome. She couldn't stop smiling and she felt beautiful.

"Martha! I'm so glad you're home. I want to tell you all about my lunch … Oh! Hello, you two little sweeties!" Esther reached down and kissed Katie and Danny's cheeks. "Martha, I'm so sorry! I completely forgot we were taking care of them tonight."

Martha sniffed covertly.

"We were just getting ready to fix some dinner. Katie was going to help me crack the eggs for pancakes, weren't you honey?" Martha smiled in her direction.

"Pancakes! Oh, that's my favorite dinner." Esther clapped her hands. "Danny, what's your job?"

"I'm setting the table!" he puffed out his chest in pride.

"I'm sure you're a pretty good table setter." Esther smiled. "Do you need a chair to get in those top cupboards?" She pulled one over to the counter for him. He climbed up, opened the cupboard door, and looked at the plates. He crinkled his forehead.

Esther watched him puzzle out the dilemma, and finally said, "Oh, Danny, we need four plates."

He stared at the plates and then jumped off the chair and ran in the living room.

"What?" Martha turned from the counter where she was mixing pancake batter with Katie. She and Esther exchanged puzzled looks.

"Danny? What's wrong?" Esther sat on the couch next to him.

"Nothin'!" he folded his arms across his skinny chest and clamped his lips tightly closed. His cheeks were red. "Doncha got any TV here? I wanna watch TV."

"We have TV, but right now we're fixing dinner and I need you to help me set the table." Suddenly Esther realized that Danny didn't know how to count. "And since I know where everything is, I'll get the dishes down and you can put them on the table, how 'bout that?"

Esther got up and started into the kitchen, hoping to keep things casual and not embarrass the boy.

He scooted off the couch, scowling. "Yeah, ok."

****

Laura finished reading Psalms 4. Her throat was getting scratchy and she needed some water. She took a little drink of nasty tasting tap water from the sink in the room. Mentally she began to make a list of things she would need. Some bottled water, a small tape player with some praise and worship tapes, a more comfortable chair certainly, and some snacks. She didn't want to waste time running to the cafeteria every time she got hungry, not that she felt that hungry, but food would be needed. When Dale got here tomorrow with the car and the luggage, she'd ask him to go to the local drugstore and find some of those things. She heard a soft knocking and turned to find a tall man, older with graying hair wearing black rimmed glasses. She assumed he must be the doctor, with his tie and white coat.

"Hello?" she asked.

He held out his hand. "I'm Dr. Rylands, and you are …?" the question hung in the air.

"I'm Laura McKenzie, Liz's mother. I just got here a few hours ago." They shook hands.

"Good! I want to fill you in on your daughter's condition." They both sat down, Laura on the chair and the doctor perched precariously on the railing attached to the foot of the bed. He held a steel chart in his hands, but he never opened it.

"Liz has mostly bruises and lacerations. She has a few cracked ribs, which will heal fine. The thing that concerns me the most is her state of unconsciousness. It's only been a little over twenty-four hours and I'm not quite ready to call it a coma, but if she doesn't wake up soon, I will. We've done some MRIs and there are no internal injuries. There is some swelling of her brain, consistent with a concussion. At this point it's a wait and see situation." He paused, wondering if Laura had questions.

"Go on." She nodded. She would wait to hear everything he said before she started asking questions.

"OK, well, we are giving her oxygen, it helps in healing. We also have an IV in her arm, to give her fluids. We had to insert a catheter, since she is unable to get up and go to the bathroom. We will also be giving her nutrients, as of course she is not able to eat. She doesn't have any bruising on her legs, the bruises are contained to her face, arms, and upper torso. I understand this was a domestic violence situation?"

Laura nodded again.

He continued, "Well, I don't know any more about the situation than that, but we don't want him to come here visiting. It could be very upsetting to her. Even though she is, to all appearances, asleep, I believe she can hear what's going on. And I'm having this conversation with you here in this room, because she's probably wondering what happened to her. Liz," he turned and looked directly at her, "now you know. You just concentrate on resting and healing. We'll deal with everything else." He turned back to Laura. "Now! Do you have any questions?" he smiled warmly.

"I agree with you that she can hear us, and what goes on in this room. I've been reading my Bible to her since I arrived, and I'm going to get some music tomorrow for her to listen to. I'm so amazed that her injuries aren't more severe, Dr. Rylands, it's a miracle! I believe in miracles, do you?" she tipped her head looking him in the eye.

"A miracle? Well, who can say?" He smiled politely and rose as if to leave.

"I see." Laura smiled warmly, her mind already adding him to her prayer list. "Her father will be here tomorrow. I flew in, but he's driving up."

"Fine. Oh, and if she doesn't awaken in the next 12-18 hours, we'll begin some physical therapy. A therapist will come in and gently move her muscles, stretching them and keeping the blood circulating. We'll take care of every aspect of her health until she is able to do it herself."

"I never would have thought of that." Laura shook her head.

"That's why we get the big bucks!" he smiled. "I'm just going to check her over before I go home. I'll be back in the morning and of course the nurses will be in and out all night long. No rest in the hospital you know!"

He tapped the steel chart with his other hand and left.

Laura sat back and thought about all that he said. Maybe Liz would wake up soon, and there would be no need for this physical therapy. Liz could be walking around here tomorrow by herself. Laura felt positive about this, that God hadn't brought them this far just to let Liz lay there in a coma or unconscious as the doctor called it.

Laura reached for Liz's hand and held it, squeezing it warmly and softly. "Don't worry honey, everything is going to be fine. You have a good doctor, even if he doesn't recognize a miracle when it's staring him in the face."

Mom, I'm so glad you're here.

Laura sat back in her chair, closing her eyes, saying little bits of prayer for Liz and the doctor and whoever else the Lord brought to mind.

Chapter 52

Finally, the bus came to a stop at the corner. It was dusk already and would be dark if she didn't hurry. Eleanor picked up her suitcase and started down the street. It was only about a half a block, but the distance stretched forever. Every step jarred her whole body and her feet were screaming with pain.

"Just a few more steps," she told herself. "Just a few more now, come on now, Eleanor, don't give up. You've traveled across the country, you survived the bus station and you can make it this last little bit home. Come on ... there's the door. Get your key now." She set her suitcase down and fumbled in her bag, and finding the key, opened the door and reached to the side of the door to turn on the light.

She entered her cottage, not even looking at anything around her. What was there to look at anyway? Just the same old junk. She stepped inside the living room and her foot felt carpeting underneath. Her brow wrinkled. Carpeting? And she looked around and saw the new couch, and beautiful wool rug, the new tables, a writing desk ... what in the world? She took a sudden deep breath as she realized she had forgotten to breathe.

Lord? What happened here? This isn't my home. All of sudden she wondered if she had the wrong house. There was a cottage right next to them, similar in appearance. Oh my gosh, she had entered the wrong house. She grabbed her suitcase and prepared to leave, feeling so thankful no one had been home when she glanced through to the kitchen and saw the curtains she had made two weeks ago.

"What in the world?" she said softly. She walked around the room, touching everything, taking it all in. How had this happened? Her painful feet were forgotten as she looked around, and gentle tears slipped from her tired eyes. How wonderful her Heavenly Father was to have done this for her. In her mind there was no other explanation. She knew Alfred hadn't gotten out of rehabilitation and done it. She knew her cranky old landlord hadn't done it. It had to be her Lord. How? No explanation occurred to her, so she sent her thanks heavenward and with a light heart began a new evening.

****

Alice leaned against the kitchen counter. Her little charges were safely in bed sleeping and the evening stretched before her. Long and lonely. Added to that was her worry over Liz and her horror over Dennis. How could he have done such a thing? Every time she thought about it she grew sick to her stomach over the violence. The phone call from Laura had done little to calm her.

She looked around the kitchen, finding it clean. There was nothing to do in here. She snapped off the light and went into the living room. A few toys and books scattered around the comfortable room, which she left. They made the room look friendly, rather than lonely. She glanced at the television, but she had never had much interest in it and didn't have any now. She turned to the bookcase looking for an interesting book. Nothing caught her eye.

She sat down in the armchair. Was this to be a picture of the rest of her life? Exhausting work all day long, followed by excruciating loneliness all evening, and then followed by a long nights sleep in an empty bed? Bud, I wouldn't wish for you to leave our Lord, but oh I wish you were here!

Alice flipped open her Bible and read a few verses, but nothing seemed to speak to her heart. She closed her eyes and tried to pray but no words came. She thought of Liz and tried to pray but could not form any sentences. "Oh Lord ... Help!" finally ended up being the extent of her prayer. And having nothing else to do, nor the energy to do it, she walked slowly down the hallway to her room and went to bed.

****

Events finally settled themselves into a routine of sorts. The doctor finally declared a formal coma and Laura and Dale spent their days and nights at the hospital with Liz. They read Scripture and books to her, they played praise and worship music, and they talked to each other and to her all day long. They laughed and told jokes, they prayed and talked to her about love and forgiveness, they simply sat and held her hand. They ate hospital food and occasionally sent out for a pizza. The nurse brought in a leather recliner and a fold away cot for the two of them to use at night.

Katie and Danny spent their days with Esther and Martha, and their nights with Carrie's family.

Dennis continued reading his father's Bible and meeting with Joe at least twice a week. He grew in the Lord by leaps and bounds, having nothing but time on his hands. He was finally listening to the things the Lord was teaching him. His ears had been opened to hear and his eyes to see. It was not all joy, there was much torment as his former life was continually before his eyes and in his mind. His failures in every area of life replayed over and over in a loop. Disciplining his thoughts and breaking down strongholds was not an easy thing. He was accustomed to following his thoughts wherever they led him.

Again, the ladies began to hold twice weekly quilting meetings to complete Liz's quilt so they could take it to her in the hospital. Every day at least one of them went by the hospital to visit Laura and Dale. They would sit with Liz and talk to her about Katie and Danny and what they were doing and learning. They would also give respite to Laura and Dale, although they never stayed away for long.

Esther was seeing Cliff nearly every day. Her cheeks were blooming roses and her eyes danced. She was in love with her first love. Life was full again and the only time she was lonely was when she was apart from Cliff. Fate may have torn them apart when they were young, but the Lord had brought them back together now, in this most wonderful and glorious time.

Gert was busy harvesting what little she could from her jumble garden. There was nothing worth canning. A few beans for a meal, a little lettuce now and then, and one stalk of corn that provided a plentiful four ears. She was trying to be faithful and attend church regularly but was so bored by the services and irritated by the people that she continually looked for excuses not to go.

Chapter 53

Carrie took her broom to the front porch. They had all agreed to put Liz's quilt in the frame today, hoping to finish it quickly. They wanted to give it to her in the hospital. They believed this quilt, made by loving hands, would be healing. Carrie moved all the chairs back, so there would be room for the frame. As she swept her mind turned to Abby, as it so often did these days. Never a mention of the baby's father, never a mention of her plans. Abby stayed in her room except to eat. She did what was asked of her, but nothing more. Carrie knew there were no baby clothes in her drawers, no cradle in the corner and no boxes of diapers. Abby had refused the offer of a baby shower. What in the world were they going to do with this baby when it came home, put it in a drawer? Or a laundry basket? Carrie and Joe talked it over many a night before sleeping and could think of no solution. So, they did the only thing they could do – take it to the Father. If He knew when a sparrow fell, surely He knew what to do with Abby's baby.

Across the street, Gert stood in her jumble garden, straddling corn plants, looking for green beans. She mumbled under her breath as she searched through green leaves of every size and shape. She glanced in her bucket and secretly swore under her breath. Barely enough for a meal, let alone any sizable amount of canning. Her hand at her back, she slowly straightened up and stretched. She was too darn old to be scrambling around in the dirt anyway, and who wanted to be stuck in the hot kitchen canning quarts of green beans till the cows came home? How many green beans could an old woman eat anyway? She grumbled her way to the back door, kicked off her rubber garden boots and reached for the screen door. Stomping through the kitchen, she stepped on an uncooked macaroni noodle, crunching it good.

"Good grief!" Gert hopped to the kitchen table, propped her foot on her knee and proceeded to pick noodle pieces out of her foot. They didn't actually break the skin, but they smarted pretty good. Finished with noodle picking she sat in the chair and stared at the wall.

Absolutely nothing was going right. "I thought You said You were going to make my rows straight. What's the deal? I was nice to Carrie, I rescued Liz, I even prayed out loud ... what more do You want?"

Everything.

Gert stood up. "Everything?" Her face turned red as anger burned its way from her heart to her mind. "Everything? I have a mind you know, why'd You give me a mind if You just wanted me to be a robot?" She sat down again, hard on the kitchen chair. And tried to listen for that voice. She went to the back door and looked again at the mess she called a garden and knew she was still looking at a picture of her heart and life.

"But I tried to straighten my rows, just like You said. I tried to do good things. I'm going to church, I'm trying to be nicer to people. I don't get it." Uncharacteristically she listened once more.

I will straighten your rows.

She sighed impatiently. "I know, You said that already. You think I'm hard of hearing?" and then flinched slightly as she remembered she was talking to Almighty God. "I'm sorry, I didn't mean to be sassy." She bit her lip.

I will straighten your rows.

There He goes again, she thought. Well, this is getting nowhere. I've got to get cleaned up, for quilting today. And off she went, still not listening.

Down the street three houses, Connie finished making the bed and headed for the shower. Ron had left early for work, as usual. The boys were sleeping in, taking advantage of the last couple weeks of summer vacation. Nothing had changed, except for the worse. Ron left early and came home late. More often than not, he slept in the family room with his new best friend – the television. He wouldn't talk to her unless it was necessary. She'd ask him about a bill and he'd answer. She'd ask him what he wanted for dinner and he'd say, "Whatever you're fixing is fine." He used to say "Hey babe! Would you make me some of that lasagna like you made last time? I'm dying for some!" and he'd hug her and kiss her. It seemed that time in their life was over and she had no idea why. Tears mixed with water as she shampooed. Her heart ached and she considered one more time if he was seeing another woman. She stood under the water stream and wondered if it were possible to drown in a shower. After a few minutes she stepped out, wrapped her hair in a towel and caught sight of herself in the mirror.

"Oh my gosh, Connie! Look at yourself!" She cringed from the picture, she had put on so much weight in the last few months, no wonder he didn't want anything to do with her. She glanced at herself again, through squinty eyes, not wanting to look, yet unable to. She didn't even recognize herself.

"Well, that settles it! Today, you go on a diet and start exercising. No more runs to the bakery, no more pizza, no more seconds, no more food, period!" All of a sudden, she felt hopeful. If she lost the weight she gained, and maybe ten pounds more than that, he'd be interested in her again. She smiled. Just to make sure she'd stick to the resolution, she chose a pair of pants that were slightly tight around the waist. Well, who was she kidding, they were all tight around the waist. But she promised herself she wouldn't undo the top button. Quickly she dressed, combed her wet hair, and ran downstairs to a nice diet breakfast of rice cakes and tea.

A stone's throw from Connie's house, Martha and Esther sat down to late morning coffee and mail.

"Esther, would you be able to run Danny down to register for school this morning, before quilting? I promised to run by the hospital for an hour or so, so Laura and Dale can do some laundry."

"Oh!" Esther hesitated, "Well, ok, sure that's no problem. Cliff was taking me to the new antique store downtown, but we can take Danny to school too. That'll work!" Esther smiled.

Martha barely disguised a sigh and a roll of her eyes.

"What does that mean?" Esther crinkled her forehead.

"Can't you do anything without Cliff anymore? Does he have to be here all the time, every night for dinner? You did have a life before he came along you know." Martha tapped her pen on the tabletop.

"Martha! I'm surprised at you. You know how much I love him, and how this is just the answer to my prayer. Remember? We talked about this." Esther was incredulous.

"Are you so sure he's the answer to your prayers? When does he ever pray over our meals? How come he doesn't come to church with us? I never hear him saying anything about the Lord ... is he even a Christian?"

Esther stared, mouth open. "Is he a Christian? How can you even ask? Of course he is! He always has been, since were in high school."

"Well, then how come he doesn't come to church with us? Or pray? Do you two talk about the Lord together? Esther, I'm surprised at you, you're more the Christian than I am, but you haven't even noticed."

Esther was quiet. "I guess ... well, I guess he goes to his own church on Sunday."

"And what church would that be?" Martha questioned.

Esther waited a few seconds before answering. "I ... I don't know." Her face was pale. Tears formed in her eyes as she answered. "Martha ... I don't know what church he goes to!" As the implication of that sunk in, the tears slipped down her cheeks. Thoughts raced through her mind too fast to capture. All their conversations replayed in the blink of an eye. They had never talked about the Lord. No, *she* had talked about the Lord, *he* had smiled and told her she was beautiful. He bowed his head while she prayed. But he never prayed.

She raised her tear-filled eyes to Martha's face. "There has to be some kind of mistake. Why would the Lord send him to me if he wasn't the one for me to love? He wouldn't give me this wonderful man who loves me, just so I had to give him up! God isn't like that! Martha, there is just a mistake that's all. I'll get it straightened out, I'll ask him, I'll talk to him, today!" and she pushed her chair away from the table and ran upstairs.

Martha sighed again and shook her head.

Chapter 54

In the hospital room, Laura and Dale held Liz's hands and prayed for her healing, they prayed for Dennis and thanked the Lord for the good friends who were helping them through everything.

"Mom, Dad, I wish I could talk to you. I wish I could tell you I'm okay. I just can't seem to wake up for some reason – I wish I understood what was going on. Whatever the reason, I'm so very glad you're here. Please play some more music ..."

Late one Wednesday afternoon, as Laura was sitting at Liz's bedside, she noticed the sheet covering her legs move just slightly. Instantly, she sat straight up, her eyes focused on that spot. Had she really seen it? Or was it a hopeful vision? She held her breath, waiting for another movement, however small.

Then, Liz's finger twitched. Tears formed in Laura's eyes, and she covered her mouth with her hand. Quickly she pressed the nurse call button, several times.

****

"Lydia! Did anyone call you? Liz is waking up." Carrie's voice was rushed and breathless.

"Ohhhh!" Lydia gasped, "Is she ok?"

"All I know is that she's moving and beginning to wake up. Call Connie ok? And spread the word."

And so the telephone lines buzzed with good news and the answer to many prayers. Just as quickly a small meeting was called to arrange the presentation ceremony. They firmly believed the presence of Liz's quilt would aid and speed her healing. Only the binding needed to be finished.

****

Esther sat in her favorite chair, eyes filled with tears. She tried to remember their high school days, and the time Cliff had accepted the Lord as his Savior. As near as she could remember, it was during summer camp, when he had gone forward with several other kids. Yes, she was pretty sure that's when it happened. And wasn't *saved* the important thing? Was it so very important if he wasn't living for the Lord? Didn't we all go through hot and cold times?

There had been no opportunity for them to discuss this issue. Cliff's grandchildren were visiting for the week and while they had certainly spent time together, it was time with children. She could see in his eyes, he knew something was wrong. Sunday, when they went home, they would have time to talk. Esther was confident in Cliff's faith. Not everyone wore their heart on their sleeve like Esther did, and she was sure he was simply a quiet, reverent man, content with his own love for the Lord. She smiled and dried her tears. Everything would be fine in the end.

****

Martha hurried to the mailbox, seeing a package hanging from the handle in a white plastic bag. Maybe the CDs were here! Quickly she brought the package inside and set it on the kitchen table.

"Esther! Our CD's are here ... come and open the box with me." Martha called. She took a knife from the kitchen drawer to cut through the packing tape. This was quite exciting, getting all the music they loved and paying only pennies for it!

And there they were. Thirteen neatly wrapped slim CD cases with all their beloved music. They spent some minutes devouring the covers, delighting in seeing the smiling faces of their favorite artists and groups. Opening that first CD and slipping it into the player. It was all so high tech and slick. They held their breath as Martha pushed the Play button and thrilled to hear the music filling the room.

"Oh Esther, this is so much better than our records, and even our tapes! It's so clear!"

They listened quietly for a few minutes, joining in on a few choruses, "… nothing but the blood of Jesus …"

They smiled at each other. Martha thinking, "What a great deal!" and Esther thinking, "I told you so!" But neither saying a word. Ralph twined around their ankles, flicking Martha's knee with the tip of his tail.

Absentmindedly, Martha began to gather up all the papers, brochures and advertisements that had filled the box of CD's. Systematically she went through it all, deciding what to keep and what to throw away, concentrating more on the music than on what she was reading.

"Sign up three friends and get 12 free CD's." Hmmm, who could she get to sign up?

"Accumulate fifty points and receive 5 free CD's!" How do you accumulate points?

She threw away a few shiny, colorful pieces of advertising and then picked up the bill. Ha … that would be easy! Write a check for a penny, she chuckled to herself.

Suddenly her face turned white and she sat on the kitchen chair with a thump.

"27.95?" she whispered, barely able to form the numbers on her lips.

She stared at the bill, but it was written in Chinese. None of it made the least amount of sense. 27.95? There must be an error.

"Martha, what's wrong? You look like you've seen the proverbial ghost." Esther returned from changing the CD.

"It's ... it's the bill. Look!" she thrust the paper at Esther.

"What?" Esther read it, wonderingly. "Well, here's the penny charge for the CD's, then there is a $10 membership fee, and then $17.94 for shipping ... all adds up to $27.95." She looked up.

Martha blinked and stared. After a minute, she got up from the chair and wandered into the living room mumbling something about highway robbery and train wrecks.

****

Connie pulled the meatloaf out of the oven, putting it on the stove to settle while she set the table. The boys were in the family room playing their new X-Box game. Techy sounds of all kinds reached her ears. Ron would be home for dinner in about ten minutes. She gazed wistfully at the meatloaf, wanting just a bite. No, a salad waited for her. Granted it was yummy with chicken and cranberries, but it was no meatloaf. She sighed and tried to be encouraged with the three pounds she'd lost.

"Whoopdee-do…" she said to herself, "A whole three pounds."

"Come on boys, let's eat!" she yelled down the hall. "Dinners ready!"

They hit the ground running, shaking the glass vases in the china cabinet on their way to the table.

Connie said a quick grace, with less than a full heart. Ron was late, again. She half-heartedly listened to the boys re-hash the video game. They ate their food at the speed of light, hardly chewing. The game was on pause and they were ready to go to battle. In what seemed like seconds, their plates were emptied, seconds had been eaten and they were looking at her expectantly. She nodded and half closed her eyes. They ran down the hall and techy sounds resumed.

She picked at her salad. She was so sick of salad she could spit. Spearing a chunk of chicken with a little extra salad dressing for fun, she took a bite. Ugh, it was awful. Considering this was the eighth chicken salad she'd eaten in three days, she didn't figure it would get any better.

Quickly, before she could think about what she was doing, she took Ron's plate and loaded it with meatloaf and mashed potatoes, green bean casserole with lots of melted cheese and three pieces of French bread. Every bite was ambrosia. It was simply the best meatloaf she'd ever made. She closed her eyes and savored every bite. The bread was crispy and dripping with butter, the potatoes couldn't have come up with a lump if they were paid money. Lost in her own little reverie of comfort, she ate every bite, feeling full in a way which couldn't be explained by the simple presence of food. Her world felt exceptionally wonderful and good. Her eyes closed and she enjoyed the moment.

Which ended all too quickly when she realized what she'd eaten and Ron got home at the same time.

They said not a word to each other. She got him a plate and he dished it up, taking it to the living room where he could watch TV. Connie watched him go and her comfort disappeared in a flash. There were two more pieces of French bread on the table and she ate them both.

Chapter 55

Joe had just said the blessing when someone knocked on their door. Carrie rolled her eyes and said, "It figures!"

There was a quiet conversation at the door, male voices rose and fell.

"Abby, do you know this young man?" Joe stood at the doorway with a tall good-looking man wearing jeans and cotton shirt. "He says he knows you."

Abby looked up, her mouth dropping open in surprise. "Randy?" her voice cracked.

"Abby." His eyes settled on her, unflinching, waiting.

Abby swallowed and fiddled with her napkin. Normally so sure of herself, she was as self-conscious as a schoolgirl. "Uh ... let's go out on the porch." She glanced at her parents, but offered no introductions, and no explanations.

****

Laura held a cup of juice with a straw up to Liz's lips. Every day Liz became more and more alert and able to move about, even doing some very simple things for herself. Bruises had healed, fading to yellow. Stitches had been removed.

They were able to have short conversations, before Liz tired, slipping off into healing sleep.

Today, Laura could barely contain her excitement. This was the big day. Carrie was bringing the quilt. They had unanimously decided Carrie should present the quilt – it had been her idea in the first place to make it for her.

"Mom? You look like you can't sit still!" Liz smiled, wondering what was going on.

"Oh, do I?" Laura said, trying to hide her smile busying herself folding a blanket.

"Helloooo!"

Liz looked to the doorway and saw Carrie's head, leaning into the room with a big grin. "How are you feeling today, Liz?" Still not entering the room.

"I'm fine, why don't you come in?" Liz crinkled her forehead.

Carrie laughed and entered the room, holding something behind her back. She and Laura exchanged conspiratorial grins.

"Ok, now what is going on?" Liz tried to look stern.

"We won't keep you in suspense any longer sweetie, I've brought you a gift, from all your quilting friends. We hope it will become dear to you." And she brought a suit box from behind her back, laying it on the bed.

Liz sat up a little, wondering, and then astonished as Carrie lifted the lid and there was the beautiful jewel tone quilt, sparkling and reaching out to her in ways she couldn't explain. Carrie unfolded the quilt and laid it over Liz's lap.

"Oh!" she gasped, "Why … why this is the quilt I worked on with you." her hands caressed the quilt.

"Yes, it is. We were making it for you when you showed up that first time." Carrie laughed and sat on the edge of the bed. "When you showed up that day, I don't know if you noticed or not, but none of us knew what to say. We felt like we'd been caught! But we couldn't turn you away, not when we'd been praying for you like we had."

"Praying for me?"

And so Carrie had to tell her the whole story of how God had moved their hearts to pray for her, and to become involved in her life. Laura hadn't heard most of this story, only bits and pieces. Now, with all the pieces woven into the quilt, it was a testimony to God's love and attention to even His smallest and most worn out little lamb.

Tears welled in Liz's eyes. She tried to talk but the only thing that came out was a cross between a laugh and a sob.

Carrie reached over and hugged her. "It's ok. Words aren't necessary."

Chapter 56

Cliff's grandchildren had gone home, and they had plans for a lunch in the Italian restaurant that had become *their place*. Esther's stomach was tied in knots. She tried to pray for peace and the right words. But her stomach continued to churn, and her mind had not a thought in it. And she was having a bad hair day to top the whole thing off. Her hair felt flat and limp. It wouldn't curl the way it usually did. And she realized her hands were shaking.

What if Cliff left her? Decided to break up with her? She remembered life before Cliff and it had been lonely. Hadn't it? She closed her eyes and thought back to the months before Cliff had reentered her life. There were good times with her friends. She enjoyed the Wednesday night church services. And when was the last time she'd attended? She couldn't remember. When was the last time she and Martha had read the Bible together before bed? Again, she couldn't remember. Her life now revolved around Cliff.

"Lord have I wandered away from You?" She prayed, "I always looked at Cliff as Your gift to me, Your answer to my prayer for a companion, perhaps a husband, but if he draws me away from You …" her prayer trailed off. Her head began to ache. The thought of giving him up was like a physical pain in her chest.

****

Abby sat on the porch, rocking. Her hands rested on her stomach, large with child. Every so often she wiped a silent tear from her face. She stared at nothing. Thoughts and emotions flew around her mind like birds leaving the telephone wire.

How have I managed to mess up my life this badly? She wondered to herself. A baby she didn't want, a man she did want but now wasn't so sure he wanted her, living in her parent's home at her age, no money, no assets, no future – what had gone wrong? The tears fell faster, and she was unable to keep them inside.

Abby hadn't cried in years. It accomplished nothing, it left the eyes swollen and made a person seem weak. Abby was not weak, but she had no strength.

Randy wanted her to make a decision. Marry him and let them make a home together. In some way it appealed to her, the whole white picket fence thing. On the other hand, then she'd be exactly like her mother and that wasn't going to happen.

Joe and Carrie watched from the kitchen window. They could see Abby crying, and Randy was not talking. They knew it was time to talk and so, went out to the porch and prayed that God would put words in their mouths.

Joe opened the conversation, "Randy, I know we just met, but obviously you've known Abby for a while. I don't think we need to worry about formalities, do you?" He spoke warmly, wanting to win Randy over and hopefully Abby.

Carrie gave Randy a short hug, "Am I correct in thinking this is your baby?" she smiled.

"Yes, this is my, er, our baby. I love your daughter and want to marry her, but so far she's refused me." Randy spoke to them, but he looked at Abby. Abby, tears still falling fast, looked the other way.

"Abby?" Carrie carefully sat on the porch seat next to her, "I think it's time to 'fess up." Carrie handed her the box of tissue she'd brought out with her.

Abby sighed, and wiped her tears. She was boxed into a corner, with no way out. "Fine, yes, he's the father of the baby. Yes, he has asked me to marry him, and yes, I do ... love him," she admitted after a slight pause. "But the whole marriage thing, I just don't think I can do it. It's so ... I don't know, limiting I guess."

"Limiting?" Carrie asked, wonderment in her voice. "How do you figure?"

"You know, one person to live with for the rest of your life. Tied down to the house like it's your whole life, no more options to even change your mind about anything at all!"

"You make it sound like a prison!" Carrie said.

"Well, isn't it? Aren't you and Dad *bound for life* to be parted only when one of you dies?" Abby did have the grace to flinch when she said that.

Carrie and Joe were silent for a moment.

"Abby," Joe took over. "Do you think Mom and I are unhappy? Do I keep her barefoot and pregnant and in the kitchen all day? Have you ever seen me treat her badly in any way?"

Abby looked startled. "Well, no …" she said slowly. "But don't you ever feel like you just want to go or do something else?"

"Of course I do, everybody does. What does that have to do with marriage? Do you mean do I ever feel like I want to go with another woman or do something with another woman? Then the answer is no."

Abby blushed, and was furious at herself for doing so, she was much more sophisticated than that.

"Dad!"

"I think the time for niceties are past, Abby. I love your mother, very much, more so every day, every year. It's not a relationship I can explain, or even understand. But we are very content just with each other."

"That's it!" Abby stood up quickly, "That's the very thing. I don't want to be *content*. I want excitement and life and experiences. Passion! Not contentment in the burbs! What?"

All three of them were staring at the puddle on the porch. "Abby, it's time to go to the hospital."

Joe ran into the garage for the car, Carrie went in for a towel and that left Abby and Randy alone on the porch.

"Oh no," Abby whispered, "This is really happening?"

Randy put his arm around her shoulders, "Yes, babe, it is. And now. Come on, let's get down the steps and into the car, this is the day!" He gently helped her down the porch steps and into the waiting car, as Carrie appeared with towels, and tried to help Abby feel more comfortable. And for once, Abby was thankful for her mother.

Chapter 57

"Hello Esther." Cliff was suddenly at the table and here Esther thought she had been watching for him.

"Cliff!" her hand flew to her heart, "you startled me." Esther tried to laugh naturally.

"I'm sorry, I didn't mean to startle you, but I think it's time we talked, don't you? I know something is bothering you, but we haven't had a spare moment to talk about it. Now," he spread his hand over the nearly empty restaurant, "we have all the time in the world. Tell me what's wrong Esther, please?"

Tears sprang up in her eyes, and truthfully, that was the last thing she wanted. If she was crying her voice would come out crackly and it would come and go, making this conversation so much harder. His kindness and evident love in his voice would break her resolve if she let him speak any longer.

Esther held her hand up, "Just wait a minute," she croaked. Taking several deep breaths, and silently calling upon her Lord for help this minute, she began to speak of her concerns.

Cliff listened intently for a few minutes, and when he realized where the conversation was going, he held his hand up. "Esther, I hear what you're saying, I truly do. But this is not a deal breaker. Yes, many years ago at summer camp, I did accept the Lord as my Savior, but that was long time ago. A youthful decision based on emotion. I've grown up a lot since then and have come to realize that there are many ways to God. I respect your right to believe as you do, and I love you for it. But, it's just not my way."

He reached for her hands, but she drew them away. His brow crinkled, "Esther?"

Silent tears were streaming down her face. Though there were few other diners, they sensed this was not a good moment, and respectfully did not look in their direction.

"Cliff," Esther whispered, "It is a deal breaker for me. God tells me not to be unequally yoked with an unbeliever. And I can't go against His word, I just can't. Oh, but I don't want to lose you again, I don't!" Her head fell into her hands and she cried quietly.

Cliff got up and sat in the chair next to her, taking her into her arms

They sat together, in each other's arms for a few sections, and then remembered they were in a public place. The restaurant owners, Tony and Maria, stood at a distance, surreptitiously watching. They had watched this romance unfold from the very first meeting and been happy to see their many visits. Now, it looked like it was over. Tony reached over and squeezed Marias hand.

"Esther," Cliff said, "I don't want to lose you again either. I lost you once because of my own stupidity and short-sightedness; I don't want to make the same mistake again. Maybe I'm wrong in the way I believe." Esther looked up at him in surprise.

"Well, I know you well enough to know that if you believe something this strongly, there is reason for it. What if I start coming to church with you? Would you give me the time to reconsider all this?" His eyes were pleading with her.

Esther realized she was holding her breath, and let it out in one whoosh. "Really?"

Cliff took a gold cloth napkin off the table and gently wiped the tears from her cheeks. "Yes, really! I'm willing to admit I could be wrong. I've been wrong before – a few times anyway." he grinned. "No, I am very serious. If it is this important to you then there must be something to it. Do we have a deal?"

Esther laughed, "Oh yes, we have a deal. Thank you!" and they hugged once more but it was a happy hug. Tony and Maria smiled at each other and realized they too, were holding their breath. "Phew!" Tony whispered to Maria.

****

Joe and Carrie sat in the hospital waiting room, nervously waiting for news of the baby. They flipped through old magazines, they watched other families waiting.

"I wish I'd brought my quilting, at least I'd have something to do with my hands." Carrie said. "I just feel all fidgety."

"I know, I do too." Joe patted her knee. "It could be awhile. I'll go home and get it for you …?"

Carrie smiled at him, "Thank you, I really do appreciate that, but I don't want to wait here alone. I'll just stick it out!"

And so, they waited for news of their first grandchild.

****

Gert had called the local handyman, Tom, to come and plow under her garden. He had arrived early in the morning and his comments on her *weed patch* had not been appreciated. But she could hear the rackety sound of the rototiller, breaking hard ground, and turning it over, exposing the underneath, the worms, the roots, and all the things that had not been seen before.

A few times she had watched from the kitchen door window and again felt like she was seeing something important, but she couldn't put her finger on what it was.

But as she watched, she remembered a phrase from the sermon a few Sunday's ago. It was only a phrase, *breaking down strongholds*, and she no idea what that meant. There must be importance to it, or else why would she think of it now? To tell the truth, she had barely listened to it the first time. By now, Gert had been thinking of this *row straightening* she was supposed to be doing just about every day.

It suddenly dawned on her that she was not straightening the rows of her garden, Tom was. What was it God had told her? *I will straighten your rows.*

I.

Oh, the realization was like a bucket of cold water. HE would straighten her rows, it wasn't something she had to do. She groaned, what a ninny she was!

There was a knock at the kitchen door. Tom was finished.

"Thank you Tom, here's your money." Gert handed over two twenty-dollar bills.

"I appreciate the work, ma'am. Uh, could I ask you a question?" he scratched his head.

Gert nodded.

"Was that your garden?"

She nodded again.

"Well, I don't know what happened to it, but you might think about putting a fence around it next year. Keep out the dogs, cats and kids."

Now Gert was not normally a woman of few words, but at this exact moment, everything was perfectly clear, and she was speechless. She simply nodded again, and Tom left her house, wondering. Well, she always had been one odd duck!

Of course! It made total sense now. God was the One – not her. He would straighten out the rows of her heart, and build a fence around it, keeping out the marauding thoughts and desires. Then it reminded her of another bit of Scripture she'd heard, something about taking your thoughts captive – well, what good was a fence if it couldn't keep something captive? A rare grin appeared on Gert's face. The burden was lifted, it was not her job. She felt a surge of joy in her freckled chest and headed over to the kitchen door window to look at her garden patch again. Freshly tilled soiled, ready for whatever she wanted to plant, and her, with a freshly tilled heart, ready to let God plant what He wanted to plant.

As she looked out the door, instead of seeing her lovely patch of newly turned earth, what she saw was that dog from next door – who had started this whole thing in the first place – taking a poop. In her new dirt!

Crimany! That fence had to be built pronto!! She yanked open the kitchen door and clapped her hands loudly. "Bad dog, bad, bad dog!" She started toward the garden patch. The dog, still pooping, hopped on off to his own yard.

"Tom!" She waved her kitchen towel in the air as she yelled. Tom was just pulling out of her driveway. "Tom, wait!" He slammed on the brakes. Now what?

Gert reached the driver's side of his pick-up truck, red-faced from the exertion. With a quick mop of her towel, she dried her face, "Tom – how fast can you build a fence around my garden?"

"Oh," he scratched his head, eyeing the patch he had just plowed, "probably wouldn't take more than a day or so."

"Well, put yer truck in Drive and head on back to the garden and get started. I want that fence up today! And clear out that dog poop while yer at it!" Gert marched back to the kitchen, not even waiting to hear Toms answer.

Tom shook his head, yes, she was one odd duck. He put his truck in Drive and did as he was told.

****

The door to the waiting room swung open and there stood Randy, with a little bundle in his arms.

Joe nudged Carrie, who had fallen asleep on the hard little couch, and she jumped up, instantly awake. Together they went forward to meet their little grandchild.

Randy's face beamed with pride. "Grandpa and Grandma – if I may – I'd like to introduce you to Joey. Joey, this is your Grandpa and Grandma…" he carefully pulled the blanket away from Joey's little face so they could meet him properly.

"Oh!" breathed Carrie, "he's so beautiful!" She touched the blanket carefully, really wanting to hold him, but not so sure Daddy would let him go yet.

"Grandma?" Randy held out his little bundle, "would you like to be the first?"

Tears welled in Carries eyes, as she took little Joey and held him close. It was then that memories of Teddy flooded her mind, of that last time she had held him, he was just this size. Joe understood without words, and hugged her shoulders. It was complete now, the circle had closed.

Randy seemed a little confused at what appeared to be an over-emotional Grandma, but he had learned a while ago, he couldn't understand a woman. Especially in this family!

"Congratulations Dad!" Joe shook his hand, "got any cigars?" he grinned.

"Thank you! No, no cigars. I think those went out of vogue a few years back," but he smiled as he said it and Joe knew he had a son in law, of sorts.

"How is Abby?" asked Carried, as she swayed back and forth in that way that Grandmas and Mama's do when holding a baby.

"She's sleeping, she had a pretty hard time. But she did it! Kissed Joey, and me! and promptly fell asleep." Randy laughed, and his happiness was plain to see as he took Joey from his Grandma, carefully supporting his little head. "I better get him back before she wakes up." He started for the door.

"Randy, wait!" Joe called. "Is he ... is he named after me?"

"I guess so. After he was born and we knew he was a boy, Abby said his name was Joey Theodore. It sounded fine to me."

"Ok, tell her we'll come by in the morning. Tell her we love her!" Joe called after him.

"Will do." came Randy's voice from the hall.

Carries knees were suddenly weak. Theodore? Where had Abby gotten that name? It wasn't a family name. Teddy was simply a nickname for Theodore. Was it a coincidence? She sat down, her mind racing.

"Carrie?" Joe sat down next to her. "What's wrong?"

She was quiet for a minute and then said, "Well, the baby ... you know, the first baby?" he nodded, "In my mind or my heart, I don't know which, I named him Teddy."

"Oh!" Joe said, knowingly, instantly seeing the connection. "Hmm ... I guess it could be a coincidence. We don't know anyone named Theodore or Teddy."

Carried nodded her head, almost sadly. *I don't know if this is a good thing or a hard thing,* she thought. *Will seeing Joey always remind me of Teddy or will Joey be the blessing that Teddy couldn't be? Well, to be fair, Teddy was and is a blessing to someone, just not me.*

And it was in that moment that she realized how free she really was from her past. Names were just names. Babies were blessings no matter what. Grandchildren were blessings, of that there was no doubt.

"You know what?" she smiled up at Joe. "It really doesn't matter. That's his name and it's a beautiful name. And I'm choosing to think positively – that she did name him after you."

He put his arms around her and kissed her. "I do love you so much."

May 22, 2020

Hello Reader!

I hope you enjoyed this little story I wrote so long ago. While it was intended to be a short story for a newsletter, it blossomed into a full-length novel and two more books in the series. These women have a story to tell and they weren't going to be told otherwise.

When I started this book, I was living in Idaho raising my children. By the time I finished the series, I was divorced, remarried, and moved to Missouri, widowed, moved back to Idaho for a few years, remarried and moved to California where I am right this minute. My desire is never to move again, and certainly I'd like to keep my husband! ☺ This series has seen me through a lot of life, and you know what I've learned through all of it? That God is good – all the time. In every circumstance, He is good. He is in control of circumstances, circumstances can not be allowed to control us. Keep your eyes on Him.

If you enjoyed Morningshine, you can read more of the Spring Street Quilters story in Morning Glory, and then in Morning of Grace. I'd love to hear from you. My email address is karensaari144@gmail.com and my website is http://karensaari.com

If you noticed the date at the beginning of this letter, you know what a crazy time this is … or was. Or has it gotten crazier? Only God knows, and once again, I'm so thankful He is in control.

Would you do me a favor? If you liked this story, would you leave me a review? I'd sure appreciate it. And tell your friends! Links to the next two books are on the next page.

Morning Glory https://www.amazon.com/Morning-Christian-Fiction-Spring-Quilters-ebook/dp/B00HADMVMA/

Morning of Grace https://www.amazon.com/Morning-Grace-Spring-Street-Quilters-ebook/dp/B078QC5JLY/

All my books are included in Kindle Unlimited. I love using KU to read books, so I think other people do to!

My next book is The Neighbor's Club. You can find out more on my website karensaari.com Sign up for my newsletter for updates. I hope to see you soon!

Made in the USA
Coppell, TX
28 February 2024

29513801R00198